Love, Lust
and Pixie Dust

W9-BNT-289

Love, Lust and Pixie Dust

LuAnn McLane

A SIGNET ECLIPSE BOOK

SIGNET ECLIPSE

Published by New American Library, a division of Penguin Group (USA) Inc.,
375 Hudson Street, New York, New York 10014, USA • Penguin Group (Canada),
90 Eglinton Avenue East, Suite 700, Toronto, Ontario M4P 2Y3, Canada
(a division of Pearson Penguin Canada Inc.) • Penguin Books Ltd.,
80 Strand, London WC2R 0RL, England • Penguin Ireland, 25 St. Stephen's Green,
Dublin 2, Ireland (a division of Penguin Books Ltd.) • Penguin Group (Australia),
250 Camberwell Road, Camberwell, Victoria 3124, Australia (a division of
Pearson Australia Group Pty. Ltd.) • Penguin Books India Pvt. Ltd., 11 Community
Centre, Panchsheel Park, New Delhi - 110 017, India • Penguin Group (NZ),
cnr Airborne and Rosedale Roads, Albany, Auckland 1310, New Zealand
(a division of Pearson New Zealand Ltd.) • Penguin Books (South Africa)
(Pty.) Ltd., 24 Sturdee Avenue, Rosebank, Johannesburg 2196, South Africa

Penguin Books Ltd., Registered Offices: 80 Strand, London WC2R 0RL, England

First Published by Signet Eclipse, an imprint of New American Library,
a division of Penguin Group (USA), Inc.

First Printing, October 2006
1   3   5   7   9   10   8   6   4   2

Copyright © LuAnn McLane, 2006
All rights reserved

SIGNET ECLIPSE and logo are trademarks of Penguin Group (USA) Inc.

LIBRARY OF CONGRESS CATALOGING-IN-PUBLICATION DATA:
McLane, LuAnn.
Love, lust, and pixie dust / LuAnn McLane.
p. cm.
ISBN 0-451-21950-3 (trade pbk.)
1. Country musicians—Fiction.   2. Love stories, American.   I. Title.

PS3613.C5685L68 2006
813'.6—dc22

2006014514

Set in Sabon   •   Designed by Elke Sigal

Printed in the United States of America

Without limiting the rights under copyright reserved above, no part of this publica-
tion may be reproduced, stored in or introduced into a retrieval system, or trans-
mitted, in any form, or by any means (electronic, mechanical, photocopying,
recording, or otherwise), without the prior written permission of both the copyright
owner and the above publisher of this book.

PUBLISHER'S NOTE
This is a work of fiction. Names, characters, places, and incidents either are the
product of the author's imagination or are used fictitiously, and any resemblance to
actual persons, living or dead, business establishments, events, or locales is entirely
coincidental.
The publisher does not have any control over and does not assume any responsi-
bility for author or third-party Web sites or their content.

The scanning, uploading, and distribution of this book via the Internet or via any
other means without the permission of the publisher is illegal and punishable by law.
Please purchase only authorized electronic editions, and do not participate in or
encourage electronic piracy of copyrighted materials. Your support of the author's
rights is appreciated.

✴ *This book is for my mother and father,*
for your unending love and support.
Thank you for always believing in me.

✳ Acknowledgments

$\mathcal{I}$ want to extend a special thanks to my editor, Anne Bohner. Your insight and enthusiasm keep my creativity flowing and my hands on the keyboard. Also, I want to extend a big thanks to production editor Rachel Granfield for your excellence and attention to detail.

As always, thanks to my wonderful agent, Jenny Bent, who has been the driving force behind me from the beginning.

Contents

Crazy

1

✦

Honky-tonk Angel

119

✦

Walkin' After Midnight

213

✦

Crazy

✳ Chapter One

Mary Jane Barone slipped her deck of tarot cards into the red silk bag and drew the strings together before tucking the bundle safely away in her desk drawer. With a huge yawn she tilted her head from side to side, causing her big hoop earrings to gently tap her cheeks. God, she was tired and so ready to call it a day. Recent media coverage had caused her "Psychic Love Connection" business to boom and while M. J. wasn't complaining, she really needed a soothing glass of red wine from Logan's, the little honky-tonk bar next door.

Although M. J. wasn't much of a party girl, Logan's had become her hangout since she'd moved to Nashville six months ago. She enjoyed people watching and listening to the country-singer hopefuls, especially Savannah Parks, the bar owner's talented sister. M. J. stood up and stretched while wondering if she had the energy to walk the short distance to the bar. Leaning over, she blew out the vanilla-scented candle and turned to switch off the overhead light but paused when a big cowboy suddenly pushed his way through the multicolored strands of beads dangling in her doorway.

Having to crane her head to look up at the guy, M. J. said, "Sorry, but I'm not taking any more clients tonight."

Tipping his black Stetson back with his thumb, he blinked at her as if confused while the beads tinkled softly behind him. "Clients? Wh-where am I?" he asked, hooking his thumbs in the belt loops of his jeans.

"The Psychic Love Connection."

"The chick . . . *love* connection?" He paused for a second and glanced around, taking in the candles and the beads. His eyes suddenly widened. "Love connection," he repeated. "Hey, this isn't . . . you aren't . . . a h-hooker, are you?"

"Sorry, cowboy, I'm a *psychic*," M. J. answered drily. By rights she should be offended, but something about the situation made her grin.

"A side . . . kick?"

"*A psychic*," she said slowly. Okay, she knew her Brooklyn accent was sometimes confusing to these Southerners, but couldn't this cowboy understand English? "No, a—whoa there, big guy." M. J. had thought that he was rocking back on his heels, but then realized that he was actually swaying. It dawned on her that this guy had probably stumbled over here mistaking it for to the bar next door. She would have immediately asked him to leave, but there was something familiar about him that tugged at her memory. "I, uh, think you're in the wrong place."

" 'S-kay. I wasn't lookin' for a hooker anyways. Don't need to pay for . . . you know. . . . Whose sidekick are you?" He gave her a lopsided grin that shouldn't have been so sweet since he was obviously tipsy, but he had a dimple in his cheek and charm that oozed past the alcohol.

M. J. just shook her head. "Do I know you from somewhere?"

"You flirtin' with me, girlie?" The words were slightly slurred but teasing.

"No," M. J. answered firmly. The truth was that she wasn't very good at flirting. "I'm just tryin' to place ya, that's all."

The cute cowboy took a step toward her. He angled his head, causing his hat to slide sideways, and said, "Shame 'cause you sure are sexy."

"Cowboy, you've got your beer goggles on," M. J. said with a grin, but felt the heat of a blush creep up her neck to her cheeks. She had never been very good with sexual banter, especially when she felt a pull of attraction.

"Do *not*." He stood up straight and squared his shoulders, trying to look sober but failing miserably.

M. J. swallowed a laugh but then wondered again how she knew this guy. "Have you been in heah before?"

The cowboy wagged his finger at M. J. and grinned. "Th-there you go flirtin' again." He held his thumb and forefinger about an inch apart and said, "I'm Brody Baker and just a tiny bit famous."

"Brody Baker?" M. J. snapped her fingers. "Oh,

now I rememba. You play bass for Travis Mackey. I saw you in concert last summer."

He smiled, showing off that sexy dimple again. "Yep, and I have my very own single coming out this week. Oh, damn, I'm s'posed to do this interview right 'bout now." He tried to slap his thigh but missed.

"How about a cuppa cawfee or a Coke first? I hate to tell ya, but ya need to sober up."

"I'm fine," he insisted while shaking his head. "Whoa, maybe I'm not so fine."

"Follow me, Brody."

" 'Kay."

M. J. led him to the back of the shop, behind which she had a small apartment. If she didn't try to sober him up, he was going to make a complete fool of himself. "Have a seat." She gestured toward the tiny kitchen table flanked by two wooden chairs. "I'll put on a pot of cawfee."

"Thanks," he said, and took off his black Stetson, revealing shaggy blond hair. "People kept buying me shots of Wild T-Turkey to celebrate my single debut," he explained slowly as if trying not to slur his words. "I stood up from the bar and *damn*, I was shit-faced. . . . Oh, sorry 'bout the language."

M. J. waved a hand at him. "Don't worry 'bout it." She thought it was kind of cute that he didn't want to curse around her. "The cawfee will be ready in a few minutes. I'm going to make sure the front door is locked."

" 'Kay. I'm not going anywhere."

M. J. grinned as she headed to the front door. She

remembered now watching Brody in concert last Labor Day while she worked at Wild Ride Resort. Travis Mackey was the lead singer, but Brody had been the funny crowd-pleaser that kept the show lively. Up until then, M. J. hadn't been much of a country-music fan, but that night the music and lyrics had spoken to her in an almost spiritual way. It was the very same night that she had dreamed that she had been singing a duet with Patsy Cline, of all crazy things, and not long afterward, she had decided on a whim to leave Florida and move to Nashville, Tennessee.

M. J. flipped the sign on the front door to read CLOSED, disappointing a few people who were forming a line outside. At her sister Sophia's suggestion M. J. had taken her business from simply reading the tarot cards to using her odd but true psychic talent. Put quite simply, M. J. could read emotion, especially love. She could tell almost immediately if a couple was destined for true bliss or dismal failure. This gift, however, had played havoc with M. J.'s own love life. Knowing right off the bat whether a guy was the real deal or just after a booty call tended to put a damper on a first date. Oddly, she had felt a strong vibe of attraction toward the cute cowboy and she suddenly wondered if her intuition was a bit off.

The aroma of coffee in the air reminded M. J. that she had better get back to Brody Baker. Taking a last look around to see that everything was in its place and locked up, she hurried back toward the kitchen. "Brody?" A little sizzle of alarm snaked down her spine when she saw that the chair he'd been sitting in was vacant. Had he gone out the back door? Was he slurring his words to some snarky reporter?

"Brody?" M. J. called again a bit louder as she entered the kitchen. With a little squeal of alarm she all but fell over his long-legged body lying on the floor. *How in the world did he end up there?* "Brody," M. J. said again, and knelt down next to him. "Wake up! You're gonna miss your interview."

Brody mumbled something, sighed and snuggled into the crook of his arm.

With a groan M. J. was about to shake him awake but paused a moment to check him out just a teensy bit. After all it wasn't every day a girl from Brooklyn had a celebrity sleeping on her kitchen floor. For a minute she thought about taking a picture so she could prove this to Sophia, but then she decided that would just be wrong. She did, however, allow herself to look.

Fancy-looking boots peeked out beneath his denim-clad legs. Her gaze traveled up his calves to his thighs and with her hand over her mouth M. J. peeked over his shoulder to get a glimpse of his very fine butt. A Western-cut brown shirt was tucked into his jeans and he had the customary wide leather belt sporting a big silver buckle. The first three mother-of-pearl buttons of his shirt were open and when Brody suddenly shifted his weight M. J. was treated to a pie-shaped slice of tanned chest lightly dusted with tawny hair.

Biting her bottom lip, M. J. gazed at Brody's face, taking in the dark blond stubble on his cheeks and his straight nose with just a bit of a bump at the bridge. High cheekbones and sexy longish hair held her attention for a minute . . . *oh*, but it was his *mouth* that made her swallow. Perfectly shaped with a slightly fuller bottom lip. M. J. wondered with a little shiver what those lips would feel like pressed to hers. . . .

She rocked back on her heels and whispered, "What's gotten into me?" Feeling foolish, she decided to wake him up. "Brody?"

He didn't move a muscle.

"Hey, ya havta wake up," she encouraged in a louder tone.

He rolled to his back, but his eyes remained shut.

"Come on, cowboy," M. J. said with a moan. She leaned in closer and patted his cheeks. "Ohmigawd!" It was as if a bolt of electricity shot from her hands straight to her heart. With a little shriek M. J. crab-walked away from Brody and looked at her hands, half expecting to find them singed.

"Wow, what was up with *that*?" she whispered as she stared over at Brody. M. J. crossed her hands over her chest where her heart was thumping wildly, and swallowed. "Could this be . . . is he . . . my love match?" She had waited her whole life for this magic moment to happen . . . but then she frowned and angled her head at Brody.

"Waida minute. *This* guy is my one and only?" Narrowing her eyes, she scooted a tad closer. While Brody certainly was a hottie, he wasn't the type of guy M. J. had always daydreamed about. Her soul mate was supposed to be tall, dark and Italian . . . not a shaggy-haired blond cowboy who was passed out drunk on her kitchen floor! No, this magic moment was supposed to happen beneath a star-soaked sky or while she was walking on a sugar-sand beach or when her eyes met her special someone from across a crowded room.

"Well . . . well, *damn*!" This sort of ticked M. J. off. As magic moments went, this one sucked. In her fantasy her soul mate was supposed to kiss her sweetly or maybe toss her over his shoulder like in a sexy historical romance novel. M. J. nibbled on the inside of her cheek, thinking that she just had to be mistaken. Okay, she had preached to clients that your soul mate wasn't always whom you expected, but *this* psychic love connection had to be all wrong. "Maybe it was just static electricity or somethin'," M. J. mumbled. She scooted closer, wondering if she should touch Brody again to see if she got the same reaction. Hey, so she got a bit of an electric shock from touching him . . . so what? This guy was her soul mate? "Yeah, right."

Still, M. J. slowly inched her hand toward Brody until she almost touched his cheek, but then jerked it back. She swallowed hard, licked her lips and then ever so slightly grazed her fingertips down the soft yet tickly stubble on his jaw. Instead of the jolting shock like before, M. J. felt a warm rush of tenderness. "Oh . . . ," she said with a breathless bit of wonder. Unable to stop herself, she brushed a fingertip over the smooth, moist skin of his bottom lip. Brody sighed and mumbled something, somehow managing to catch her fingertip between his lips. *Oh my* . . . M. J. held her breath. The touch of his tongue, the heat of his mouth, made her shiver and then imagine once again what it would feel like to kiss him.

While initial psychic intuition was always an indica-
tor, M. J. knew from personal experience that a *kiss* was
a determining factor in a love connection. What if she
just leaned in and pressed her mouth to his? Just a brief
light-as-a-feather touch would do it and then she would
know. Making her decision, M. J. took a deep breath of
coffee-scented air, bent over and lightly touched her lips
to his.

Instant longing, liquid and warm, had her sucking in
a breath, but when M. J. would have pulled away, Brody
cupped his hand to her head and opened his mouth for a
full-blown kiss. His lips were firm yet pliant, soft but de-
manding. He tasted of bourbon and man . . . hot and
potent. The stubble of his beard grazed her cheek, sending a tingle down her spine that had M. J. opening her
mouth for *more*. Her head swam, her breasts swelled,
and heat pooled in places that had been cold for way too
long. Needing to feel more bare skin, M. J. tugged at his
shirt until the mother-of-pearl snaps started popping
open. She moaned into his mouth when her hands en-
countered warm smooth skin, silky hair, firm muscle
and the bump of a nipple. . . .

But then Brody's hand fell away from her head and
slid to the tile floor with a soft thump. His mouth went
slack and the magical kiss ended with the sound of a
long sigh and then light snoring.

What? M. J. felt like smacking him. Rocking back
on her heels, she wasn't sure whether to laugh or cry.
With her hands pressed to her cheeks she muttered,
"Ohmigawd," thinking that this was just too weird, and
in her family weird was *normal*, so that was definitely

saying something. Still a bit shaken, she felt as if her legs were made of wet noodles as she stood up, but she managed to walk over to her tiny closet and locate a pillow and a blanket. Coming back into the kitchen, she knelt down next to Brody, slipped the pillow beneath his head and then tucked the knit blanket around him. As an afterthought she tugged off his boots . . . no easy task, but he slept like the dead. With a weary sigh M. J. moved Brody's boots over to the corner and glanced at the digital clock on the microwave.

Although it was just after ten she decided to turn in for the night. She paused in the doorway and looked down at Brody, hoping that the reporter wouldn't be too ticked that he was a no-show. His white socks peeked out from the too-small green blanket that M. J. usually snuggled into while watching TV. It felt kind of intimate to see him wrapped in something that was usually tucked around M. J.'s own body. Shaking her head at the crazy turn of events, she reached over to the wall and turned out the light.

As she tried to go through the normal routine of getting ready for bed, M. J. kept thinking about the stranger sleeping on her kitchen floor . . . a stranger with whom she had shared a long hot kiss . . . a *stranger who could very well be the man of her dreams*. M. J. blinked at her reflection in the small mirror while swishing mouthwash around. Of course she *could* be wrong about Brody Baker, but her psychic love-connection intuitions were usually spot-on.

The trouble was, though, would a country-singing, bourbon-drinking, big strapping cowboy ever believe that an off-the-wall psychic chick from Brooklyn could be *his* one and only? M. J. spit the mouthwash into the sink and blew out a minty-fresh sigh. Her clients were always amazed when she hooked them up with someone unexpected, but that's because in her experience people tended to look for love in all the wrong places while ignoring the obvious. Just last week M. J. had floored a client when during their session she had envisioned a brown truck, a clipboard and brown shorts. Suddenly her client realized that she was in love with her UPS guy, who had been delivering packages to her for over a year.

M. J. shook her head as she entered her bedroom. Psychic powers weren't as extraordinary as most people might think. Feelings, intuitions and signs . . . they were all *there* but all too often either ignored or dismissed. But M. J. was a big believer that there were no coincidences and that everything happened for a reason. Something had drawn her to Nashville, Tennessee, and M. J. believed that her *something* was sleeping on her kitchen floor.

Chapter Two

The smoky aroma of bacon frying curled into Brody's brain, making his stomach rumble. He forced open heavy eyelids, wincing and blinking in the bright morning light. *Wait a minute*, Brody thought with a frown. *It's morning?* The last thing he remembered was tossing down shots in Logan's bar.

So then where the hell am I?

Brody realized that although his head was on a sweet-smelling pillow, he was lying on a hard floor in a small kitchen. While he had ended up in some strange places the day after partying, lately he had been trying to reform his wild ways, so this was a bit of a surprise. A woman dressed in a long, flowing purple skirt and a billowing white blouse was in the process of making coffee. With her back to him the woman reached up on her tiptoes and retrieved two coffee mugs. Brody noticed that she was barefoot, with shiny red toenails and two gold toe rings adding to her Bohemian appearance. Long black hair . . .

lots of it . . . fell in glossy waves halfway down her back. Several gold bracelets encircling her wrists jingled as she worked and for some reason this made Brody smile in spite of his pounding hangover. When she turned to grab a skillet, he finally got to see her profile and although he didn't recognize her, he felt an instant attraction. While she wasn't traditionally pretty, she had an exotic sex appeal that had his heart thumping in tandem with his throbbing headache.

Brody wondered how he could politely ask who she was, how he got here, and what, if anything, occurred between them. He closed his eyes and concentrated. Surely he would remember if they had slept together. Snippets, images, floated and swirled in his brain . . . floral perfume, silky hair . . . her mouth covering his. . . . God, what had he done? Well, he might as well face the music.

"Uh, excuse me?"

"Oh!" She dropped the skillet to the stove with a loud clank that made Brody wince, and turned to face him.

Still wincing, Brody pushed up to a sitting position. "This may sound crazy, but would you mind telling me who you are and where I am?" His voice sounded husky, as if he had just finished a two-hour concert, and his mouth felt like it was filled with cotton.

Her dark eyebrows rose a fraction as she answered, "I'm Mary Jane Barone and you're at the Psychic Love Connection."

Who, what . . . *where?* Brody tried to swallow, making his tongue stick to the roof of his mouth. *The psychic love connection? What the hell is that?* He blinked at her in confusion. "I'm . . . where?" She had a funny accent. God, he was still in Nashville, wasn't he?

"The Psychic Love Connection," she repeated slowly. "Well, technically you're in my apartment behind my shop." Turning around, she opened the refrigerator and pulled out a bottle of water. "Thirsty?"

Brody nodded absently and accepted the cold bottle while trying to make some sense of what she had just said. After unscrewing the cap, he guzzled most of it and was embarrassed when some of it dribbled down his chin. He wiped it away with his hand and then mumbled, "Thanks."

"Hungry?"

"Uh, yeah." Who *was* this woman? She seemed a little nervous and that couldn't be good.

"Have a seat and I'll scramble some eggs." She opened the refrigerator again and pulled out a carton of eggs and a bottle of orange juice. Pouring him a generous amount, she handed it to him and said, "Drink all of it. The potassium in the juice will help chase the hangover away."

"Thanks," Brody answered lamely as he settled into the chair, really wishing that he could remember how he'd ended up in Mary Jane Barone's kitchen. While drinking the tangy juice, Brody watched Mary Jane work efficiently in the small space. Cracking the eggs with one hand, she whisked them in a bowl, making her bracelets clink. Again, Brody thought how different she was from the type of woman he went after, so he had to ask, "Um, just how did I end up here?"

She paused in her whisking and turned around to face him. "By mistake. Logan's is right next door."

"Oh." This was becoming as clear as mud. "So you just let me stay here?"

She shrugged. "I have really good intuition where people are concerned. After all, I *am* a psychic," she added with a small grin. "Besides, I remembered you from when you performed at Wild Ride Resort, so I knew ya weren't a serial killer. And since you passed out on my floor I was kind of stuck with you."

"I passed out?" he asked, feeling heat creep up his neck. "How humiliating."

"Whadevva." She waved a dismissive hand at him. "From what ya told me it wasn't entirely your fault," she gently assured him. "It seems that you were being given an endless supply of Wild Turkey shots to celebrate your new single."

Brody groaned and slapped his hand to his forehead. "I was supposed to do an interview with *Nashville Now Magazine*." He shot Mary Jane a look. "I didn't . . . did I?"

"I was trying to sober ya up when ya passed out on me."

"I guess I owe you."

"It was nothin'." She blushed a bit as she waved the whisk in his direction. "Don't worry 'bout it."

Brody chuckled at her nasal accent. "You're not from around these parts, are you?"

"How'd ya guess?" she asked with a smile. "No, I was born and raised in Brooklyn. Besides, I look like a putz in a cowboy hat."

"Aw, I bet you'd look cute."

She blushed a pretty shade of pink and lowered her eyes. Brody thought again about how she wasn't at all his type, but he felt another strong pull of attraction. He had this crazy notion to stand up, tug her into his arms and kiss her senseless. "Lord have mercy," he said, and ran his fingers through his hair.

She looked over at him. "What?"

Embarrassed at his wayward thoughts, he said, "Um, would you mind if I used your bathroom?"

"Oh, sure. Down the hallway on the left."

"Thanks."

After Brody left the room M. J. let out a breath that she didn't realize she had been holding. She was usually a person who was pretty sure of herself, but Brody made her trip over her own tongue and blush like a schoolgirl. Just looking at the man made her all hot and bothered. It sure didn't help that his shirt had been unbuttoned almost to the waist, and neither did the memory of her tugging those snaps open while kissing him. Luckily Brody didn't seem to remember those little details. "What had I been thinkin'?" M. J. whispered. "I had been thinkin' that he was my soul mate," she answered herself as she poured the eggs into the sizzling skillet. M. J. often wondered out loud, a habit that had never ceased to annoy her brother; her sister; her college roommate; and various other people who tended to answer her seemingly off-the-wall questions when in reality she was simply talking to herself. "What does one say to one's potential soul mate?" she mused while scrambling the eggs.

The sound of a woman chuckling had M. J. spinning around, although she knew she wouldn't see anyone in the room. This had been happening for a while now. "Ask him where he's been all your life," the soft Southern voice answered, and then chuckled again.

"Pixie?" M. J. saw a shadowy flicker of light zip through the room and then disappear. At night her Southern ghost sort of glowed in the dark, always exiting the room with a shimmer of light that reminded M. J. of pixie dust, so M. J. dubbed her ghostly friend "Pixie." Of course most people would have been weirded out by Pixie, but M. J. was no stranger to psychic phenomena, so she took it all in stride . . . well, almost everything. This business with Brody Baker had her all shaken up.

Just as M. J. was placing a garnish of an orange slice on a plate heaped with fluffy eggs, crisp strips of bacon and two slices of golden wheat toast, Brody entered the room. M. J. felt her heart kick it up a notch and she hoped he attributed the warmth in her cheeks to the heat of the stove.

"Wow, this sure smells good," Brody commented as he folded his big frame into the chair.

M. J. smiled, feeling ridiculously pleased with his compliment. She noticed that his hair was wet around the edges and his shirt was buttoned up and tucked into his jeans. M. J. found it a bit endearing that he had attempted to tidy up for her. "Cream or sugar?" she asked as she handed him the steaming mug of coffee.

"A little bit of cream, if you don't mind."

"Not at all." M. J. turned to the small refrigerator

and opened the door. Because she was so nervous, she was finding it difficult to read Brody's emotions. She sensed curiosity, but was he attracted to her? Maybe she was mistaken about this whole thing.

Just then a shimmering light flitted around in the refrigerator and the Southern voice scolded, *Believe, Mary Jane Barone.*

"Pixie?" M. J. hissed softly, but of course Brody heard her.

"Excuse me?"

"Uh, nothin'."

"If you can't find the cream, that's okay. I can drink it black."

The light landed on the butter and M. J. gently swatted at it to get to the cream.

"Hey!" Pixie protested in her throaty Tanya Tucker voice. "Y'all be careful! These wings are delicate!"

"Sorry," M. J. said automatically.

"It's okay really. I'll drink it black." He gave her a curious look when she turned around with the carton in her hand. "Or with cream . . . is fine too."

With a nervous smile M. J. handed him the carton. "Here ya go."

"Thank you."

M. J. felt a warm presence tickling her ear. "Oh, such a polite young man," Pixie crooned. "He's smokin' hot. And that blond hair? I've got to fly over there and cop a feel against my wings."

"Don't you dare!"

"Uh, dare what?" Brody asked.

"B-burn your mouth. The cawfee is hot." M. J. almost groaned, thinking she was making a very poor impression on the man of her dreams.

"I'll be careful," Brody assured her with a smile.

M. J. returned the smile, but her eyes widened when she noticed light flickering through his hair. "Stop!"

Startled, Brody sloshed hot coffee over the rim of the cup onto his fingers. "Yeeow!"

"Oh, sorry!" M. J. handed him a napkin.

"Listen," Brody began with a polite nod, "I appreciate all of your hospitality, but maybe it's best if I get going."

"Oh." M. J. felt a sinking sensation in her stomach.

Pixie flitted out of his hair. "Don't let him go!"

"Stay and eat your breakfast, Brody. You'll feel better with something in your stomach."

"Okay, but how about you relax and eat with me?"

M. J. smiled. "I'm not really hungry, but I'll have a cuppa cawfee."

Brody's eyebrows rose. "So you cooked this just for me?" He took a bite of the eggs. "It's very good."

M. J. felt the warmth of another blush creep up her neck as she nodded. "I thought ya might need it."

Brody leaned back in his chair. "Well then, let me repay you with dinner tonight."

Pixie zoomed around his head and shouted, "Yes!"

"Oh, ya don't have ta do that."

Pixie stopped in her tracks and sputtered, "Are you crazy, Mary Jane Barone?" She flitted over and hovered in front of M. J.'s nose. "Take it back right now!"

$\mathcal{B}$rody knew that he was hungover, but it seemed like M. J. was looking at him a bit cross-eyed. "Are you okay?"

Her head snapped up to look over at him. "Uh, yeah, sure," she answered, but swatted her hand through the air.

Brody glanced around. "Um, is there a fly or something in here?"

"Nah," she answered, but then narrowed her eyes and batted in front of her face before turning to pour herself a cup of coffee. "Just a little *pest*."

Brody didn't see anything, but he politely refrained from commenting. He was beginning to think that the little psychic was one taco short of a combo. Still, he was intrigued and there was also that strong sexual pull that he couldn't deny, making him feel torn between getting the hell out of there and kissing the woman senseless.

Kissing her . . . wait a doggone minute. That thought cut through the whiskey fumes in Brody's brain. Closing his eyes, he recalled the sweet floral scent of her perfume filling his head. Yeah, and his fingers had threaded through her hair, and oh man, his mouth had locked with hers for a long, *hot* kiss that had rocked his senses. . . . God, but then what had happened? He squeezed his eyes shut more tightly and concentrated but got nothing. "Damn."

"Excuse me?"

Brody opened his eyes, wanting to ask her if they had shared more than a steamy kiss, but he was too embarrassed. Instead he pointed to the chair opposite him and said, "Have a seat and tell me all about this psychic love-connection thing that you do."

"Oh." She sat down, waving her hand, making her bracelets jingle. "It's boring, really."

Brody crunched through a bite of toast. "I'm curious. Enlighten me."

"Well . . ." Without looking at him, she traced her finger over the rim of her coffee cup. "I help people find their true love."

"Really? Their true love, huh?" Brody tried hard to hide his amusement. "Just how do you manage this?"

She gave him a small shrug but kept her eyes downcast. "I, um, have always been able to read emotion, especially strong feelings like love. I sorta know when people are meant for each other . . . *or not.* Let me tell ya, people *really* don't like when ya tell them that they're barking up the wrong tree."

"Interesting." Brody took a sip of coffee, hiding his

smile. "Tell me more." He watched her trace the rim of her cup again. When she angled her head a cascade of long dark hair fell over her shoulder, making Brody want to reach over and run his fingers through the soft-looking waves.

"Well, sometimes I do readings for couples, but more often than not, I get singles coming in to ask me how to find their soul mate."

"And you think you really do?"

She finally looked over at him. "Yes."

Brody sat up straighter in his chair. He gave her a polite nod, even though he wasn't buying any of this love-connection stuff. Not knowing what to say, he gave her a lame, "Wow."

She shrugged again and looked a bit uncomfortable but then raised her chin a notch. "I don't know how or why I have this power. I just *do*."

"So how do you perform this . . . gift? Turn over those cards or something?"

"Tarot cards? Sometimes, just to give me a starting point. I don't always need them, but it makes the client somehow think that I'm more accurate if I use them. The cards, *however*, are only as good as the person reading them. For example, the Death card is rarely about death but freaks people out. Ya know, it's more about how you interpret them than what cards are actually turned over."

Brody nodded like he knew what the hell she was talking about. "So how does it work? Do you see the future? Give them a phone number? Names?"

"I can't usually give them names, but when I hold

their hands . . . I *see* things . . . clues. Brown shorts and a big brown truck led one client to her UPS man. It's sorta like when my sista, Sophia, helps the police solve a crime. She can give them clues, but she is only as good as the detectives who are on the case."

"Your sister is a psychic too?"

"Runs in the family. She's a medium . . . a bit different than me."

Brody had no idea what a medium was but nodded again.

"See, what most people don't realize is that if we listen to our hearts, we're led in the right direction . . . maybe to a certain city, for example. Most of the time, though, your soul mate is very near. . . ."

"Go on," Brody prompted when she fell silent. He took a sip of his coffee and waited.

"No, you're not taking me seriously."

"Okay, Mary Jane, I'll admit that I find the whole idea rather far-fetched, but I'm willing to listen."

"For your own amusement." Her words were sharp, but her brown eyes misted over, making him feel like a jerk. When she blinked he thought for a panicky moment that she was going to cry. She might be a little off-center, but he liked her and sure as hell didn't want to be the cause of her tears.

"Oh, don't feel so bad," she assured him with a wave of her hand. "Most people are nonbelievers. I just hoped maybe ya wouldn't be one of 'em."

Something in the way she looked at him got to Brody in a way he couldn't explain. "Make me a believer, then. Do me."

"D-do you?"

"Yeah." With a smile, he offered her his hands to hold. "Tell me who my soul mate is."

"Y-*your* soul mate?" Her eyes widened a fraction and she visibly swallowed. She looked at his hand like it was a snake.

"Yes." He wiggled his fingers and gave her a grin. "Come on. Lay it on me. Is she blond? Long-legged?"

"Is that whatcha want? A leggy blonde?"

Brody shook his head, a bit confused at her reaction. Damn, he had been only teasing. What was she getting so riled up about? "You tell me, Ms. Love Connection."

She pursed her lips. "I'm not in the mood."

"You have to be in the mood?"

"Yes."

"But it's your business. You can't just say that you're not in the mood."

"Well, as ya can see I'm not *open* for business. This isn't a friggin' 7-Eleven."

Brody frowned. Hadn't she been ready to cry a moment ago? What was up with this chick? He was about to ask her just that when his cell phone rang. "Excuse me," he said, reaching in his pocket. Flipping the phone open, he answered, "Hello?"

M. J. pushed away from the table and busied herself by pouring another cup of coffee while Brody talked on his phone. She knew that he must think that she was crazy, but how in the world was she supposed to give him a reading? M. J. shook her head. She couldn't just tell him that *she* was his love connection, now, could she? Plus, that whole thing about the leggy blonde had just ticked her off. Again she wondered if her psychic radar was way off for some reason. Maybe the cute cowboy wasn't her soul mate after all.

"Mary Jane?"

She turned around from the sink. "Yes."

"I know this is bold of me to ask, but that was *Nashville Now Magazine* on the phone and the reporter wants to meet me in thirty minutes. I don't have time to go to my place, so would you mind if I showered here?"

An instant visual of bare-naked Brody with hot water streaming down his body left M. J. momentarily speechless.

"I'm sorry. . . . I shouldn't have asked."

"Oh, uh, no. I mean sure. You can use my shower."

He grinned. "Thanks. I owe you yet again."

"There are fresh towels in the linen closet. Help yourself. . . . Oh, and you'll find a new toothbrush in the medicine cabinet. You're welcome to it."

"You're an angel," he said over his shoulder as he hurried down the short hallway.

"An angel," M. J. muttered. "Right." A moment later she heard the rush of running water, and the picture of Brody in the buff returned with a vengeance. "Oh, stop," she said with the heel of her hand to her forehead. But then she suddenly realized that this wasn't just about lusting after a hot guy; this was her psychic power kicking in. The same thoughts, images, feelings, that M. J. relayed to her clients during a reading were now materializing for herself. But *this* was intensely strong, vividly real.

"Mmmm." When she shut her eyes, it was as if she

were suddenly in the shower stall with Brody. M. J. could feel the hot spray of water and smell the almond-scented shampoo. Unable to resist, she ran her hands over his warm, wet skin. He was sleek with soap and yet hard with muscle. M. J. let her hands slide downward until she heard his sharp intake of breath.

Although Brody's face had been turned upward in the pelting spray, he suddenly opened his eyes. Blinking, he stepped back against the tiled wall and turned around as if expecting to see someone. M. J. lightly massaged his thighs, coming closer and closer to her goal. She was surprised and yet delighted that he could somehow sense her touch. Feeling bold, M. J. cupped his sac and watched him grow thick and hard. Aroused and curious, M. J. wondered how much he could actually feel . . . and just how far she could take him before this unexpected magic faded away. Dipping her head, she decided to find out. . . .

Brody's heart pounded and his dick throbbed with the mother of all erections. He moaned, wondered what the hell was happening. He felt as if he were being oh-so-lightly touched, *stroked*, and yet his own hands were fisted at his sides. Okay, so he had been thinking about the little psychic chick, but good God . . . what was happening? Before he could even begin to wonder Brody felt something warm and soft encase his dick.

It felt like a woman's mouth.

Brody sucked in a breath that eased back out as a moan when it felt as if the tip of a tongue encircled the head, then took him in deep and then slowly back out. He could feel the light tickle of teeth, warm, wet pressure and the laving of a tongue. Bracing his hands on the opposite sides of the wall, he gave in to the exquisite torture.

This was wild.

This was crazy.

Just what in the hell was happening here?

Hot water pelted his back and cascaded over his shoulders. Fragrant steam clouded the small space while the sweet pleasure increased. "God." Brody moaned, wondering again how this was happening, but he was beyond caring now. He felt pressure as if hands cupped his ass and the soft licking heat became faster, harder, almost frenzied. Pressing his shoulders against the tile, Brody thrust his hips upward and exploded with a long, delicious climax that left him limp and panting.

"Holy shit." Brody opened his eyes, which had been squeezed shut, and half expected someone—*Mary Jane* perhaps—to someway, somehow be in the stall with him. He could have sworn that he felt wet tendrils of hair clinging to his thighs, but when he reached down he came up with nothing but air. Taking a deep shuddering breath, he said, "Damn, what was up with that?" A dream? Wishful thinking? Pent-up sexual frustration? Was he still drunk?

Still a bit astonished, he looked down at his dick, which remained ruddy red and steely hard. "Good God." While his little fantasy or whatever the hell it was had been amazing, Brody had to get to this interview and arriving with a hard-on would make about as good of an impression as showing up loaded. With a groan, Brody turned the nozzle to cold, hoping that the icy blast could cool his overheated body.

Chapter Four

"Whoa!" Blinking and shivering, M. J. felt as if she had been doused with an icy blast of water. A bit dazed, she fell back on her butt, realizing with a hot blush that she had been on her knees. With her hands to her warm cheeks, M. J. knew that although she had experienced some really strange and mystical occurrences in her twenty-six years, this one had been extraordinary. She wondered how much of this interlude Brody had felt, but she couldn't exactly ask, now, could she? M. J. grinned, thinking that perhaps the evidence would show on his face . . . or maybe elsewhere.

She pushed up to her feet, not wanting Brody to see her sprawled on the kitchen floor. Still feeling shaky and more than a little aroused, she gripped the edge of the cool sink while sucking in deep breaths. "So maybe my psychic powers aren't on the fritz after all," M. J. whispered. She blinked when a flickering light swirled before her eyes. "Pixie?"

"Damned straight," Pixie said in her gruff voice. "I told you to trust in yourself. Don't you go turnin' down his dinner invitation, you hear?"

"Go away," M. J. said, swatting the air.

"Pesky fly again?"

M. J. whirled around to see Brody standing in the doorway. "S-somethin' like that."

He leaned one shoulder against the door frame and said, "I want to thank you for everything."

"My pleasure," she automatically answered, and then felt her cheeks grow warm. *How much of the shower incident did he experience?*

He looked at her for a long, hot moment, making M. J. think that he was going to ask her something, but then abruptly straightened up and said, "I've got to run. I'm late."

"Oh, well, good luck." M. J. felt a sinking sensation when he didn't say anything about having dinner or even indicate that he was interested in seeing her again. A soul-mate love couldn't be one-sided, could it? Man, that would suck.

Pixie flitted in front of her face. "Don't let him leave, for pity's sake! Flirt or crack a joke! Do something!"

Nibbling on her lip, she racked her brain for something funny or flirty to say but came up blank.

"Remind him about dinner," Pixie hissed. "Quick!"

"Um, are we still on for dinner?" Oh, where did she get the nerve? M. J. tried to smile, but she was sure it looked like a wince.

Brody paused but then said, "I'll check my schedule and call you, okay?"

"Oh . . . sure," M. J. answered with false brightness. "Call me."

After another slight pause Brody smiled at her but then left. For a long moment M. J. just stood there looking at the vacant spot where Brody had been standing. She felt like crying. Or maybe throwing something.

"Why are you lookin' so down in the mouth?" Pixie asked from her perch near the coffeepot. "He said he'd call."

M. J. slowly shook her head. "Yeah, well, that's kind of difficult to do, since he didn't bother to ask for my number."

"Well, hellfire."

M. J. chuckled without much mirth. "Yeah, hellfire."

"I'm sure that he simply forgot."

"Oh, thanks for trying, Pixie, but I've learned over the years that guys don't dig girls who have psychic powers." M. J. closed her eyes and swallowed. "I had just hoped that he would be different."

"He *is* different! He's your danged soul mate."

"Yeah, well, here's the thing. Soul mates pass each other on the street every day, which is a crying shame. But even if you're lucky enough to find your soul mate, you still havta want the relationship. Even though I could feel that Brody was attracted to me he was fighting it tooth and nail. I'd bet everything I own that it's the psychic thing that turned him off." M. J. refrained from explaining just *how* attracted Brody had been to her during their steamy shower encounter.

"I hear giving-up noises coming from you, Mary

Jane Barone! I thought a girl from Brooklyn would be made of sterner stuff."

M. J. thought about this for a moment. Finally, she straightened her shoulders and said, "You know something, Pixie? You're right. I am!"

Pixie flitted around in a happy circle. "Now, that's what I'm talkin' about. Woohooie! Now go for it."

"But I don't know Brody's number or where he's staying. That's not likely to be common knowledge, since he's a celebrity."

Pixie stopped in midtwirl and hovered in the air. "Well, duh, you *are* a psychic, are you not?"

"Yeah, but—"

"No buts! You can do this, Mary Jane. Use your gift. You deserve to be happy too."

"Pixie, am I ever going to find out who you really are? Where'd you come from, anyway?"

The bright little light faded, but M. J. could hear the gruff laughter and then the cryptic words, "Patience is a virtue, girlie. All in due time."

M. J. sighed. Her life certainly had taken a wild turn since her move to Nashville. It had been a whim, nothing more than blind intuition based on that weird dream that she had been singing a duet with Patsy Cline. Maybe she had it all wrong. "Could that shaggy-haired singin' cowboy really be the one?"

"You talking to yourself again?"

M. J. turned around at the sound of Savannah Parks's voice. "Hey there."

"Hey there? I do believe you're trying to talk

Southern. But you have to say it like *hay*, not *hey*. I hope I didn't startle you. Your front door was open."

M. J. laughed. She really liked Savannah, the younger sister of Logan, who owned the bar next door. Shy but friendly Savannah was the opposite of her outgoing brother. "What brings ya over here?"

Savannah held up two fingers. "First I wanted to let you know that I'm singing at the bar tonight about eight o'clock. Second," she said, and clasped her hands, "guess who just told me that I have a golden voice."

"Brody Baker?"

Savannah's blue eyes opened wide. "Wow, those powers of yours are amazing. He was at the bar to do an interview and I had been rehearsing when he walked in."

M. J. just laughed, thinking that it was too complicated to attempt to explain. "I'll come on over after I close up. Savannah, you have a soulful and yet powerful voice. You're gonna be a star."

"Really? Is this a psychic prediction?"

M. J. shook her head. "Nah, this is simply my opinion from hearing you sing."

"Oh."

She seemed disappointed, so M. J. said, "Look, I know your brother doesn't exactly approve of my shop, but come on over if you want to and I'll read your cards. No charge."

Savannah wrinkled up her nose. "Logan can be so stuffy sometimes. By the way, he likes *you* even if he is a skeptic." She tipped up a can and took a long drink.

"What are you drinkin'?"

"Slim-Fast."

"You don't need to diet."

Savannah pursed her lips. "Yeah, I do. I can never seem to shed these stubborn fifteen pounds. It doesn't help that I'm so darned short. You know, country stars nowadays have to not only be good singers but be sexy too." She sighed. "Shania Twain I'm not."

"Oh, come on. You're a cutie!"

Savannah rolled her eyes. "I don't need to be cute. I need to be smokin' hot. Doggone Logan sucked up all of the tall, athletic, outgoing Parks genes, leaving me short, pudgy and shy. Not a good combo for becoming a star."

M. J. wagged a finger at her. "Yeah, but can Logan sing?

"Oh, he sucks!"

"Well, if it's any consolation, I've got a gorgeous, outgoing athletic brother too."

"Is he psychic like you and your sister?"

"No, and he doesn't want to be. He's the only normal one in the family, or abnormal, depending on how you look at it." Pouring herself another cup of coffee, M. J. said, "It wasn't easy for him growing up in working-class Brooklyn with a psychic family. My parents run this little shop where they sell a variety of books on the paranormal, lotions, potions, candles and so forth. Lucio always wished that we owned a butcher shop instead."

"So what does he do?"

"He's a personal trainer. Darn, I wish he lived around here."

"Ohmigawd, me with a personal trainer? I'd trip over my own two feet." Savannah crooked one eyebrow. "Oh, I just bet your brother is a hottie."

"Well, let's put it this way: He's graced the cover of a few fitness magazines."

"Wow."

"Yeah, and he goes through women like water through a sieve."

Savannah wrinkled her nose. "Ew, a womanizer?"

"No, he's not like that. Women chase after *him*. But he can't ever seem to find someone who captivates him." M. J. was about to go on when Savannah suddenly looked a bit uncomfortable. "Hey, are you okay?"

"I'm fine," Savannah said with a shaky little laugh.

"You can tell me if something is bothering you, Savannah."

"No . . . really . . ." She shrugged. "Something kind of weird just hit me."

"Do I need to remind you that there isn't anything weird that is likely to faze me?"

Savannah swallowed and then said in a whisper, "I just got the strongest feeling that my deceased grandma was here in the room with me. Can you, *you know*, talk to her or something?"

"I'm sorry, Savannah. I'm not a medium. That's my sista's expertise."

"Really?"

"Yes. She's promised to come in for a visit. If she does, I'm sure she could help you contact your grandma."

"Logan would have a fit," she answered with a groan.

"Uh, no offense, Savannah, but you don't need his permission."

"I know. Ever since Mom and Dad retired to Florida and left Logan to run the bar, he thinks that he has to parent me. He just doesn't get that I'm almost twenty-three years old."

"I'm sorry. I shouldn't be butting into your family business."

Savannah shook her head. "Not only are you right, but you're my friend."

"Yes, we certainly are friends and I value that, but feel free to tell me not to be a buttinsky."

Savannah nodded. "So, you're coming to hear me sing tonight, right?"

"Ya betta believe it."

"Speaking of that, I'd better get going. I'm sure Brody Baker is finished with his interview by now and I need to rehearse."

M. J. felt a warm tingle at the mere mention of his name. "Uh, do you know if Brody Baker lives in Nashville?" She tried to keep her tone casual.

Savannah shrugged. "I think I heard him tell Logan that he recently bought a farm about an hour from here, but then again I thought I heard him mention a hotel. Why do you ask?"

M. J. felt a blush warm her face.

"Oh, I get it. You're a fan. Hey, Logan might be able to get you an autograph. Do you want me to ask?"

"Oh, no . . . *no*." She waved her hands in protest. I was just curious."

"Yeah, right." Savannah wagged her eyebrows. "I heard that Brody's going to be in town for a while promoting his new single. He always comes to the bar to hang out. Logan usually gets him to sing at least one song. Maybe you'll get lucky and he'll drop by tonight."

"Yeah, maybe I'll get lucky." Oh, *that* would be something.

"Don't be afraid to approach him. He and Logan have been friends for a long time. Brody's a really good guy . . . a little crazy but nice." She looked at her watch. "I've really got to go."

M. J. followed Savannah to the door and locked it. Since she didn't open until noon, she still had a couple of hours to kill. With a nervous little shiver, she knew that she was going to utilize the time by concentrating on finding Brody. "Oh, but if I figure it out, what excuse am I gonna use for showin' up on his doorstep?"

M. J. looked around the kitchen for the familiar flickering light. Usually talking to herself was like an open invitation for Pixie to show up, but the room remained quiet. All of a sudden M. J. spotted Brody's black hat beneath the table where it must have slid to the floor. "There's my answer."

She supposed that if her powers failed her, she could ask Logan if he knew where Brody was staying, but she really didn't want to go that route. Plus, M. J. figured that if she was able to *see* where Brody was staying, it would be another sign that the cowboy was indeed *the one*. With that in mind, she headed to her bedroom with a notepad and pen. After pulling the shades down, M. J. sat on the bed and eased back against the huge mound of pillows. She took a cleansing breath, closed her eyes and let her powers go to work.

For a few minutes she got *nothing* but then realized

that she was just too nervous. Determined, though, M. J. concentrated on breathing deeply. Starting with her feet, she tensed her muscles and then let them relax until she got a boneless, weightless out-of-body feeling that let her mind take over. Images started materializing in misty black-and-white fog, but just out of reach. M. J. sifted through the fog looking for clues. Finally, the initial *M* became clear and then a door with the number 508. Quickly, she jotted this down on paper.

Then, M. J. saw the interior of a room. The drapes were drawn, letting in only a slice of sunshine. She spotted a desk and a nightstand next to a huge bed. Creeping closer, M. J. realized that she wasn't just seeing the room but feeling as if she were actually *there*.

And a man was sleeping beneath the covers.

With a thumping heart she knew that that man was Brody Baker. Although she didn't know exactly where she was, she had found her man. And she couldn't take her eyes off Brody.

With a sigh he rolled onto his back, causing the sheet to slide to his waist. M. J. had to suppress a moan when a mound of clothing on the floor confirmed what she already sensed. Brody Baker was naked. Feeling a little guilty at this invasion of his privacy, M. J. knew she should try to identify his location and exit the room . . . oh, but then he shifted, causing the sheet to dip farther south. Unable to help herself, M. J. crept closer and her breath caught at the sight of him.

His shaggy blond hair was bed-head sexy, but he looked younger and a bit more vulnerable in his sleep. Dark blond stubble, though, shadowing his cheeks was pure masculine beauty and in stark contrast with the soft fullness of his mouth. Her eyes were drawn to the slow rise and fall of his chest—hard muscle without too much bulk and lightly dusted with tawny hair. M. J. thought that he was sheer perfection and had to sigh. When he stirred she wondered if he could sense her presence.

Her fingers itched to stroke his bare skin. Swallowing her nervousness, she inched forward, but when Brody suddenly mumbled and stirred, M. J. put her hand to her mouth and froze in her tracks. Well, she didn't suppose she actually had tracks because she wasn't here in body, was she? Still, she couldn't leave until she touched him. Maybe a kiss would do something wild and special. A little kiss wouldn't hurt, would it? What was the harm in that?

*B*rody sighed in his sleep when he felt something warm and soft touch his lips. With a moan, he opened his mouth for more, but just as quickly the feeling was gone. He shifted, searching, *needing* the sensation to return. Oh, but then a light tickling sensation trailed across his chest . . . fingers, tendrils of hair? Wanting more, Brody tried to lift his arms, but he felt trapped in some sort of limbo between slumber and wakefulness. A familiar perfume, floral and exotic, filtered into his semiconsciousness, stirring his senses. With a sigh, Brody sank into the delicious dream, welcoming the silky heat that seemed to caress his entire body. He became aroused, hot and thick against the smooth cotton sheet. Moaning, he arched up from the mattress, seeking the source of this sensual assault.

And then Brody heard a soft tinkling sound near his ear . . . bracelets . . . ? "Mary Jane?" With his heart thumping, he struggled to open his eyes. He felt pressure and the sensation of a warm body on top of his . . . but how? This was too real for a dream and yet he couldn't seem to wake up. Suddenly, he felt the sweet pressure of soft lips pressed against his.

What was happening?

With a groan Brody struggled to open his eyes and then pushed up to a sitting position. A shriek and a thump had him instantly alert. Brody squinted in the dark room and then flicked on the light. After jumping to his feet, he scrubbed a hand across his face and muttered, "What the hell just happened?"

"Darned if I know."

Startled, Brody looked down. "M-Mary Jane?"

"Yes?" she answered meekly, and was blushing to the roots of her hair.

"How did you get in here?"

"I . . . um—" She swallowed. "I'm not sure."

"Not sure?" Brody stared down at her. "What do you mean, you're not sure?"

Blinking up at him, she stuttered, "I—I was only t-trying t-to find you . . . but not . . . not *literally*. But when I kissed you I was suddenly, well, *here*."

"Suddenly here? I'm confused."

"You're, um, also naked."

"God." Brody glanced down at his big boner and grabbed a pillow to shield himself. "Now tell me who let you in here."

"No one," she said as she pushed herself up on her elbows.

"Yeah, right." Brody narrowed his eyes at her. "So you just materialized out of thin air?"

Her eyes rounded and she looked at her hands as if surprised. "Y-yes, I suppose I did. After we kissed. *Wow . . .* "

"Oh pul-ease. Listen, if you have any pictures, hand them over. I'd hate to have you arrested." He shook his head, thoroughly disappointed. "I had a much higher opinion of you, Mary Jane. Now, tell me who the hell let you in my room. Heads are gonna roll over this one."

With an outraged gasp, M. J. scrambled to her feet. "I don't have any pictures!" Stretching her arms akimbo, she said, "Frisk me if ya want to!"

God help him, he wanted to rub his hands over her delectable body but for reasons other than frisking her. His damned dick twitched behind the pillow at the thought. Angry with himself, he lashed out, "Okay then, so what were you doing in my bed? Hoping to brag to your friends?"

"Of course not! How could ya say such a thing?"

"What am I supposed to think?" He threw his hands up in the air and the pillow slid to the floor.

With a shriek M. J. put her hands over her eyes. "Look," she said quietly, "I've invaded your privacy and for that, I'm sorry. I won't breathe a word of this to anyone. Good-bye, Brody." With her hands still covering her eyes, she turned toward the door. "I'm sorry," she repeated in a shaky tone.

"Wait," Brody pleaded. Feeling like a heel, he tried to think of something redeeming to say, but the words died on his lips when he looked at the door. "I hooked the chain through the lock. I remember. I did. I—I know that I did." He blinked at the locked door for a moment. "How *did* you get in here?"

M. J. swallowed. How could she explain something that she didn't understand? "Um . . ." She was trying to think of a plausible explanation, but Brody chose that moment to turn and look at the window, exposing his bare backside to her. How she could be admiring his very fine bum under these crazy circumstances was beyond her, but wow, it was nice . . . muscular and firm. She angled her head for a better look.

"We're on the fifth floor, so . . . hey, were you checking out my ass?"

"No!" She knew her face was flaming. "I can't help it if you're parading around naked."

"It's my doggone room."

"Still . . ."

"Oh, I get it." Brody chuckled and then pointed at her. "I'm being punked. Come on out, Kutcher!" He looked around. "Where's the camera?"

"Um, there's no camera."

"Yeah, right," Brody scoffed while backing up toward his clothes. M. J. averted her gaze while he tugged on his pants. "So who's behind this, anyway? Travis? Logan? Come on. Fess up. Wow, I have to admit that this is good."

"Brody, I know this is hard to believe. I mean, even I'm having a hard time with this, but I'm telling ya, I was concentrating really hard on locating you, getting foggy bits and pieces, a few clues . . . but then . . ." M. J. bit her bottom lip, reluctant to reveal the rest.

"Go on." He folded his arms across his chest and

waited, the very essence of a rather amused nonbeliever. This wasn't going to be easy.

"Okay, but do you mind if I sit down?"

A flicker of concern crossed Brody's face and he gestured toward the bed. "Sure."

"Thanks." M. J. didn't realize how wobbly her legs were until she crossed the room and sort of collapsed onto the mattress with a little bounce.

"You okay?"

M. J. nodded, but she realized that she wasn't anywhere close to being okay. Her hands trembled at the thought of trying to convince Brody that she had vaporized from her apartment and somehow materialized in his room. He was going to think she was insane.

Maybe she was insane. Or maybe this was a dream and she'd wake up any moment now in her own bed. Taking a deep breath, she closed her eyes and hoped to be snuggled up beneath her comforter. When that didn't work she did the old pinching-herself trick. "Ouch."

"What in the world are you doing?" He stared at her as if she were wacko.

"I was tryin' to pinch myself awake."

The looking-at-her-like-she-was-wacko expression intensified.

"Quit looking at me like that."

"Like what?"

"Like I'm a nutcase."

"You just tried to convince me that you somehow appeared in my room. How am I supposed to react?"

Okay, he had a point. "I think I should just go."

"Oh, no, you don't. I deserve an explanation. If this

isn't a prank or some sort of groupie-stalking thing, then just what the hell is going on here? Just what are you up to, Mary Jane Barone?"

"I'm not up to anything!" She sprang to her feet. "I can't explain what happened because I don't know!"

"Maybe . . . ," he began, but couldn't come up with anything remotely plausible. "Maybe you were sleep-walking? My sister used to do that."

"But how did I find you? And how did I get in here?" M. J. shook her head but then looked him in the eye. "Look, psychic phenomena can't be explained. But Brody, our minds, our spirit . . . our *hearts* are so much more powerful than we know. Sometimes you have to take a leap of faith and simply believe."

Instead of answering, he looked around the room.

"What are you doing?"

"Looking for the camera."

M. J. felt her heart sink and her anger rise. "There's no damned camera!" Taking a step closer to him, she said, "Just for the record, you wanted me here."

"What?"

She poked him in the chest. "You heard me. You were thinking of me, or the connection wouldn't have been so powerful just like in the—" She stopped and clamped a hand over her mouth.

"In the *what*?" First he squinted and then his eyes went wide and his eyebrows shot up. "Holy shit . . . in the shower?" He swallowed and took a step backward. "You were . . . that was . . . ? *No!*" His Adam's apple bobbed and his mouth moved, but nothing came out. Finally in a husky voice he said, "So it *was* you?"

Feeling heat in her cheeks, M. J. nodded.

"I tried to tell myself that I was imagining you, or maybe still drunk. . . . Hell, I don't know." He ran his fingers through his hair. "But you *were* in the shower. With me. I could feel you . . . hot and misty, and yet you weren't really there . . . physically, were you?" He took another step backward and came up against the wall. "Are you a witch or something? How in the hell did you do that to me? How did you get in *here*?" He glanced at the latched door and then back to her. "Did you drug my coffee? Mix something into my eggs?"

"You wanted me here, Brody. You were thinking about me."

"Yeah, I was thinking about you." He flushed a little. "I admit it. But I was thinking about how I'd like a cheeseburger earlier and one didn't just appear in my hands. So now you're trying to tell me that I conjured you up like a genie in a bottle? That this is somehow my doing?"

"Stop shouting."

"I wasn't shouting, Mary Jane."

"It felt like it. And don't call me Mary Jane. Only my mother calls me that." She felt ridiculously close to tears.

His expression softened, making her feel even closer to crying. "What should I call you?" He took a step forward and she took a step back.

"Nothing." She backed up another step and her legs hit the edge of the bed. "This is all wrong," she whispered more to herself than to him. "Some sort of cosmic wires must have gotten crossed."

"What are you muttering about? What wires?" He glanced around the room and then narrowed his eyes at her. "You're wired? Taping this whole thing? I knew it! So this *is* a prank."

M. J. gasped. She wasn't quick to anger, but when she did get pissed she was hell on wheels. And now she was pissed. With a little shriek she stepped forward and actually took a swing at him.

"What the . . . ?" Brody ducked as her fist whizzed past his head. "Are you crazy?"

"Don't call me that!" M. J. took another swing and connected with his shoulder, making her bracelets jingle and her wrist throb. "Ouch!" she shouted, grabbing her hand, but a little pain didn't stop her from swinging again. "Damn!" She realized that she was hurting herself more than him, but she didn't care. "I'm not crazy! I get so sick of being called that." Sort of *not* proving her point, she started swinging with both fists, coming up mostly with air. She knew she was being unreasonable, but M. J. had been taunted and teased about her powers and her psychic family since childhood. She mostly shrugged or sometimes even laughed it off, but coming from Brody, it hurt so damned much that she just lost it.

"Ow!" Brody hissed when she landed a punch to his gut. "Stop!"

"Oh, God, did it really hurt?" She put a hand to her mouth.

"Well, yeah, a little." He rubbed where she'd hit him. "What the hell is wrong with you? First you break into my room and now you attack me."

Her remorse vanished in a flash. "I didn't break into your room. And there is *nothing* wrong with me!" She swung again, but this time he was ready for her and grabbed both of her flailing fists. Not one to give up, she tried to knee him in the groin.

"Why, you little hellcat!" He sounded surprised and a little amused. It somehow pissed her off even more that he wasn't taking her seriously. She sensed that he still thought this was some sort of elaborate joke.

"You big . . ." She twisted her wrists while trying to come up with a name vile enough, but sputtered a lame, "Jerk!"

"Calm down and I'll let you go," he offered in a voice laced with laughter. "Then you can tell me who put you up to this. There must be electronics involved . . . computers."

"I'm not a damned hologram, Brody. I'm real," M. J. ground out through clenched teeth while trying to ignore the fact that her breasts were crushed to his chest and that he smelled really good. Frustrated in more ways than one, she yanked her wrists away from him, sending them off-balance and tumbling backward onto the bed with a big bounce. Brody landed on top, squishing her into the mattress. "Get off of me," she tried to shout, but her words came out muffled against his chest. Silky hair tickled her nose and she tasted salty-sweet skin. "Move this minute," she attempted, but the effect was more like she was licking his chest and moaning than speaking.

"Sorry . . . what the . . . ?" He shifted and she suddenly had a nipple against her tongue.

Good God.

This time she bucked her hips instead of trying to speak, sending him a different message via his lower anatomy. "Let me up," she said, totally licking his nipple.

Sucking in a breath, he said, "So instead of hitting me you're licking me? Boy, you're fickle."

"I'm not licking you!"

"Kissing me, then?"

"My mouth is pressed against your chest! Let me up, damn it, or I'm gonna bite you!"

Chapter Six

"You wouldn't dare," Brody challenged. A sharp nip at his chest was her answer. "Ouch," he complained, but in fact it turned him on. "Tell me who put you up to this and I'll let you go." She nipped at him again and bucked her hips. "Okay, that's it. Nobody bites Brody Baker and gets away with it."

"Oh really? Just whadaya gonna do 'bout it?" Her chest was heaving like she had run a marathon. Color rose high in her cheeks and her dark hair was in wild disarray. Brody had never seen anything sexier.

"Maybe I'll bite you back." Transferring both of her wrists into one of his hands, he tugged them above her head. Arching one eyebrow, he said, "Then again, I think I might just have to kiss you."

"Let me go, ya big . . . bully!" She glared up at him, but her dilated pupils indicated that she wasn't as opposed to the idea as she pretended to be. Brody didn't know how or why she was here in his room, but she was right about one thing.

He wanted her there.

When he dipped his head slightly she warned, "Don't you even think about it." She would have been more convincing if her voice hadn't been thick with desire.

"Okay, maybe I'll do this instead." He unbuttoned the top button of her billowy blouse.

"I'm gonna scream," she threatened, but arched her back and moaned when he nuzzled her neck. "I m-mean it."

"Oh really?" Brody unbuttoned another button, revealing the crest of her breasts. "I hope so."

"Why, you arrogant—," she began, but sucked in a breath when he kissed and nibbled on her neck. "I didn't mean . . . oh, stop . . . right this *mmmm*-minute. Don't you dare . . . ohhh!"

With a low moan Brody tugged on her earlobe with his teeth while he made quick work of the rest of her buttons. When he felt her body relax he trailed kisses over to her mouth. He kissed her deeply, melting into the moment while feeling an intense reaction that went well beyond sexual desire. He didn't just want her; he needed her.

But not like this. Not in anger or frustration. Reluctantly ending the kiss, Brody released her hands and rolled sideways to his hip. Bending his elbow, he propped his head up with his hand and gazed down at her.

"Wassamatta?" she asked in a husky voice that had Brody wanting to kiss her all over again.

"You told me to stop."

She swallowed and gazed at him in confusion.

"You meant it, right?"

"Of course," M. J. lied. She averted her gaze from his knowing eyes. "Oh . . . sorry," she said when she noticed the small red bite mark near his nipple.

"For what?"

"B-biting you."

"I deserved it."

"I should go, Brody."

He tucked a finger beneath her chin, gently forcing her to look at him. "Do you really want to leave?"

M. J. hesitated to answer. She could feel confusion and disbelief rolling off of him in waves. But stronger than his skepticism was a deep longing that took her breath away. He wanted her. He needed her. Maybe, just *maybe*, if she stayed and made love to him, it would be so magical that he would have to believe . . .

But what if he didn't?

M. J. sighed. If he didn't, then at least she would have this memory to keep, to treasure. After all, most people weren't lucky enough to ever find their soul mate, so if making love to him right here, right now, was all she ever had, then she'd better take it.

Okay, that's a bunch of hooey. Admittedly it was a sad and sucky thought, but M. J. decided that was better than running away. "Call me M. J."

"What?"

"You wanted to know what to call me," she said shyly.

"M. J." He nodded. "It suits you . . . feisty and cute. So, M. J., may I kiss you?"

She nodded, whispering, "Yes."

With a slow smile he dipped his head and captured her mouth in a tender kiss that made her throat tighten with unshed tears. Anger was much easier to deal with than tenderness. And God, now she was nervous. This might be her only shot to impress him in the sack.

Gawd. She searched her brain for lovemaking skills and came up blank.

"Why are you frowning?"

"I'm not frowning."

"M. J., it looks like you're trying to solve a math problem in your head." He rubbed his fingertip over her bottom lip. "We don't have to do this if you're not ready."

She knew he was being a gentleman, but his voice held just enough impatience to tick her off. "I'm *ready.*"

"Okay, now you sound pissed."

"Maybe *you're* not ready," she challenged, lifting her head from the bed for emphasis. He moved against her so that she could feel the steely hardness of his erection. "Okay, I stand corrected."

He laughed. "So if you're ready and I'm ready, just what are we waiting for?"

Oh, this was so much easier when she was invisible. She closed her eyes and swallowed. "Just kiss me, Brody."

"Now you're talkin'." Brody dipped his head and captured her lips in a long heated kiss. He realized then that she wasn't some seasoned groupie. She trembled beneath his touch, making him want to say soothing words in her ear. "You taste so sweet . . . smell so good . . . you're driving me nuts." Okay, that wasn't exactly smooth, but damn, he was just a good ol' boy from Texas. He must have been doin' something right, though, because she sighed and arched her back so that her breasts grazed his chest. "You know you're wearin' way too many clothes." With a flick of his wrist he unhooked the front clasp of her bra. "God . . ."

Her eyes flew open. "What's wrong?"

"Your breasts are beautiful." He cupped them in his hands. "So full, so soft . . . ," he murmured, and then dipped his head and took a nipple in his mouth.

"Ya know, you're right."

"That your breasts are beautiful?" He pulled back and gave her an amused grin.

She laughed. "No. That I'm wearing way too many clothes."

Brody grinned. She seemed to be relaxing. "You take care of that while I take care of business."

"Business?"

"Protection."

"Oh . . . sure, protection." She blushed, making Brody realize that this wasn't something that she normally did. He headed to the bathroom and fumbled around for a condom. He was so excited and nervous that he could hardly get the damned thing on. It had been a while since he had been with a woman . . . quite a while. He had been trying to settle down, concentrate on his music, hell, just grow up. But still, this felt different. She was different. Brody paused and then scrubbed a hand down his face. Okay, that was an understatement. The woman was a psychic, or so she thought. She had also claimed that she sort of vaporized into his room . . . *so just what was he doing making love to her?* She was a nutcase. With a long sigh he put his forehead against the cool mirror and wondered what the hell to do. He felt such a strong connection to this woman and yet he couldn't risk his career by getting involved with someone so *out there.*

M. J. waited stark naked in the middle of the bed practicing what she hoped were seductive poses. Finally, she realized that Brody was taking way too long to simply roll on a condom. Staring at the closed door, she concentrated on trying to pick up his emotions. It took only a second to discover a mixed bag of feelings, the strongest of which was regret. He no longer wanted her there.

Oh no . . . he wanted her *gone.*

And here she was trying to decide if a smile or a pout was sexier. Oh God. She put her hands to her cheeks. "Oh God, oh God, *oh Gawd.*" Scooting to a very unsexy on-all-fours position, she looked down at her pile of clothing on the floor. "Oh, Scotty, please beam me up," she whispered, wishing it was that easy.

To her surprise, M. J. suddenly felt a tingling sensation in her fingers. The feeling radiated all the way to her toes, making her body began to feel light, like she was made of foam. Through a misty fog she saw Brody open the bathroom door wrapped in a towel. He looked over at the bed and gasped her name.

And then everything faded to black.

Chapter Seven

"What the . . . ?" Brody stared at the bed with his mouth hanging open while M. J. faded to a silvery white and then vanished.

Vanished!

And didn't she just ask Scotty to beam her up?

Brody stood there for God knew how long blinking at the empty bed while trying to let it all sink in. Finally his legs gave out and he slid to the floor. "What the hell?" He swallowed and ran his fingers through his hair while repeating, "What the hell just happened here?"

If this was a prank, it was of David Blaine quality. With a frown he reached over and picked up her white blouse, evidence that she *had* been in the room. The floral scent of her perfume lingered, filling his head and rekindling his desire. He twisted around and saw that the door was still locked. "Maybe I'm suffering from exhaustion," he mumbled. Tapping his head, he said, "Think, man, think. There's got to be an explanation."

Of course no explanation filtered into his brain because there was none.

Brody remembered that M. J. had said that psychic phenomena had no explanation, but that you just had to take a leap of faith and simply believe. "Maybe I should . . . ," he whispered, but then tossed her blouse to the floor. "Yeah, right. I'm being played." Pushing up to his feet, he stomped over to his clothes and tugged on his jeans. He located a hotel plastic laundry bag and stuffed M. J.'s clothing into it. With a muscle ticking in his jaw he headed out of the room and jabbed his thumb onto the elevator button. He and Ms. Mary Jane Barone were going to have a heart-to-heart and she was going to come clean and explain all of this psychic bull once and for all.

Blinking in the afternoon sunlight, he headed over to Broadway, hardly nodding to a few people who recognized him. Normally he would smile at the sounds and sights of downtown Nashville and maybe pop into Tootsie's or the Stage for a beer and to listen to the country-star hopefuls who played all day long for tips from tourists. But today he walked with his head down as his feet ate up the pavement. He came to a stop at the Psychic Love Connection and took a deep breath. The sign on the door read CLOSED, so he headed around to the back door to M. J.'s apartment. Taking another deep breath, he raised his fist and rapped sharply on her door.

Brody waited, tapping the toe of his boot on the concrete. When M. J. failed to answer he knocked again and then pressed a doorbell that he hadn't noticed. Nothing. Frustrated, he stepped closer to the door and peeked between the gap in the curtains. He felt a bit foolish doing this, but he wanted some answers and he had the sneaking suspicion that M. J. was home. He rang and knocked and buzzed the bell again and waited.

"Ah, damn," Brody muttered. With a sigh he thought about leaving, but something compelled him to turn the doorknob. He was so surprised when it opened that for a moment he simply stood there. Thinking that it was odd that the door would be unlocked but that M. J. wouldn't answer his persistent knocking, Brody silently crept into the kitchen. His gaze flicked over to the table, where a fat candle burned, sending the scent of vanilla curling into the air. Alarm fluttered in his chest at the thought that M. J. could have come to some kind of harm. He was about to call out her name when he heard her shout at someone.

"No, I won't! Oh, don't even go there!"

Brody charged down the short hallway and burst into a small bedroom with his fists cocked. Adrenaline pumped into his system. Anyone who tried to hurt her would be one sorry sucker.

M. J. screamed at the sound of him entering her bedroom. Still screaming, she picked up the closest available weapon, which, fortunately for Brody, happened to be a stuffed animal. Whirling around, she winged the big purple pig at him. It bounced off of his head, but she had a huge supply of pillows and a stuffed menagerie at her disposal. She kept them coming one after another, in rapid-fire succession. A pink teddy bear, then a monkey, followed by a heart-shaped pillow.

"M. J., stop! Look up, damn it! It's me, Brody!"

M. J. was in the middle of a full swing with a big feather pillow, so the law of motion kept her going and she smacked Brody in the head so hard that he fell sideways onto the bed. Several white feathers burst from the seam and floated through the air in gentle contrast with her onslaught. Finally realizing who the intruder was, M. J. said, "Oh my Gawd, did I hurt you?" She peered down at him.

"I'll live," he said with a sigh. "Remind me to wear a cup when I'm around you."

"Oh, did I hit you *there*?" She put her hand over her mouth and made the mistake of gazing at his crotch.

"Yeah, with a big purple thing."

"Oh, Charlie. My stuffed pig."

He picked up a green monkey. "These things have names?"

M. J. grabbed it from him and hugged it to her chest. "Yes. My parents were fortune-tellers at many a carnival. My daddy won these for me. I named them when I was a child, so stop giving me that *She's crazy* look again."

"I'm not giving you that look."

She narrowed her eyes. "Are too." She thought about throwing Pete, the green monkey, at him but refrained. "What are you doing here?"

He gave her a guilty look but didn't answer.

"Oh, I get it. You came to demand answers."

His guilt became more pronounced, but he came up to his elbows and said, "As a matter of fact, *yes*. I do believe you owe me one."

"I don't owe ya a thing, cowboy. And by the way, how did you get in here?"

"I knocked, but you didn't answer. The back door was open."

M. J. frowned. "No, it wasn't. I'm sure I locked it."

"Unlike you, I don't have the *power* to materialize into someone's place. I came in through the back door!"

"Keep your sarcastic comments to yourself!" M. J. threw Pete at him. "Really? Well, let's just see. Follow me." She stormed away from him and into the kitchen. She heard the click of his boot heels on the tile floor behind her. Stopping in the doorway of the kitchen, M. J. pointed to the back door.

"Holy shit." The dead bolt was clearly locked. "B-but I came in through the damned door and didn't lock it behind me." He took a couple of deep breaths. "What the hell is going on here, M. J.?" he asked in a hushed voice. "How did I walk in here through a locked door?"

She turned around to face him. "With some help, I suspect."

"From who?"

"Pixie."

"Just who is Pixie?"

"I'm not quite sure. She won't tell me."

"She won't tell you . . . ?" Brody shook his head.

"You're givin' me the *look* again."

Brody lifted his hands skyward. "Do you blame me? Damn it, woman, you could try the patience of Job! Now, give me some answers. This prank or game or whatever the hell it is has gone way too far. I want the truth."

M. J. had to bite her bottom lip to keep it from trembling, but that didn't keep a tear from sliding down her cheek. Soul mate or not, this was never going to work.

"Oh, no, you don't. Waterworks don't move me," he tried to say in a stern voice. Bullshit. Seeing her cry tore at his gut. "Just tell me what's going on here, M. J." Taking a step closer, he gently swiped at a tear. With a shaky intake of breath she leaned her cheek into his palm, and God help him, in spite of it all he just had to kiss her.

Brody lowered his head and captured her mouth with a soft, sweet kiss. Her lips trembled, but she accepted him, wrapped her arms around him, melting into his embrace. He could feel the heat of her skin through the silky robe she wore and he wanted nothing more than to slip the robe over her shoulders and make passionate love to her.

But first, they needed to talk.

Brody reluctantly pulled his mouth from hers. "I've never wanted a woman more than I want you, M. J., but I'm having a hard time comprehending all of this. Help me understand what's going on here, okay?"

Splaying her hands on his chest, she looked up at him. "Okay, but first I want you to open your heart and your mind. Believe me when I say that I'm not playing any games. This isn't a prank, Brody. Ya gotta trust me on this, please."

Brody looked into her luminous brown eyes and saw sincerity. "I trust you."

She gave him a smile that went straight to his heart and then she grabbed his hand. "Okay, then, let's go sit down and talk." She tugged him into a small living room and gestured toward a faded floral-print sofa. "The place came furnished," she said, wrinkling her nose.

"It's okay," he lied as he sat down on the lumpy cushion.

"I didn't want you to think this was my taste." She made a sweeping gesture with her arm, causing her breasts to jiggle beneath the silky green robe.

"Um, you might want to take that robe off if we intend to get anywhere."

M. J.'s eyes widened. "Off?"

"Okay, that didn't come out right. What I meant . . . at least what I meant to *say* is that maybe you need to change into something less distracting."

"Or maybe we can talk later." Her cheeks turned a rosy shade of pink. "Oh my *Gawd*." *I can't believe I said that* was written all over her face, but she stood her ground. "I have this really bad habit of voicing my inner thoughts."

Brody swallowed and then said, "Honesty is a good thing in my book." He needed answers, wanted explanations . . . but more than that, he needed *her*. "Come here," he said gruffly. When she stepped closer Brody reached out and tugged on the ends of the green sash holding her robe together. Threading his fingers through the silk, he untied the knot and then slid his hands around her waist, parting the edges of the material as he drew her to him. As he had suspected, she was naked beneath the green silk. She drew in a shaky breath but didn't protest.

"You're beautiful, M. J.," he said, and then ran his hands up her thighs and encircled her waist again, pulling her even closer.

"Do you think so, Brody? Truly?" She caught her bottom lip between her teeth while pulling the edges of her robe together. "Oh, there I go again . . . thinking out loud."

Angling his head, Brody said, "You have no idea how appealing you are, do you?" When M. J. lowered her eyes Brody lifted her chin with his finger. "Do you?" he repeated more forcefully. M. J. shook her head while blinking rapidly like she might burst into tears. "Hey, what did I say?"

With a smile that trembled around the edges she said, "No one has ever called me beautiful before, Brody. Well, except for my mother and father and my nana, but they don't count."

"I find that hard to believe."

"Yeah, right, Mr. Blond and Leggy." When he frowned at her she did a little head bop and added, "That's what ya said ya wanted, remember?" She nudged his shoulder and tried to smile but didn't quite make it.

"I want *you*," Brody said, surprised at the emotion he felt while saying it. He pulled her onto his lap and threaded his fingers through her fabulous mane of hair.

"But—" She searched his face while unanswered questions hung between them.

He put a finger to her lips. "Shhh. We'll talk later."

Dipping his head, he captured her mouth in a heart-pounding kiss—slow, sweet, deep and then hungry. He soon had her beneath him on the sofa. The green silk fell open, baring soft skin to kiss, nibble and suckle. Leaning against the back of the sofa, he let his hand slide up her smooth thigh and skim ever so lightly over her mound . . . back and forth featherlight until she shivered and arched her back.

"Open up for me, M. J.," Brody coaxed. She answered by parting her legs. While watching her face, Brody increased the pressure, letting one finger delve into her wet heat. He slid his finger slowly in and out, deeper and then deeper still, until with a long, throaty sigh M. J.'s eyes fluttered shut. With his drenched finger he circled her clitoris lightly . . . barely touching her until she whimpered and then thrust her hips in search of relief.

"Brody . . ." Her plea was throaty and desperate, but instead of giving her what she wanted, Brody stilled his hand and turned his attention to her breasts. He laved one nipple and then the other, licking and tasting in slow circles. Her perfume, her scent, floral and musky, filled his head.

Brody was painfully hard, straining against his jeans, but all that mattered now was giving her exquisite pleasure. While Brody had never had any complaints from women, this intense desire to please her first was new. Normally he would already be taking care of business, but with M. J. he wanted to make being with him special—no . . . make that *unforgettable—so that no other man could measure up*. When that thought registered in his brain, it rocked him to the core. But before he could dwell on the intensity of his feelings for a woman he barely knew—a woman who claimed to be psychic, for God's sake—he needed to hear her cry of pleasure.

"*B*rody . . . *please*," M. J. shamelessly pleaded, but her body felt as if she were a bow stretched to the limit, needing the arrow to be released. Brody's hot mouth and softly abrasive tongue circled her nipple as he slipped his finger into her once again. She arched her back and felt as if she were being pulled even tighter as her desire mounted even higher. Then, when she felt as if she couldn't stand it any longer, he nipped at her sensitive nipple while caressing her clitoris. Intense pleasure, hot and sweet, unfurled and then soared. When she cried out Brody leaned in and kissed her deeply as if pleasing her was all that mattered to him.

Wrapping her arms and legs around him, M. J. kissed him back while shuddering with little aftershocks. A warm and sated feeling of sexual satisfaction made her laugh low in her throat. "We're not done yet, cowboy," she whispered in his ear.

Brody pulled back and gave M. J. a lopsided smile

that took her breath away. "I was hoping you'd say that." He moved sensually against her so that she could feel the steely hardness of his erection.

"I want you naked," she said, and then laughed.

"Yep, you said that out loud." He stood up and slowly unbuttoned his shirt.

"You are such a tease," M. J. complained. When she tried to grab him he took a step backward just out of her reach. After unsnapping his jeans, he oh-so-slowly lowered the zipper. She swallowed when the head of his penis poked out. "You're not wearing underwear."

"I dressed in a hurry."

"Yeah, well, then *undress* in a hurry."

With a grin he crooked one eyebrow and then slid his jeans halfway down his hips. His penis sprang forward, long, hard and ready for her.

"Come here, Brody."

"No, I want to striptease for you," he said, but when he tried to slowly slide his jeans down his thighs, he lost his balance and fell to the floor with a thump and a curse.

With a laugh, M. J. sprang from the sofa. "You forgot to take your boots off. That's why you lost your balance." She tugged them off and then made quick work of his jeans. "Just what are you trying to accomplish?"

"I was trying to be memorable."

M. J. thought Brody was joking, but when her gaze met with his, her heart started thudding in double time and she swallowed. "Unforgettable?" she asked softly.

"Yeah." He actually blushed. "But falling on my ass wasn't *quite* what I had in mind."

If M. J. hadn't already known that Brody was her soul mate, she could have fallen in love with him right then and there.

"Oh, please quit giving me the *He's a cute dork* look."

M. J. pushed his boots out of the way and scooted closer. "You're mistakin' it for the *I want to make love to you* look."

"Oh."

"Yeah, oh. But not on this yucky carpet." She stood up and crooked a finger at him. "Follow me."

"Anywhere."

They hurried to her bedroom and fell onto the bed in a fit of laughter. "One minute," M. J. said, holding up a finger, and then hurried to the bathroom to find protection. *Oh, please let there be condoms beneath the sink.* She had bought them, hadn't she? A while back just in case? Pushing past cotton balls, Q-tips, tampons, hair conditioner and toothpaste, she finally spotted a lonely box of Trojans hidden in the corner. "Yes!" She hurried back into the bedroom with the condom in her hot little hand. That taken care of, Brody propped pillows behind his back and said gruffly, "Straddle me."

"S-straddle you?" She glanced at his erect penis and swallowed. God, she wished she were more experienced at this. With a determined nod, M. J. swung her leg over his hips. He put his hands around her waist and helped her ease downward, taking him inch by inch. Her experience with men was limited, but God, he felt big . . . hot and oh-so-hard, but she loved having him this way, face-to-face and buried deep. The feel of him inside of her like this was so erotic that it made her gasp.

"You okay? You're so tight. . . . I don't want to hurt you."

"I'm fine," she assured him, touched that he was so concerned. "You feel . . . good. Hot. *Powerful.*" She looked at him, into his eyes, which were dilated to a deep, dark shade of blue. *I've waited so long to find you,* M. J. thought, and barely restrained herself from saying this to him. He cupped her breasts, lightly thumbing her nipples. She moaned, letting her head fall back when he took her into his mouth. With her hands on his wide shoulders she began to move, but Brody stopped her.

"No, wait. One more move and I'll lose it," he pleaded with a weak laugh. "I want you that badly, but I want to prolong the moment. Just kiss me first, okay?"

"Okay." M. J. leaned forward and pressed her mouth to his and remained still, even though the urge to make love to him was strong. She kissed him with a deep passion that showed how much she needed him, wanted him. But neither of them could keep the kiss from turning wild, hungry . . . a tangle of tongues, a nibble of teeth. Her beaded nipples grazed his chest, sending a sharp sizzle of longing that made her want to ride him hard, but he held her securely around her waist.

"God, M. J., I can't wait any longer. *Love me now,*" he pleaded hotly in her ear, and then released his hands.

With a little cry, M. J. came up to her knees and sank back down . . . hard. Gripping his shoulders, she rode him frenzied and fast. Steely hard, long and thick, he stretched her, filled her. He was almost too much, making her whimper even as the pleasure began to build. With his hands around her waist, he helped her, guided her until M. J.'s heart pounded and her breathing became reduced to gasps.

With a hoarse shout Brody climaxed an instant later, thrusting his hips upward, going deeper than M. J. thought possible. She arched her back when she came with a sharp intensity that had her squeezing his shoulders and calling his name. After catching her breath, M. J. leaned against him, burying her face in the crook of his neck. With a low chuckle he wrapped his arms around her, making her feel safe and loved.

This is how it is supposed to feel, she thought, but instead said, "That was amazing, and Brody, I meant to say that out loud." She put her palms on his cheeks and kissed him tenderly.

Yes, the sex *had* been amazing, Brody thought, but incredibly, it was her kiss that blew him away. Soft and sweet and yet somehow so intense that the kiss tugged at his heartstrings. For a hell-raiser like him this was so emotionally moving that he threaded his fingers through her hair and kissed her back with all he had. "Hey," he said when the kiss ended, "you wore me out, lady. Are you up for a long nap or do you have to open up your shop?" He really wasn't all that tired. In truth this was a thinly veiled excuse to cuddle with her, but he was too much of a guy to ask if she wanted to spoon.

"I make my own hours. I wasn't really kidding when I said that I had to be in the mood to do readings.

Sometimes I'm just not focused and I'm thinking this would be one of those times."

Brody chuckled. "Good." Kissing her lightly on the nose, he said, "I need a moment in the bathroom and then let's snooze for a while. After that, I'll go get us some take-out barbecue sandwiches from Jack's downtown and we can feast in bed."

"You don't want to leave this bed, do you?"

Tucking a wavy lock of midnight hair behind her ear, he admitted with a grin, "No."

M. J. kissed him again and then murmured against his lips, "Me neither."

Once in the bathroom, Brody leaned his hands on the cool sink and gazed at his reflection. He tried not to think about the paranormal event that had rocked his world that morning, but he was hoping that M. J. would soon fess up to the trick she had used to make it happen. Pushing that thought to the back of his head, he decided to enjoy the afternoon. Once he got to know her better, surely she would confess that her Psychic Love Connection shop was just a fun but harmless tourist attraction and that the rest of the psychic phenomena could be explained away with smoke and mirrors.

When Brody reentered the bedroom M. J. was already sleeping, curled up beneath the blanket. She shifted when he came closer, revealing one bare shoulder, which he suddenly needed to kiss. Brody slid beneath the covers and pulled her close, burying his face in her hair. She sighed and then mumbled something that sounded like "I love you." Brody's heart pounded and he held his breath, waiting for her to say it again. When she didn't

Brody gave himself a mental shake, thinking that perhaps he was mistaken. Besides, he reasoned, he really didn't *want* her to be in love with him. They were little more than strangers . . . and there was so much she needed to explain before he could even think of having a serious relationship with her.

And yet she felt so damned good in his arms. With that thought Brody pushed all else from his mind other than having her snuggled against him. At this moment in time it seemed like the only thing that mattered.

Chapter Nine

"Hey, sleepyhead, you hungry?"

M. J. answered with a moan but opened her eyes a slit. Her cheek rested against a firm bicep, and her hand nestled in the center of his chest. "Mmmm," she breathed, thinking that he felt warm and solid and smelled so good. "Hungry for what?" When she nibbled on his arm he chuckled.

"A big pulled-pork sandwich from Jack's Bar-B-Que."

"Can I have *you* for dessert?"

Brody laughed. "You betcha. Just drizzle me with chocolate."

M. J. pressed her face against his arm. "Oh, I can't believe I just said that!"

"Oh, but you did and I intend to hold you to it." After kissing her on top of the head, he scooted from the bed, giving M. J. a nice view of his muscled backside. "Um, M. J., where are my clothes?" He looked over his shoulder at her with a grin. "Ah, I remember. In the other room. No need to get up . . . or even move from the bed. I'll be back in a bit with dinner. Oh, and chocolate sauce."

M. J. giggled. After Brody left she sat there in the middle of the bed trying to absorb everything that had happened in the past couple of days, but it was too much to comprehend. But still, a big smile spread across her face and she said, "I've found my man. My soul mate." M. J. put her hands to her cheeks and then bounced a little on the mattress. "I've *really* found him." Coming up to her knees, she bounced a bit more and then came up to her feet and started jumping trampoline-style up and down and then twirled. "I've found him!" she shouted, not caring that she was stark naked. "I've finally found him!" Her boobs bounced and her hair flew up in the air, but she jumped a bit more until her heel landed on a stuffed animal and she lost her balance, falling against the pillows in a fit of laughter.

Happiness washed over her like warm spring rain. Breathing hard, she smiled up at the ceiling, daydreaming about Brody and chocolate sauce until the sound of her cell phone ringing made her just about jump out of her skin. "Eeek!" Grabbing the phone from her nightstand, she flipped it open, dropped it and finally managed to say, "Hello?"

"M. J.! Hey, little sis, what's up?"

"I've found my soul mate, Sophia." There was no sense beating around the bush, since her sister would get it out of her eventually. Sophia always called when she sensed something was up.

"Shut up!"

"No, I'm serious." She bounced a little.

"You found your soul mate in *Nashville, Tennessee*? Please don't tell me he wears a cowboy hat and chews tobacco."

"Well, yeah, hello! Of course he does. Well, not the tobacco part. But he wears a cool hat and looks amazing in it. His name is Brody Baker and he's the bass player for Travis Mackey."

"Wow, I love his music."

"Yeah, well, get this. . . . Brody has his very own single coming out this week. So yeah, he wears a hat and boots and the whole nine yards."

"And this . . . this bass-playing, hat-wearing singing cowboy is okay with you being a psychic?"

M. J. frowned, wishing she had a phone cord to curl around her finger. She reached up and twirled her hair instead. "Well, okay, there are a few issues we have to overcome. But Sophia, the man is my *soul mate*. We'll deal with the details later. . . ."

"Oh, baby sis," Sophia said in a sad tone that made M. J. bristle. She crossed her legs and squeezed the tiny phone way too hard.

"Why are you being such a downer? God, mediums are such killjoys. You seriously need to stop talking to dead people for a while. I was jumpin' on the bed a minute ago and now you've murdered my moment. Wham." She snapped her fingers. "Just like that."

"You were *jumping* on the bed? God, that is so Tom Cruiseish. You're scaring me, M. J."

"Oh, okay, *you* talk to the dead and dream about

murder victims, and me jumping on the bed scares you?"

"Hey, you're my *sista*," she protested in her Brooklyn accent. M. J. imagined her pounding her chest with her fist. "I care 'bout ya, ya know? I didn't mean a frightened kind of scare. It's almost impossible to frighten me. I meant a I'm-scared-you're-gonna-get-hurt kinda scared."

"Sophia, I appreciate your concern. I really do. But you havta admit that you're a bit jaded. And I warned you that jerk Mike Morgan wasn't the one for you. But see, the difference here is that I know that Brody *is* the one for me."

"M. J., we both know that finding your soul mate doesn't guarantee a happy ending. You might have traveled to Nashville to find this guy, but it sounds like you're still worlds apart. A good ol' boy country singer? Come on, M. J., will this guy ever accept what you do for a living, not to mention the rest of our family? God, Lucio is the only so-called normal one and even he has trouble accepting us. And we're his family! Soul mate or not, be ready for him to ditch you."

"Gee, tell me how ya really feel. Don't hold back."

"I'm just giving ya fair warning."

M. J. closed her eyes and blew out a long sigh. "Sophia, I don't need your warning. I need your love and support. Just be happy for me!"

"Aw, baby sis, you know I love ya and want you to be happy. But it will take a special guy to deal with our family."

"I know and Brody is special."

"Okay, okay. You sound like you're head over heels."

"I am, Sophia. I didn't know I could feel this way about someone."

Sophia groaned. "All right already. Just promise me one thing."

"What?"

"Promise me that you won't settle for love alone. This guy might be your soul mate, but he has to believe in you and your psychic abilities . . . not just accept but believe."

M. J. twirled her hair around her finger. "That's a tall order."

"Could you be truly happy with anything else?"

"No," M. J. admitted, and realized that it was true. She refrained from telling Sophia about the recent unexplained phenomenon when she'd somehow materialized in Brody's room. With a groan, M. J. wondered how she was supposed to get Brody to buy into something that she didn't fully comprehend.

"*Hey*, what was the groan for?" Sophia asked in a tone thick with suspicion.

"Somethin' I wanna talk about, but I don't have time right now. Call me later, okay?"

"You got it."

"Hey, when are you coming to Nashville for a visit? Isn't your show on hiatus right now?" M. J. asked, referring to Sophia's cable talk show, *Seeking the Other Side*.

"I'd love to come for a visit, but my agent wants me to write a book, so I've been busy doing an outline. As soon as I get it finished I'll drive on down. Maybe I can

get Lucio to come with me and we can hang out together."

"That would be great. Give Luc my love and Mom
and Pop too, okay?"

"You bet. Talk to ya soon."

M. J. smiled when she ended the call. Granted, her
family might be a bit off-the-wall, but she loved them
dearly. Knowing that Brody would be back soon, she
headed into the bathroom for a quick shower and then
changed into a zip-up hoodie and pair of low-slung gray
sweatpants. After pulling her hair up into a sloppy bun
that she hoped looked sexy, she brushed on some mascara and a bit of peach-colored lip gloss. She dabbed a
hint of perfume on her wrists and then tried not to be
nervous. Deciding that it was late enough in the day for
a drink, she headed into the kitchen in search of a bottle
of red wine to soothe her nerves.

M. J. was three sips into a glass of Merlot when
Brody knocked on the back door. Just seeing him gave
her a little zing of excitement. He entered with a grin
and sat the brown bag on the kitchen table. "Sorry I
took so long. The line at Jack's was huge. Then I was determined to find chocolate sauce, but there aren't any
grocery stores on Broadway, but I got a flash of genius
and bought some in an ice cream parlor. They don't actually sell it, so I had to promise to sing for my chocolate sauce."

"Ya gotta be kiddin' me. They have a stage in an ice
cream parlor?"

"This is Music City, USA, M. J." He gave her a grin.
"But the bottom line is that I got the sauce."

M. J. smiled back, but she hoped that this wasn't all about sex for Brody.

"Hey," he said softly, and then snagged her around the waist, drawing her close. "Let's go have our dinner in bed."

M. J. shrugged as she played with a button on his shirt. "The sandwiches are sloppy. Do you mind if we eat at the table?" She gazed up at him and held her breath.

"No, that's fine," Brody answered with an easy smile. He was about to tease that they could have dessert in bed, but he sensed that M. J. was upset about something and refrained. "Damn, I'm going way too fast for you, aren't I?"

She responded with a small frown. "I'm not into meaningless sex, Brody."

"Is that what you think of me?" He was surprised at how much her comment hurt. "Of what we shared?" God, he sounded like a girl, but he didn't care.

"No, but—"

"Shhh." Brody gently stopped her with a finger to her lips. "Let's slow things down and eat our sandwiches here."

M. J. gave Brody a shy smile. "I'd love to go over to Logan's later and listen to Savannah sing. Would you take me?"

God, he wanted to just gobble her up, but he gave her a kiss on top of the head. "You betcha."

"Thanks," she said, and gave him a peck on the mouth, but she lingered just long enough that he had to swallow a groan. This slowing-things-down idea sucked, but he understood her reasoning and respected her wishes.

"Hungry?"

"Famished," she responded. "I really miss the deli sandwiches from Brooklyn, but this smells heavenly."

Brody pulled the Styrofoam boxes from the brown bag and nodded. "Yep, this is different from the Texas barbeque that I grew up with, but it's melt-in-your-mouth good. What else do you miss about Brooklyn?"

"Pizza!"

"Aw, come on. There is pizza everywhere."

M. J. shook her head while removing the sandwiches from the packaging. "Not like in Brooklyn. There is a little Italian restaurant called L&B Spumoni Gardens that has the best Sicilian pizza in the world. Mmmm, homemade crust that's crispy in the bottom and soft in the middle, and the thick layer of cheese is under the sauce. Totonno's is a Coney Island tradition and supposedly, like, the oldest pizzeria in the United States or whatevva. It's more old-school with amazing sauce and homemade mozzarella, but Spumoni Gardens is my favorite. Ah, my mouth *wattas* just thinkin' 'bout it."

"What is spumoni?"

"Italian ice cream. My favorite is pistachio. You want somethin' to drink?"

"A beer would be great."

"Hmm, I might have one or two hidden in the fridge." She opened the door and bent over to rummage around. Although Brody knew she wasn't intentionally trying to be provocative, her little ass was so damned cute and damned if he didn't go and have to notice that there were *no* visible panty lines. Just when he was breaking out into a sweat she turned around with a triumphant smile. "Found one!"

When M. J. handed the beer to him the little bit of breast jiggle let him know that she was braless as well. God, he suddenly wanted to press the cold bottle to his forehead. Instead he twisted off the cap and took a healthy swig. "So what else do you miss besides the food?"

She sat down at the table and said, "I could go on about the food *forevva* . . . Terrace Bagels, cheesecake from Junior's . . . but I miss the shopping at the Fulton Street Mall the most. Sophia and I could shop until our legs were like lead." She nodded. "Brooklyn is the kind of place that nevva gets out of your system, ya know?"

"I'd like to go there with you. See you in your element."

"Think ya could keep up with me, cowboy?"

He shook his head while picking up his fork. "No way. Remember, I'm a slow-movin' Texan."

She laughed and they tucked into their food in companionable silence . . . another thing that he liked about her. She didn't chatter just to fill the void. She did, however, turn him on with every little move she made, from chewing her food to swallowing her wine to dabbing the paper napkin against the corners of her mouth. When her knee accidentally brushed against his, Brody just about tipped his chair over.

"Oh, are you okay?" She gave him a curious look.

Feeling like a love-struck fool, Brody nodded. "I'm

fine, just getting a bit full. How about a long walk before heading over to Logan's?"

She gave him a sweet smile that sent a shot of pure longing straight to his heart . . . and then down to his groin. He shifted in his chair, trying to keep his libido under control.

"I'll just put away these leftovas and then change."

Brody waved her off. "You go get ready. I know my way around a kitchen. I'll clean up."

"You are so nice!" She gave him another smile and he shifted uncomfortably. His jeans were getting tighter by the minute and it had nothing to do with the food. "I'll be back in a jiffy."

After M. J. left the room, Brody groaned. "Let's slow things down," he muttered darkly, wondering just what in the hell he had been thinking.

"*Y*ou havta quit buying me stuff," M. J. told Brody as they strolled hand in hand down Broadway. She was wearing a red cowboy hat that he had insisted that she try on, and then had purchased under her profuse protest that at one hundred dollars the hat was way too expensive. Plus, M. J. really didn't consider herself a cowboy-hat-wearing kind of girl, but Brody told her that she looked hot wearing it, so of course she kept it on.

"Let's go in here," he said, tugging her inside of Trail West, a Western-apparel shop.

"Brody . . . ," she protested, shaking her head, when he held up a pair of snakeskin red and black boots.

"Oh, come on. Just try them on."

M. J. glanced at the price tag and sucked in a breath. "No!"

"Please?" he pleaded low and sexy in her ear.

M. J. rolled her eyes but had to laugh when he tried to pout. "Stop that. You look silly. Do I *look* like the kind of girl who wears cowboy boots?"

He made his pout bigger and tried to make his bottom lip tremble. "You'll never know unless you try them on."

"Oh, okay! Just stop with the fish lips, already. I'll try them on, but you are *not* going to buy them for me. You got that?"

"Got it." He gave her an innocent smile and a happy nod.

M. J. reluctantly tried the boots on, thinking that she wouldn't be caught dead in them, but Brody insisted that she get up from the bench and parade around the store. Despite the pointy toes, they were butter soft and surprisingly comfortable.

"Do you like them?" he asked, and she made the mistake of nodding. "I'll take them," he said to the salesclerk.

"Brody!"

"I'm buying them for *me*. . . . I just want *you* to wear them."

M. J. narrowed her eyes, but her mouth twitched at the corners in her effort not to grin.

"Look," he said, putting his hand on her knee, "I make way more money than I know what to do with and this is fun for me. Indulge me, okay?"

"But—"

He put a finger to her lips. "But nothing. There aren't any strings attached, M. J. You're not thinking that, are you?"

M. J. gazed down at the floor. "I'm not used ta men buying gifts for me. I don't know what ta think."

"Then don't."

"Don't what?"

He tapped her temple. "Think. No thinking, no worries. Let's just have fun."

"Don't worry; be happy, huh?"

Brody grinned. "There's the attitude."

By the time they were finished in Trail West, M. J. owned two pairs of boot-cut Wranglers, a snowy white Western-cut shirt with red piping on the pockets and a leather belt with a big silver buckle. Quite an ensemble for a girl from Brooklyn and yet she couldn't wait to put it on because she knew it would make him happy.

"Thirsty?" Brody asked once they were back outside in the warm sunshine.

"A little."

"Good, then let's go grab a beer at Tootsie's."

M. J. grinned. "The famous little honky-tonk that's painted orchid on the outside?"

"The one and only Tootsie's Orchid Lounge. I played there a few times," he said, and took her hand in his once again as they walked, while he lugged the shopping bag with the other. Although no one had approached Brody for an autograph, M. J. could tell by the curious looks they were getting that people passing were recognizing him. While M. J. felt a bit like a princess on the arm of a rising star, at the same time she knew that this was also another complication in their relationship.

Because of the late-afternoon hour Tootsie's wasn't

crowded. Still, Brody ushered her to the back of the bar to a round table tucked into a little alcove away from prying eyes and flashing cameras.

"How about a beer?" Brody asked after storing the big shopping bag beneath the table.

"Sure." M. J. was usually more of a wine sipper, but a cold tangy beer sounded refreshing. When Brody stood up and kissed her on the cheek she was touched. His tender gesture made her feel as if they were really a couple and she liked that feeling. "Make it somethin' light, okay?"

"You got it." Brody walked over to the bar, which took up one side of the long narrow room. In the front corner next to the window there was a stage barely big enough to hold a few musicians. A young guy sporting a snazzy black hat and very tight jeans was warming up right now, even though there were only a half dozen patrons in the place. M. J. thought it a bit sad that there were so many hopefuls and so slim a chance of ever making it.

"Here you go," Brody said when he returned with a longneck bottle. He slid onto the tall stool and clinked his bottle to hers. "You look so darned cute in that hat."

"Oh, you are so full of it," she chided, but felt the heat of a blush in her cheeks.

"Hey," he said, leaning close, "you're going to have to get used to my gifts and compliments. I just can't help myself." He gave her that cocky grin of his, but there was a serious expression in his eyes that made M. J. feel warm all over. He swallowed and for a moment she thought he was going to kiss her, but then he drew back and took a long pull from his beer as if trying to cool himself down.

"So," M. J. began, and swept her hand toward the wall laden with pictures, "are you up there somewhere?"

Brody raised his eyebrows. "On the Wall of Fame? Maybe someday . . . if I'm lucky. Just look at all of the legends up there," he said, pointing with his beer bottle. "Hank Williams, Loretta Lynn . . . man, how I wish these walls could talk. You know, it's rumored that Roger Miller wrote 'Dang Me' while sitting here in Tootsie's."

Roger Miller? M. J. racked her brain but came up blank, but luckily Brody didn't seem to notice.

"You know Willie Nelson got his first songwriting job after singing here."

"The old guy with the ponytail who does Farm Aid?"

Brody chuckled. "Yes. He's also a gifted songwriter. Did you know he wrote the song 'Crazy' sung by Patsy Cline?" Brody pointed to the Wall of Fame where Patsy's picture was hung. Shaking his head, he said, "She died in a tragic plane crash at the age of thirty. She had just finished singing at the Grand Ole Opry. Damn, she was in her prime."

Patsy Cline? M. J. felt a little shiver travel down her spine.

"What?" Brody asked with a frown. "You look like you've seen a ghost."

"It's nothing."

"Tell me, M. J."

After a deep breath, M. J. said, "I had this wacko dream when I lived in Florida that I was singing a duet with Patsy Cline. It sort of prompted me to move here to Nashville."

"You moved here because of a dream?"

"I was feeling restless and needed a change of atmosphere," M. J. defended herself. "But yes, it was a factor in my decision. Dreams have meaning, ya know. I go with my gut, my intuition, Brody. It's what I do." She toyed with her beer bottle without looking at him. This was the first reference to her psychic ability all afternoon. A sudden uneasiness washed over her.

"Hey," Brody said, covering her hand with his, "I didn't mean anything by it. I was just curious. I want to learn everything about you."

M. J. gave him a small smile. "Sorry that I overreacted. People can be mean about the psychic thing."

"If anyone is mean to you, I'll kick his ass," he said with so much feeling that M. J. had to laugh and the mood was suddenly lightened. Maybe he was going to believe in her and even defend her, after all. Oh, how great would that be?

"So you were singing a duet with Patsy Cline, huh? Were you any good?"

M. J. snickered. "Yeah, in the dream I was wonderful. In reality, I suck . . . *suck*! I'm so bad that I havta mouth the hymns at church to keep people from scooting away. So I guess you were in the choir, though, huh?"

Brody shook his head and laughed. "Hell no. My voice doesn't have all that much range. I'm taking lessons to work on that."

"Ah yes, but you have a distinctive voice, Brody. Kind of smooth but rough around the edges . . . very sexy."

"You think so?" Brody looked so pleased that she had to smile.

"I know so. I was impressed when I heard you and Travis Mackey sing last summer. Something about the music moved me. The songs have stories . . . sometimes funny, sometimes sad, but always with meaning."

"It's crazy to think that you were in the audience and now here we are. Life is weird, huh?"

"No argument there. Now, tell me about yourself, Brody." M. J. learned a great deal about Brody over the next hour. He grew up on a ranch in Texas where his family raised cattle and had a little bit of oil . . . nothing huge but it provided steady income with a lot of hard work. Brody admitted that he picked up playing the guitar mainly because he thought chicks would dig it. He had an older brother who was an overachiever honor student, leaving Brody the role of goof-off, which he fulfilled very well, thank you very much. He attended Vanderbilt University, which was really a thinly veiled ploy for him to live in Nashville, and went to classes only when he wasn't writing songs or singing for tips, which was, well, basically never. Finally, his parents quit sending money and Vandy tossed him out on his ear, but he stayed in Nashville, where he ended up a studio musician and then ultimately in Travis Mackey's band.

"So, now tell me all about you, Brooklyn girl."

"Wow, look at the time." M. J. was saved from discussing her so-called not-so-normal life when she glanced down at her watch. "We need to get goin' or we'll miss Savannah singing at Logan's and I promised her I'd come."

"Okay," he agreed, and hopped down from the stool. After retrieving the shopping bag, he offered her his hand and they headed out, but he paused near the stage to toss some cash into the tip jar.

"Hurry," M. J. said, "or we won't get a seat." She tugged on his hand as they wove through the thickening crowd. When they arrived back at her place, Brody offered to go over to Logan's and save a spot while M. J. freshened up.

After touching up her makeup and brushing her hair, she took the new clothes Brody bought her out of the shopping bag but hesitated. The cowgirl outfit was so *not* her. She was about to put on her usual skirt and blouse when she felt the tingle of a presence in her bedroom. "Pixie?" M. J. called out, looking around the room for the familiar twinkling light.

"Don't tell me you're not gonna wear that getup after that handsome boy paid all that money for it."

"Pixie, where have ya been lately?"

"Oh, don't you go changing the subject on me, girlie. I didn't die yesterday," she said, laughing gruffly at her play on words. "Oh, I just kill myself."

"But you're already dead."

"Who says so?"

"You just did."

The light flitted around. "Oh, horse pucky."

"Who are you, really, Pixie?"

The light stopped flitting and hovered. "If I told you, I'd have to kill you."

"Very funny."

"I thought so."

"So, you *are* a ghost, then, right?"

"Just call me your little honky-tonk angel."

Honky-tonk angel? Something clicked in M. J.'s brain, making her gasp. "Ohmigod. Are you the ghost of Patsy Cline?"

"Why would you think that?"

"Because it's one of her songs and people sometimes refer to her as that. I Googled her after the dream I had that I was singing with her . . . *you*?" A little tingle ran down M. J.'s spine at the thought.

Pixie started flitting around the room as if she was nervous. "Naw, sorry to disappoint you, but I'm not Patsy Cline. I do love her music, though. Speaking of music, you need to get changed and go listen to my . . . Savannah."

"*Your* Savannah? Are you somehow connected to Savannah Parks?"

"I didn't mean it that way," Pixie said, bouncing around the room like a pinball.

M. J. put her hands on her hips and attempted to follow the flight of the flickering light. Flickering meant that Pixie was about to exit, so she said hurriedly, "I'm not buying what you're selling. I'm thinkin' that this whole thing—me coming to Nashville—is somehow your doing, but there is a much bigger picture, isn't there?"

"Maybe . . . ," she admitted, her gruff voice growing dimmer.

"And me materializing in the shower with Brody . . . you caused that to happen, am I right?"

"*Steamy*, huh? Oh, there I go cracking myself up again." Her light flickered and her voice sounded far-away.

"Wait! Pixie! Zapping me over to Brody's room was your doing too, right? I don't have that kind of power, do I?"

"Sorry 'bout that, but I was desperate," Pixie shouted, but her voice became even more faint. "And I'm . . . new at this . . . so I kinda *goofed*."

"Goofed?" M. J. shouted, somehow thinking that if she shouted, Pixie's voice too would become stronger. She filed away the "new at this" clue for later examination.

"Yeah . . . you . . ." M. J. had to strain her ears to hear the rest. ". . . weren't supposed to . . . actually end up there in the flesh. . . . The connection between you two was just too danged strong."

"Oh, Pixie, how am I ever going to explain that to Brody? He thinks it was all some elaborate illusion."

"You have to admit that it was really cool," she said from far away but with a bit of pride. "I'll do my best to help you," Pixie promised in a voice that M. J. could barely hear. "Now, go join that handsome cowboy . . . and wear the danged outfit!" Her light flickered once more and then in a cloud of shimmering Pixie dust, *she was gone.*

Chapter Eleven

*B*rody sat at a side table near the small stage where Savannah was setting up her gear. His eyes kept darting to the front entrance in search of M. J. while he nursed a cold beer. She should have arrived by now and Brody was becoming a bit concerned as to what could be keeping her. He sat next to the wall with his hat pulled low over his eyes in hopes that he wouldn't be recognized. He wanted to enjoy the show and not steal any of Savannah's thunder. She was damned good. So good, in fact, that he was going to give one of her demo tapes to his manager . . . secretly, not wanting to disappoint her if nothing came of it.

Savannah reminded him a little of Carrie Underwood with her sweet disposition and shy smile, but big, powerful voice. He could see her becoming a star, with a little luck and a lot of hard work.

Brody was in the middle of a swallow of beer when M. J. finally walked through the front door. He absently sat the bottle down with a clunk and almost choked. *Hot damn.* His exotic little psychic had turned into a smokin' cowgirl. She wore the tight Wranglers well and the white blouse accentuated her dark glossy hair. Brody sat up straighter and tipped his hat back to get a better look. Her eyes met his and he felt a sizzle all the way to his boots. As she made her way through the crowd she got admiring once-overs from every guy in the joint, making Brody want to march over to her and slip his arm around her waist.

He realized, though, that he didn't need to because she seemed not to notice the appreciative looks, but only had eyes for him. "Hey there," he said, wishing for something more clever to say, but his tongue was a bit tied. "Or should I say, 'Howdy, partner'?"

"Brody, do I look ridiculous?" she asked as she sat down on the tall stool, and slapped a hand over her mouth.

"You look amazingly hot." He pulled her hand away from her mouth. "I'd better be careful or I'll find myself in a bar fight. Something I've managed to avoid lately."

"A bar fight, but why?"

"M. J., every guy in here is drooling over you."

"Nuh-uh." She glanced around with a cute little frown.

"Ya-huh." He picked up a napkin and acted like he was patting his chin dry. "Me included."

"You are so full of it," she chided, but her cheeks turned a pretty shade of pink. "I feel silly wearing this hat."

"M. J., you're in *Nashville*."

"Point taken, cowboy."

"Now you're talkin', cow*girl*."

"Oh, *stop*." She shoved at his chest but then let her hand linger there just long enough to make Brody's heart kick it up a notch. He was about to ask if she wanted a beer when Logan came over to the table with a glass of red wine. "On the house because of the outfit," he said with a wink. "Hey, you two know each other?"

"Thanks, Logan," M. J. said with a smile, and then turned to Brody to give an explanation of their relationship.

"Yeah, we do." Brody nodded and covered her hand with his, realizing that he was trying to give Logan the message to back off if he had any ideas. *Man, I've got it bad*, Brody thought with a mental shudder, but kept his hand over M. J.'s.

"That's great." Logan cocked an eyebrow and gave Brody a half grin, letting him know he got the subtle message that M. J. was off-limits. This was a weird feeling for Brody, who had never been much of the jealous type. But then again he had never fallen like this for a woman, especially not so hard or so fast. The mere thought of M. J. with another guy set Brody's teeth on edge and it just so happened that Logan was quite a chick magnet. Well, Logan could have any chick he wanted, just not *this* chick.

Brody jumped when M. J. nudged him in the ribs. "What?"

"Logan asked if you want a beer."

"Oh, yeah, a Bud Light." He tipped his hat back and asked, "Is mine on the house too?"

"You're not pretty enough," Logan answered with a grin. "I might slide you a free beer if you get up there and sing after Savannah's done."

"We'll see," Brody answered. He should have readily agreed, since he was supposed to be promoting his single at every turn, but oddly the thought of getting up there and singing in front of M. J. unnerved him a bit. Crazy when he was used to playing in front of thousands. "I'm looking forward to listening to Savannah, Logan. She's getting better and better every time I hear her sing."

Logan beamed with pride. "Yeah, little sis kicks ass, doesn't she? Funny thing is that she's so shy and yet when she gets up there on stage she can really work a crowd. She seems to know just what songs to sing to get this place rocking."

Proving Logan's point, Savannah started her set with a cover of Gretchen Wilson's rowdy "Here for the Party." The small dance floor immediately filled up, mostly with women raising their longnecks while dancing, cheering and singing along.

Brody cracked up when M. J. joined in singing, "And I ain't leaving till they throw me out."

"You a Gretchen Wilson fan?"

M. J. shrugged. "I know this song from Savannah singing it. I've been sort of a regular here since I moved to Nashville," she answered close to his ear in order to be heard over the music. Her leg brushed against his and Brody wished he knew whether it was an accident or an invitation. He hoped like hell it was an invitation. *Go slow*, he mentally ordered himself. But then she placed her hand on his thigh, leaned in and said, "Savannah's amazing, isn't she?" when Savannah jumped headfirst into a powerful rendition of Martina McBride's "Independence Day."

"Yes, she's talented," Brody answered absently. His brain wasn't focused on Savannah; his mind was zoomed in on the heat of M. J.'s hand on his thigh and her breast pressed against his arm. But just when he thought she was doing some major-league flirting, her hand slipped from his leg. Her eyes rounded and she leaned back against the wall as if seeing something she couldn't believe. "M. J., you okay?"

"*No way.*"

"No way . . . what?" Brody asked, but M. J. just blinked from beneath the brim of her hat.

"No *way*," M. J. repeated when a piece of the Pixie puzzle fell into place. But just when she was absorbing the first shock, Savannah hit her with another one when she said, "Y'all, I'm going to sing the classic song 'Crazy' in honor of my granny Parks, who passed away this past winter." Savannah paused and visibly swallowed. "I've been feeling her presence lately, kinda like she's been guiding me from that honky-tonk heaven in the sky. She dearly loved Patsy Cline, so Granny Parks, this song's for you. Here's hoping that you and Patsy are pickin' and grinnin' with the angels."

"Hey, we were just talking about that song," Brody commented.

M. J. nodded absently.

"Uh, earth to M. J.? What's going on here, cowgirl?" he asked in her ear.

M. J. hesitated while taking a sip of her wine, wondering just how much she should reveal, but then decided that if Brody was her soul mate, he was going to have to accept her for who and what she was. With that in mind she took a deep breath and said in a rush, "I just had a psychic love connection."

"Whoa, really? Just now?"

She nodded.

"Okay, are you going to tell me about it?" he prompted with a grin that had M. J. wondering if it was a *You gotta be kidding* grin or a *How cool is that?* grin.

Praying for the latter, she said, "Savannah Parks and my brother, Lucio Barone, are soul mates."

"Oh," he answered, and gave her a frown that she couldn't quite read. He took a slug of his beer and then asked, "Is that all?"

"No," M. J. began, but her voice was drowned out when Savannah started singing "Save a Horse (Ride a Cowboy)," causing the crowd to go nuts.

Brody grabbed her hand and said loud enough for her to hear, "Let's go someplace where we can talk."

M. J. nodded in agreement. They waved to Savannah as they left, dropping some money in the tip jar. She grinned and waved back, looking a bit startled when she realized that M. J. was leaving with Brody Baker. Once outside M. J. took a breath of sultry night air. "Would you like to head inside my place?"

"Yeah," Brody answered. "I hope you don't mind leaving. I hated not being able to talk without yelling, even though I was enjoying hearing Savannah sing."

"No, that's fine. I'm sure she was thrilled to see you

in the crowd," M. J. answered as she unlocked her door. Brody followed her in past the shop and into her apartment. "Can I get you something to drink?"

"A bottle of water would be great."

M. J. nodded and reached into the refrigerator, snagging two cold bottles. She handed Brody one and then twisted the cap off hers and took a long swallow. Brody did the same and for a moment they were silent, but there was something alive in the air. M. J. leaned back against the sink and tried to think of something to say, but all she could think of was that she wanted him to kiss her. As if reading her mind, he took a step closer, sat his bottle on the counter and then gently took hers as well.

M. J. swallowed when he put a hand on either side of the counter. "I've been dying to do this all night," he said softly as he removed his hat and then took hers off too. Then, leaning in, he pressed his mouth to hers. His mouth felt cold from the water but heated up instantly. Their tongues met, danced, while Brody threaded his fingers through her hair and cupped the back of her head, angling his mouth to go deeper. With a moan way in the back of her throat, M. J. wrapped her arms around him, pressing the palms of her hands against his back and curling her fingers into his shirt.

"I thought you wanted to talk," M. J. said breathlessly when the kiss finally ended.

"I do. But I wanted to kiss you more."

M. J. laughed and then bumped against something behind her on the counter, almost knocking it to the floor. She turned around and caught it from sliding off . . . and then sucked in a breath when she saw what it was.

It was the chocolate sauce. Her heart hammered in her chest. Should she?

Could she?

"Hey, what do you have there, cowgirl?"

M. J. uncapped the lid and dipped her finger into the thick sauce and turned around. "I have dessert," she said, and slipped her finger into her mouth, slowly savoring the dark chocolate. She raised her eyes to his. "Or at least the garnish."

Brody's Adam's apple bobbed in his throat.

"Hmmm, I need something to slather it on, but I'm fresh out of ice cream. Any ideas?" She raised her eyebrows while licking her lips.

"An endless supply. Hey, can I have a taste?" he asked, but when she turned around with a chocolate-tipped finger Brody said softly, "No, you eat it." After she licked her finger Brody leaned his body against hers and gave her a long and lazy kiss as if savoring the flavor of her mouth. "M. J., do you have a basting brush?"

"A what?" She was a bit dazed.

"A small brush used for barbeque sauce."

"Oh, I'm not sure." M. J. shrugged and started looking in drawers. "This?"

"Yeah, perfect." Brody grabbed the brush and the sauce.

"Hey, give me that," M. J. protested with a laugh while following him out of the kitchen and into her bedroom.

"Not yet," Brody said, and placed the container and

the brush on the nightstand. "In due time." He flicked on the small lamp on the lowest setting, bathing the room in soft light.

"Oh, no, cowboy, you're not the boss." She tapped her chest. "I'm in control." With that proclamation she gave him an unexpected shove, sending him tumbling onto the bed, and then hopped on top of him. "And you, *sir*, are my dessert." She reached down, grabbed the edges of his shirt and tugged hard, making the snaps pop and give until his chest was exposed. "There, that's better," she said with a satisfied nod. Then, she scooted down and unbuckled his belt, making quick work of the button and zipper. Biting her bottom lip, she lingered there a long moment letting her hand caress his erection. He felt hot and hard beneath the soft cotton of his boxers.

"God . . . M. J." She looked up to see his eyes flutter shut. A muscle ticked in his jaw, making M. J. smile. It was a heady feeling knowing that she could affect him this way. He came up to his elbows, watching her with a grin, while she struggled with his boots. "Need some help?" he offered just as the boot slipped off.

"Whoa!" M. J. shouted as she tumbled backward, landing on the floor clutching the boot. With a shout of laughter she scooted to her feet and tugged on the other boot with the same result. She peeled his jeans off slowly, inch by inch, until he was bucking his hips in protest.

"You're killing me," he moaned, flopping back to the pillows.

M. J. answered with a low chuckle. "Oh, the torture has just begun."

He came up to his elbows again. "Aren't you gonna shed any clothing?"

"In due time," she said, mocking his earlier comment.

"Please?" He gave her a pleading smile that she just couldn't resist.

"Well . . . okay." She leisurely unbuttoned her blouse and shrugged out of it, letting him feast his eyes on her white lace demibra that made her breasts spill over the top. She tugged off her boots, leaning over to give him a teasing view. She unbuckled her belt and unzipped her jeans so slowly that Brody moaned.

"Damn, girl, you're slow as molasses in the winter."

With a shy smile M. J. shed her jeans and then stood before him in her bra and white satin thong, trying to steady her legs. The smoldering look Brody gave her took her breath away. She had waited so long for a man to look at her with love and adoration. Emotion welled up in her throat, but she swallowed it, knowing that bursting into tears would be a mood killer.

"You're *beautiful*."

Oh, God, the tears welled up again. But determined not to ruin the moment, M. J. decided to concentrate on the task at hand. Reaching over to the nightstand, she dipped the brush in the thick sauce and then climbed onto the bed. Straddling Brody at the waist, she swirled the chocolate down his chest and then followed the dark path with her tongue, stopping at his navel.

Brody moaned, clenching his ab muscles when M. J. dipped the brush again and then sat back on her haunches, eyeing him like he was edible. Her dark wavy hair was a sexy mess and there was a bit of chocolate on her bottom lip that he longed to lick off. Her breasts were all but spilling out of her bra, the dusky nipples peeking over the white lace. With a little grin, she dabbed some chocolate on his chin and then licked it off, letting her soft tongue linger on his stubble. She kissed him oh-so-briefly, just a touch of tongue and a hint of chocolate. Brody arched up for more but sucked in a breath when she scooted south, peeling back his boxers to midhip. He about came up off of the bed when the bristles of the brush grazed over the head of his dick with the cold sauce just before she lowered her head and licked it off with the very tip of her tongue, light and teasing, making him want so much more.

"Let's get rid of these," she said, and tugged his boxers off, tossing them over her head. "Now, that's better," she said, leaning over to the nightstand.

Brody held his breath while she painted his shaft with long strokes, up and down, light and slightly prickly against his sensitive skin. It felt as if all of the blood in his body had settled in his dick. He throbbed, swelled . . . becoming almost painfully hard. "God, M. J."

"You look good enough to eat," she said, and flipping her hair to the side, she leaned down and began licking the chocolate off. First, she used the tip of her tongue to catch the drips, but *then* she angled her head sideways and used more of her tongue to lick off the chocolate.

"M. J., I . . . I can't . . . can't take . . . *ahhhh*," he moaned when she took him fully in her mouth. She felt hot, and soft, loving him with deep delicious strokes, flattening her tongue and raking him slightly with her teeth. Brody sank his fingers into her hair and gave in to the intense pleasure, climaxing with a hot rush that seemed to come from his soul. M. J. scooted up into his arms and he held her close, stroking her hair. She snuggled her face into the crook of his neck and it hit him hard that he was really and truly falling in love with her. When his heart slowed down to an almost normal rate, he said, "Okay, cowgirl, your turn."

✳ Chapter Twelve

M. J. let out a shriek of laughter when Brody rolled her over to her back. "What are you doin'?"

"A little payback," he said as he swirled the brush in the chocolate.

M. J. sucked in a breath when he began painting her nipples, first one and then the other. The light abrasiveness made her shiver and arch her back in pleasure.

"Oh, they look like chocolate kisses," Brody said, and rumbled with laughter. "Mmmm, I think I need a little lick and maybe a little nibble."

M. J. sighed when the heat of his mouth covered her breast. His soft tongue licked and soothed and then nibbled, sharply sending a sizzle of heat coursing through her veins. He leaned up and kissed her, tasting sweetly of chocolate and man, heat and desire. She let her hands roam over his back, loving the feel of his smooth skin, the ripple of muscle. His mouth moved to her neck, her shoulder. She laughed when he kissed her elbow, and the inside of her wrist.

"I don't need chocolate. I love the way you taste," he said hotly. He kissed between her breasts and began a trail downward, making her belly quiver and her heart pound. He kissed the tender inside of each of her thighs, making her shake with anticipation. She could feel the heat of his breath, the tickle of his beard, the softness of his hair, brush over her mound as he kissed one thigh and then the other, coming closer and closer to where she wanted him.

"Oh!" she breathed when he finally placed his moist mouth on her sex, nuzzling her open. He kissed her there too, slipping his hands beneath her bottom to lift her higher and open her wider, and then made sweet love to her with his mouth. M. J. fisted her hands in the sheet as the pleasure mounted. With a moan Brody moved her to the edge of the bed, bent her legs over his shoulders, loving her wildly, madly taking her soaring until she let out a cry of pure joy.

And then before she had fully recovered Brody slipped on protection and came back to sink inside her with a sigh of pleasure. He rocked slowly, murmuring in her ear, "You feel so good."

"Mmmm, cowboy, so do you." M. J. wrapped herself around him, her arms around his neck and legs around his waist, loving him back with all she had. He took his sweet time, going slow and easy as if savoring each stroke, while murmuring soft, sexy words into her ear. She sank her fingers into his hair and arched up to get even closer, loving the silky feel of skin against skin.

If she didn't already know this man was her soul mate, she would know it right here and now.

He kissed her deeply as he came, taking her right along with him, and then rolled to the side, hugging her close. "I love you, Brody," M. J. said, cupping his cheek in the palm of her hand. He gave her a small smile, but she felt him stiffen. "I—I shouldn't have said that. I—I have that damned problem of speaking my thoughts out loud, you know?" She tried to laugh, but it came out sounding more like a squeak. With a groan she leaned her head against his chest.

"M. J., it's okay." He put a finger beneath her chin so that she had to look at him. "I'm falling for you too." After a tender kiss, he continued. "Let me slip into the bathroom for a minute and then we can talk."

M. J. nodded mutely as she watched his very fine butt walk into the bathroom. "He's falling for me," she crooned softly, grinned like the Cheshire cat, stretched, and then hugged a purple pig lying next to her.

"Hey, put the pig down. That's my turf," Brody said as he walked over to the bed.

With a laugh M. J. tossed the stuffed animal to the floor and held out her arms. "Not a problem."

Brody slipped between the sheets and turned to face her. He ran a finger tenderly down her cheek and said, "Okay, now let's talk."

M. J. felt a shot of alarm but nodded. "Ask me anything, Brody. I'll be honest. You can always count on that."

"Okay, then, tell me about this thing you do."

The word *thing* bothered her, but she swallowed the

hurt and nodded. "Well as I already explained, I help people find their soul mates. Tonight, for example, when Savannah was singing I saw my brother's *face*, felt a *connection*. Normally, I would need other clues, but since it was my brother I immediately figured it out. I just somehow know that they are meant for each other."

Brody remained silent, but the fact that he was chewing on his bottom lip bothered her. Finally he ran his fingers through his hair and said, "Yeah, but there was more to it than that. Tell me everything."

M. J. swallowed but then plunged forward. "While I believe that I came here to Nashville to find you, there is a much bigger picture."

"Tell me."

With her heart hammering, she continued. "Remember I told you that I had this weird dream that I was singing a song with Patsy Cline? Well, it all fell into place tonight when Savannah talked about her deceased granny. She mentioned feeling her presence lately and that's because her granny *has* been here. I've been calling her Pixie because I see her as this sort of shimmering light." M. J. paused to glance at Brody, who remained frowning and silent. *Not a good sign.*

"So she's a ghost?"

M. J. shrugged. "I think of her as being more like an angel. She claims she has wings and I suppose she does, even though all I can see is a flickering light that tends to zip around the room," M. J. said with a little chuckle, but sobered when Brody didn't even crack a smile. "Pixie wanted me here in order to bring my family."

"You mean your brother?"

"Well, I can't be sure yet, but I think there *might* be a connection between my sista, Sophia, and Logan too. Wouldn't that be cool?" she ventured weakly.

The frown on Brody's face remained and he shoved his fingers through his hair again. "Okay, but just how did you end up in my hotel room? That was some sort of trick, though, right?"

"Um, that was Pixie's doing. I don't have that kind of power, thank goodness, and Pixie . . . um, claims it was a fluke, you know, that she didn't quite understand what she was doing."

With a long intake of breath, Brody sat up in bed, resting his hands on his bent knees. M. J. scooted up as well, bringing the sheet with her, securing it beneath her breasts. "You believe me, don't you, Brody?"

He reached over and tucked her hair behind her ear. "I believe that you're sincere." When he paused, her heart sank to her toes. "I also think that you believe all of this mystical magical stuff. And maybe you have some special intuition when it comes to matchmaking, for lack of a better word, but M. J., the rest is tough for a cowboy like me to swallow. I *just can't* wrap my brain around the rest of it."

"I understand," she said, her heart breaking. "People have a hard time believing in something that you can't explain with a math equation or good old-fashioned logic. I've dealt with this all my life," she told him quietly. "But you know, I can't comprehend how a microwave works or how airplanes fly or how I can talk to someone halfway around the word with a tiny cell phone. To me that's all magic."

Brody angled his head as if trying to understand what she was saying. "That's just technology."

M. J. put her palms up. "Maybe so, but years ago it was science fiction. Man has been to the moon, deep in the sea and to the top of the world. I believe that our mind is the last frontier."

Brody shook his head as if mulling this over.

Knowing she should probably shut up, M. J. went for broke. "The sun, the earth, the moon, the stars . . . the miracle of birth? A higher power? Who can explain any of this? Sometimes you just have to have faith in order to believe in something you can't explain."

"I understand what you're getting at," he admitted, but his tone said he didn't agree.

M. J. shook her head sadly. "I made a promise to my sista this morning that I wouldn't settle for someone who couldn't believe in or support me for who and what I am. Not even love can overcome that, Brody."

With that, Brody lowered his head in defeat and slowly replied, "Are you asking me to leave?"

She put her hands on his cheeks. "No, I'm asking you to believe."

Brody closed his eyes and inhaled. "I love you, M. J. I know this because I never felt this way before. But I can't give you what you're asking . . . not honestly and you deserve honesty."

M. J. nodded, swallowing the tears clogging her throat. "Thank you for that. I wouldn't want anything less."

Brody kissed her on the forehead and somehow managed to get dressed and out the door. He wandered around the city, barely seeing the sights and sounds of Nashville at night as he walked for who knows how long before he ended up back at his hotel room. He fell into an exhausted but fitful sleep and woke up the next morning feeling depressed and wanting to call M. J. so badly that it hurt.

For the next week Brody concentrated on business, doing every interview and making every promotional appearance that he possibly could just to keep busy, but when his single broke into the *Billboard* top twenty, he didn't feel as much joy as he should have felt. Then, when his music video debuted on CMT and made it into the top ten for the week, he should have been thrilled . . . but he wasn't.

Every damned waking minute and even in his dreams, for that matter, he had M. J. on the brain.

His missed her.

He loved her.

Countless times he had picked up his cell phone to call but then thought that it would only be difficult for them both. She wanted him to support and understand something that he couldn't even comprehend, so where did that leave them?

With a sigh, Brody packed his bags, needing a break from the city and from memories of the time spent with M. J. He tossed his gear in his truck and drove to his recently acquired farm, about an hour south of Nashville. The farm was his little slice of heaven, fifty acres of woods and fields, including a stocked lake just begging to be fished.

Brody hopped out of his truck and took a deep gulp of farm-fresh air. The barn was in good condition, but the house needed major repairs. While Brody's first thought was to flatten the house and start from scratch, he angled his head at the rambling mess of peeling paint and suddenly had other ideas. With that thought in mind he grabbed his gear and hurried up the steps and went inside.

An hour later he was shirtless and sweating while scraping paint from the front-porch railing. *M. J. would love this place. It's got character*, he thought, wiping the sweat from his brow with his forearm.

And so his life went for the next month. During the day he worked on restoring the house and at night he sat on the front porch with his guitar and wrote songs . . . *sad* country songs, tearjerkers about love lost. Damn, he was *becoming* a sad country song, moping around drowning his sorrows in beer and blues, and tonight was no exception. With his guitar on his knee and sorrow in his heart he began playing.

"What the hell is wrong with you, boy?"

Brody abruptly stopped strumming his guitar, sat up straight and squinted his eyes into the dark night, looking for the source of the voice. "Hello? Who is out there?"

"M. J. misses you, you know. Been crying her eyes out," accused the gruff Southern voice.

"Hey, where are you?" Brody stood up and peered into the darkness but didn't see a thing, and since he hadn't heard a car approach and the farm was pretty remote, a little shiver ran down his spine. Brody looked down at his beer can with a frown. Damn, he had had only two, so he wasn't drunk, and he wasn't crazy, although he seemed heading in that general direction. "What the hell is going on here?" he whispered into the sultry night.

"You're a danged fool, Brody Baker."

Brody whipped around to the sound of the voice but didn't see a thing . . . or did he? Was that a firefly? Brody squinted again, searching for the flickering light, when something smacked him upside the head. "Ouch!" he shouted, but his eyes widened when he spotted what looked like a tiny ball of fire tumbling to the ground. Without really thinking, Brody reached out and caught the ball in the palm of his hand, expecting it to be hot, but all it did was tickle.

"Dang, that hurt."

Oh God. Suddenly it hit him. "P-Pixie?"

"Yeah," she said, moaning, "least that's what M. J. calls me and it's kinda growing on me. Note to self, don't ever do *that* again!"

"Do what?" he asked as if it were normal to be talking to a shimmering light in his palm.

"Well, my doggone hand is the size of a danged flea and I felt the need to knock some sense into your thick skull, so I body slammed you. Think I mighta broke a wing."

"You did?"

The light shimmered around in his palm as if she was checking herself out. "Oh, probably not. Just rattled my brains is all."

Brody sat down on the porch step. "Lord Almighty, you're real. M. J. was right."

"Course she was, you danged dummy. Look, I know it's hard for a cowpoke like you to swallow, but there's more to life than what meets the eye. You can write that down if you want."

Leaning his forearm on his knee, Brody blinked down at the little light. "So let me get this straight. You're Savannah and Logan's grandma, right?"

"Yeah, Savannah has been feeling my presence, but Logan is a tougher sell . . . a hardhead like you."

"So, are you an angel or a ghost?"

She flitted around in his palm. "I'm *not* a ghost! Ew, how creepy." She sighed. "You'd think once you made it through the pearly gates you'd be all leisurelike, but *no*, they give you tasks to do with, like, a territory and everything."

Brody frowned. "So what are your assignments?"

She chuckled. "My territory is the South—imagine that—and I'm sort of a honky-tonk cupid. My job is to get people where they need to be in order to fall in love. I asked for my first assignment to be Logan and Savannah, so that's where M. J. came into the picture. She was easy since she believes in all of this hocus-pocus . . . dreams and signs and all that."

"So you weren't working on me and M. J.?"

She left his hand and started flying around. "You and M. J. were like a sidebar, something that I had to deal with in order to complete my task, and let me tell ya, Brody, you've made my first assignment a tad difficult."

"I'm such an idiot," Brody said, coming to his feet and slapping his thigh.

"Aw, don't beat yourself up about it."

"Okay, work your magic and poof me over to her place. Come on," he pleaded, moving his fingers in a beckoning motion, "have at me."

"Um, that was sort of a fluke. I don't rightly know how I did it. I think it had something to do with how much the two of you wanted to be together."

"Fine, I want to be with M. J. now. Do your thing." He spread his arms akimbo and waited.

"But Brody, I'm not sure how much she wants to be with you, soul mate or not. You haven't called the girl in over a month. You'd best just hop in that fancy truck of yours and drive over there."

"Here I am, so you two can stop your arguing."

Brody pivoted around so fast that he almost fell over. "M. J.? How'd you get here?"

"Did I do that?" Pixie asked. "Damn, I'm good."

M. J. chuckled and pointed to her car parked over near the barn. "I drove."

"How'd you know where to find me?" Brody asked. He paused for a second and said, "Oh, I forgot, you're psychic. You know that stuff."

M. J. grinned. "Actually, I got the address from Logan and used MapQuest."

Brody descended the steps to stand next to her. "How'd you get the address from Logan? He swore not to give it out."

"Flirted," she admitted, looking down and scraping the toe of her boot across the grass.

"I'm gonna kick his sorry ass."

Her eyebrows shot up. "For giving me your address?"

"No, for flirting with you."

"You're joking, right?"

"Yeah." Brody nodded and then wrapped her in his embrace. Kissing the top of her head, he said, "God I've missed you." He pulled back and tipped her chin up. "I can't live without you . . . and those are both titles of songs I've written in the past week. I'm telling Travis that the title of our next CD needs to be *Mary Jane Barone.*"

M. J. laughed and then caught her bottom lip between her teeth. After a moment she asked, "So what does this mean, Brody?"

"Well, I've been talking to a feisty little ball of fire, so either everything you've told me is true or I'm crazier than a bedbug."

She wrapped her arms around his waist and gazed up at him with her luminous brown eyes. "Was that your macho way of telling me that you believe in me?"

"Yeah," he answered gruffly. "I'm sorry," he began, but M. J. stopped him with a finger to his lips.

"No, stop. Don't you see? I wouldn't want it any other way. You came to terms with this in your own way, unforced and honest. I couldn't ask for more."

"I love you with all my heart and soul," Brody said softly, and leaned in for a long delicious kiss. When he pulled back M. J. was crying. "What? Baby, please don't cry."

M. J. smiled, brushing at her wet cheeks. "This is

how I always dreamed it would be . . . kissing my soul mate beneath a star-soaked sky and in the light of the silvery moon."

"We can do more than kiss," Brody said with a wicked grin.

M. J. grinned right back. "You read my mind, cowboy. Just who is the psychic here, anyway?" she asked, pulling him in for another long, hot kiss.

"My work here is done!" Pixie said, and flickered off into the night. "Damn, I'm good—*ouch*," she muttered, smacking into a low-hanging branch. "Gotta work on this flying thing."

Honky-tonk Angel

"Run!" Sophia's brain shouted, but her body refused to obey. She stood frozen with wide-eyed, icy terror while her assailant bore down on her. A scream welled up in her throat just as her feet finally took flight. She blindly ran down the dark, deserted street as fast as she could until her breath came in ragged gasps. Cold sweat rolled down her back and her heart thundered in her ears.

Without looking back, Sophia knew that he was closing in. His boots clumped on the pavement, closer and closer until she could feel the heat of his whiskey-tainted breath and smell his rank odor. When his fingertips brushed against her back she willed her feet to go faster.

"Slow down, you bitch!" he growled, and then grabbed her by the hair.

Sophia screamed in pain and fear but slammed her elbow into his gut. He roared in anger and then twisted *his fist into her hair and yanked hard, making Sophia fall backward against his hot, sweaty body. With a desperate scream she bucked and writhed, ignoring the pain as she frantically tried to escape.*

"You belong to Jimmy Joe Tucker now. Time for a little payback," he said low and fierce into her ear. Sophia could feel his erection poking into her back and shuddered.

"No . . . ," she moaned while trying to arch away from him.

"Oh yeah, baby. You're gonna like it." He reached around and fondled her breasts and then squeezed hard, making Sophia's knees go out from under her. He dragged her into the nearby alley and shoved her roughly against a brick wall. With a whimper she tried to knee him in the groin.

"Bitch!" he hissed, and slapped her with the back of his hand. Pain exploded as Sophia felt her lip split open. She slithered to the ground and then he was on top of her, tearing at her clothes. . . .

With a gasp, Sophia jackknifed into a sitting position in the bed while clutching the sheet to her hammering heart. Rapid, shallow breathing made her feel light-headed and cold, even though her body was bathed in sweat. For a moment Sophia felt disoriented. She blinked, looking around the room, wondering where she was, but then remembered that she was in her sister's apartment in Nashville, Tennessee. Although everyone thought she was here to write her book and to watch over Love Connection while M. J. was on tour with

Brody, Sophia was secretly hiding out from low-life Jimmy Tucker. She had helped put the murdering slime-bag away, but he was out on parole and if her recent dreams were right, he was out to kill again.

Sophia shivered. Her dreams were always right.

With that sobering thought she tossed back the covers and scooted from the bed. Although she hadn't slept much, returning to another frightening dream didn't hold any allure, so she headed to the bathroom for a long hot shower.

Breathing in the peach-scented body wash made Sophia feel slightly queasy while she tried to scrub the feel of Jimmy Tucker's hands from her body. Placing her palms against the warm tile, she let the hot water pelt against her back and willed the nausea to pass. "The nightmare is over. . . . You're safe," she whispered, but the dream had been so vivid that her fear was hard to shake. With trembling fingers, she slicked back her hair and swallowed. "Suck it up, Barone," she said to herself. "There's no way that creep knows that you're in Nashville. No way."

"I don't know what you're getting so fired up about, Logan. Sophia Barone is a professional medium, after all."

"As opposed to a large?"

Savannah snapped her dish towel at her brother, catching him on the arm. "Ha-ha, very funny," she said, and went back to drying the beer mugs.

"Hey, that stung," he complained, rubbing his arm beneath his T-shirt sleeve.

"Wuss." She wrinkled her nose, snapping the damp towel at him again, but his reflexes were too fast and he easily caught it.

"Not hardly," he countered, and tossed the rag at her, grinning when she missed it. "Nice catch."

Savannah stuck her tongue out at him, making Logan laugh. They might be siblings, but they were complete opposites and even though Logan loved his baby sister dearly, they almost always saw things from different angles. Savannah loved all things artsy, while Logan had gotten all of the athletic genes in the family. He might be thirty-five years old, but at six feet two inches of solid muscle, Logan could still knock a baseball over the center-field fence, water-ski like a pro or climp up a mountain. You name a sport and Logan could probably do it.

Savannah turned around and leaned one hip against the bar. "You know, Logan, I'm twenty-three years old and a senior in college. Ever since Mom and Dad retired to Florida and you took over this bar, you think you need to run my life too. I know you mean well, but if I want to talk to Sophia about making a link to Granny, I damned well *will*."

"Making a link?"

Savannah rolled her light blue eyes at him, the only feature that they had in common. "*Connecting* with her, Logan. It kills me that I wasn't there when she died. All I want to do is say a proper good-bye and know that she's gone on peacefully. What's so wrong with that?"

Logan folded his arms across his chest. "I don't feel right letting you conjure up the dead. Granny is gone,

Savannah. I miss her too, but let her rest in peace." He turned away to wipe down the bar, but her next words had him spinning back around.

"I've been feeling her presence. Logan, what if she's trying to tell me something?"

Logan put his hands on his sister's shoulders. "Savannah, I see things every day that remind me of her, so I guess you could say that I've been feeling her with me too. Whenever her favorite Patsy Cline song comes on the radio it chokes me up. Time will heal, I promise."

"Whatever. I knew you wouldn't understand." She pursed her lips and turned away, wiping the mugs with jerky movements and setting them down none too gently.

Logan kissed her on top of her dark blond head, knowing that losing Granny Parks had been hard for his sister. Those two had shared a kinship and a love of music that Savannah sorely missed. While his heart went out to her, he couldn't condone having this Sophia chick trying to raise his granny from the hereafter, even if she was sweet little M. J. Barone's sister.

When Logan thought of M. J. falling in love with his friend Brody Baker he had to smile. He had heard that they were making wedding plans after Brody's latest country-music tour was over. Right now, M. J. was with Brody and Travis Mackey's band out on the West Coast, leaving her apartment open to her sister, Sophia, who was supposedly writing a book called *Seeking the Other Side*, the same name as her cable talk show, which was on hiatus for the summer. Logan knew this information from surfing her Web site. He figured since he owned the building, he should know a bit about the person who would be living next door to him for the next couple of months. Evidently Sophia Barone was well respected in the psychic world, which was sort of an oxymoron as far as Logan was concerned.

"I'm finished cleaning up," Savannah said, bringing him back from his musings. "I'll be back tonight around seven to sing."

Logan nodded. "Bring some of your friends with you, okay? Especially . . . what's her name, the stacked blonde?"

Savannah wrinkled her nose at him. "You dirty old man. Those college girls are way too young for you."

"I'm not walking with a cane yet."

Savannah shook her head. "Yeah, but you're not getting any younger. You need someone special, not some eye candy looking for a one-nighter."

"I don't do one-nighters," Logan protested, trying to look affronted.

Savannah did the rolling-her-eyes thing. "Yeah, right. Unfortunately my roomies think you're hot. *Why*, I'll never know. But hey, these girls are my friends, Logan. None of them need their hearts broken by you, okay?"

"I was only teasing, little sis. I'll keep my hands off of the Vanderbilt college girls. Too uppity for me anyway."

"Too *young*," Savannah said firmly.

"*Whatever*," he mimicked, but shot her a grin. The truth hurt, but Savannah was right. The college girls *were* too young, but he sometimes fed his ego by flirting with them. It passed the time and was basically harmless. It had been a while since he had gone on a real date, but most women Logan's age wanted to get serious and he wasn't ready to settle down. *Hell no.*

The fact was that the bar turned a nice profit but required long hours, leaving little time for the important things in life, namely sports. The last thing he needed was a woman telling him that he couldn't go golfing or fishing or hang gliding or whatever the hell he wanted to do with his valuable spare time.

Logan glanced up at the Budweiser clock above the bar and saw that it was a little past noon. Logan's didn't open until three, so he had time to go for a jog and grab a bite to eat before doing inventory and getting ready for the evening crowd. Since he was already in running shorts he tugged off his white T-shirt and then doubled over to begin stretching his tight hamstrings.

"Excuse me, but do you serve lunch?"

Logan angled his head up from his bent-over position and saw a fancy pair of sandals and a shapely pair of legs. *Damn, Savannah must have left the front door unlocked.* "Sorry, no," he answered, pushing up with an involuntary grunt.

Holy shit.

Logan was used to having to look down at women, but this chick was just shy of eye level. And she was a real looker if you were a sucker for the exotic type. . . . Dark fathomless eyes, long glossy black hair, high cheekbones and a straight nose made her look haughty and untouchable until Logan's gaze lit on her mouth. *Damn.* Plump, wide and perfectly shaped. *Oh, what a mouth like that could do to a man.*

One delicately arched eyebrow and the slight pursing

of her glossed lips told Logan that she knew exactly what she was doing to him. "There are plenty of restaurants downtown," Logan answered briskly. "Demos' over on Commerce Street serves steak and spaghetti. Jack's right down the block here on Broadway has ribs and chicken. There's a Hard Rock Cafe. . . . Just about whatever you're hungry for is within walking distance." Logan tried to sound businesslike and keep his gaze from overheating even though his dick was doing a little dance in his shorts, making him feel a bit like a horny teenager, while she appeared as cool as a cucumber. This kind of pissed him off. He wasn't one who liked feeling at a disadvantage.

"Hmmm," she said, tapping the side of her cheek with a glossy red fingernail. "I was really looking for something *quick* and *easy*. Any suggestions?"

"Oh, ummm . . . let me think." Logan knew he was at a crossroads here. He could jump on the sexual-innuendo bandwagon or blow her off. Part of him wanted to put her snooty ass in her place . . . but the other half, the half twitching in his pants, wanted to take control of the situation and give her back a little of what she was dishing out. The problem was, Logan wasn't entirely sure if she was coming on to him or just dicking with him. He suspected the latter, but then again he had lived long enough to know that women weren't exactly immune to his charms.

Logan decided to fight fire with fire.

"Let's see. . . ." Rolling his head from shoulder to shoulder, Logan stretched, pretending to be mulling the question over. He tightened his ab muscles, showing off his six-pack. Then, reaching up, he ran his fingers through his short-cropped hair, knowing it would cause a ripple of muscle. But he suddenly felt so ridiculous doing this that he almost burst out laughing. Trying to keep a straight face, he asked, "Uh, you're not a vegetarian, are you? I mean, you do eat meat, right?"

Her amazing mouth twitched at the corners and for a moment Logan thought she might crack a smile. "As a matter of fact, not often, only when I *really* crave it."

"Ah, so what are you craving right now?" He leaned his elbows back on the bar, trying for a nonchalant yet sexy pose, even though he was getting a cramp in his left calf.

She gave Logan a deadpan dude-you-gotta-be-kidding look and remained silent.

Okay, this has gone far enough. Logan felt like an idiot and she obviously wasn't buying into his crap. "You were going to roll your eyes, weren't you?"

"How'd ya guess?" One eyebrow lifted and he saw just a hint of a smile.

"My sister does it to me all the time when I'm acting like a jackass."

She smiled, softening her features, making her go from haughty and untouchable to breathtaking and oh-so-enticing. For a moment Logan could only stare. But suddenly there was something familiar about her . . . prompting him to ask, "Have we met before?"

This time she did roll her eyes. "You've gotta be kidding. That's the best you've got? I'm disappointed."

Logan laughed. "I wasn't handing you a line. You do look familiar."

Chapter Two

The low rumble of Logan's laughter washed over Sophia like warm summer rain. "Is that so?" she asked, trying her best to keep her aloof armor in place, but she was caving, big-time. Logan Parks was friggin' hot. If that wasn't enough, he had linebacker shoulders that a girl could grab on to and an amazing sculpted chest lightly covered with dark hair that narrowed to an enticing line over ripped abs. He had the long lean build of a natural athlete and it wasn't hard at all to imagine him in a cowboy hat and leather chaps. He was drop-dead gorgeous but not in a pretty-boy way. . . . Oh, no, this guy was all man, rough and rugged. Dark stubble covered a strong jaw softened a bit by a full, sexy mouth. His nose was just slightly crooked like he had seen a fight or two . . . or three. He had high cheek-bones, a wide forehead and closely cropped dark chest-nut hair mussed right now from his fingers. It was his eyes, though, that captivated Sophia—Paul Walker ice blue, but by God, they could make a girl positively melt. Those eyes were looking at her closely right now, as if trying to place her.

"Where have I seen you before?" he asked more to himself than to her.

"I'm not sure," Sophia answered, but wondered if he had seen her on television. He didn't look like the type to watch *Seeking the Other Side*, her syndicated show, but you never knew these days. "I'm new in town, having just moved into my sista's place last night. I'm guessing you're Logan?"

He nodded with a slight frown and then his blue eyes widened. "You're Sophia Barone, M. J.'s sister?"

"I know—we look nothing alike except for our eyes and hair color." She stepped closer and offered her hand. "Nice to meet ya, Logan. M. J. has had nothing but great things to say about you and your sista. As you know, I'll be living in her place for the rest of the summer."

"You sound a lot alike, though."

Sophia grinned. "Ya mean my Brooklynese?"

"Yours is more pronounced."

"Yeah, well, she's been away from home longer."

"Oh, okay, I recognize you now from your Web site."

"You visited my site?" Sophia asked, a little disappointed that his teasing manner had been replaced with a more serious attitude.

Logan shrugged. "I wanted to know more about what it is that you do."

"Oh," Sophia said, feeling a little like she was suddenly under a microscope. "I'll be happy to enlighten you."

"No, I get the general idea." He hesitated but then went on. "Listen, I have a request."

"Okay." Sophia chewed on the inside of her mouth, trying to put her aloof attitude back in place, but she felt vulnerable and exposed. She had no idea what was coming, but she didn't like the vibes she was picking up.

"My sister, Savannah, wants you to . . . to conjure up our dead grandmother. Savannah never got to say goodbye before she died and now she has this crazy notion that Granny has been trying to contact her or something."

"Oh, so you want me to make a link to your grandmother?" Sophia asked with a slight smile. "I can—"

"No!" Logan interrupted, shaking his head. "No, you're getting the wrong message. I *don't* want you to do this. Savannah is an emotional girl and she misses her granny dearly."

"But perhaps I could make a link and give Savannah some much-needed closure. If she's been feeling her presence, then it's probably because your grandmother needs this connection as well to pass on peacefully." Sophia gazed at him, hoping to see a little interest, but all she saw was a muscle ticking in his jaw.

"Look, Ms. Barone, I don't mean any disrespect, but I don't want you to do this, okay?"

Sophia masked her hurt by narrowing her eyes. *Why don't people* understand *that when they say they don't mean any disrespect, they always manage to shovel it right at you?* "How old is your sista?"

"Twenty-three." The muscle ticked again. "Look, I know that she can do this if she wants to. I'm asking you as a favor not to do it."

"Now, just why would I do that?" she asked sharply. Her hurt was quickly dissolving into anger. Most of the time she let these types of comments roll off her back, but for some reason this disbelief coming from Logan stung. Maybe it was because she had let down her guard and allowed herself to be attracted to him; *whatevva*, it hurt like hell.

Logan pushed away from the bar and took a step closer. Sophia guessed that he could usually intimidate people by towering over them, but in her heels she stood almost eye to eye. Lifting her chin, Sophia stood her ground. "*Fugetaboutit*. If your sista wants a reading with me, I'll be happy to oblige."

"Really?" He cocked on eyebrow and said, "You know technically I leased that apartment to M. J. and I'm under no real obligation to let you stay there."

Unprepared for this, Sophia sucked in a breath. "You're threatening to *throw me out* if I see your sista? You're that narrow-minded?"

Something like regret passed over his face, but he said, "I love my sister and I don't want her sucked into thinking that she's having a conversation with her beloved grandmother. I just don't want her emotions toyed with that way. Surely you can see where I'm coming from."

Sophia inclined her head. "Yeah, unfortunately, I do. You think that I'm a hack, a fake taking money from innocent, unsuspecting people like your sista. I get your point loud and clear! I swear I'd pack my things in an instant except that I promised M. J. I'd keep an eye on her place for her and I need the privacy for personal reasons."

She swallowed and said, "Look, I'll promise you that I won't seek your sista out, but if she comes to me in need, I won't turn her down even if it means being evicted by the likes of you."

"The likes of me?"

Sophia put her hand to her mouth and then said, "Oh, I'm sorry. I didn't mean any *disrespect*." With that parting jab, she turned on her heel and walked out of the bar with as much dignity as she could muster. The only saving grace was the look of horror that he had been so rude etched on his handsome face.

Sophia's appetite had vanished, leaving her feeling drained and hollow. M. J. had been so insistent that she should immediately introduce herself to Logan that she had made up that lame excuse of asking him if they served lunch when she had known damned well that they didn't. The bar's hours of operation were posted as plain as day, but when the door was conveniently open Sophia had spotted the delectable Logan tugging off his shirt and, in a moment of insanity—well, perhaps lust— had decided to walk on in.

"Wow," Sophia whispered as she entered the apartment. She tried to remember when she had been so instantly attracted to a guy, and drew a blank. But then she mentally shook herself for letting her usual guard down. In one month she would be thirty-five years old and it was becoming more and more evident that there wasn't a guy out there who wanted a psychic medium for a wife. Talking to the dead was a real mood killer, so much so that Sophia had long ago given up on marriage. Sure, she knew that guys found her sexy and she worked hard to keep in good mental and physical shape, but she got so sick and tired of first dates that she just quit dating completely and concentrated on her career. Consequently, she had shot to the top of her profession, landing her own talk show and a lucrative book contract about her psychic experiences.

Sophia reached in the fridge for a bottle of water. "Jerk," she muttered as she unscrewed the plastic cap. She took several long gulps before leaning her hands against the cool sink, blinking back tears. "Suck it up, Barone," she said tightly. *Look at the bright side.* Her career was rewarding. She had seen so many people find peace and closure after she'd linked them to a deceased loved one. She had helped to locate missing people, helped police solve cold cases. But *damn it*, she was human and she wanted the warmth of an embrace, the joy of children, the heat of passion.

Sophia wanted to be loved.

What was so damned exasperating was that men found her so physically appealing. She could have sex out the wazoo, but she didn't want sex. Well, no, she did want sex and pretty damned badly. "I want a friggin' relationship too," Sophia said, and slammed the bottle down so hard that it cracked. The fact that M. J. had found her soul mate had given Sophia renewed hope, but when Logan's flirting turned sour it was an instant reminder that a love connection wasn't in the cards for her no matter how much M. J. insisted it was.

Sophia sighed. Even if she was lucky enough to find someone to love, it wasn't likely that he would stick around after learning her profession. "Hi, my name is

Sophia Barone and I see dead people." She tossed the bottle in the trash with a little more force than necessary. "Who needs a man, anyway?" she muttered. Oh, but then a mental image of bare-chested Logan skittered into her brain and halted, refusing to budge. For a moment, just one long, heated moment, she imagined what it would feel like to be held in those strong arms. He could chase her fears away, protect her from harm.

Sophia shivered, remembering the real reason she had come to Nashville.

But then she pushed away from the sink, took a deep breath and squared her shoulders. "Get a grip, Barone. You're tougher than this," she whispered, deciding to do some relaxing yoga. What she really wanted to do was go for a long mind-numbing run, but Logan, the hunky jerk, was heading for a run and he was the last person she wanted to encounter . . . well, the second-to-last person.

✳ *Chapter Three*

Logan ran like a demon up hills over side streets, longer and harder than usual, desperately trying to get the image of Sophia Barone's hurt look out of his mind. By the time he arrived back at his apartment, sweat was pouring off him, burning his eyes and soaking his shorts. In the end he was light-headed with exhaustion but still felt like an ass.

Logan hated feeling like an ass. His mother had pounded Southern manners into his brain and being rude to a woman was just something he couldn't live with. After a shower he donned fresh jeans and a blue polo shirt with his logo on the sleeve and quickly checked on things at the bar. When Jack Shea, his head bartender, arrived, Logan turned operations over to him and walked next door to order a pizza. While his food was being prepared he returned to the bar and located a bottle of red wine. Then, armed with a hot veggie pizza, a nice bottle of Chianti and an apology,

Logan took a deep breath and lightly rapped on Sophia's door.

After a moment Logan saw Sophia peek past the lacy curtain covering the window. She hesitated long enough to make him think she wasn't going to let him in, but just when he was about to knock again the door swung open.

"Pizza delivery," Logan said with what he hoped was an engaging smile.

"I didn't order pizza," she said, and closed the door.

Logan stood there for a moment feeling a bit foolish. Since he wasn't used to getting the old turndown from women, he was suddenly at a loss as to what to do. Juggling the wine and the pizza, he reached out and knocked again. After a moment the door swung open. Without a word, Sophia took the pizza and the wine from him and then closed the door in his face.

Logan stood there blinking but then rapped on the door a bit harder. She took her time but then opened the door, munching on a slice of pizza, looking way too cute in low-rise sweatpants and a matching blue hooded top unzipped just low enough to make him sweat. She raised her eyebrows in question and tilted her head to the side, causing her ponytail to flip over her shoulder, making her appear way younger than he suspected that she was.

Thinking fast, Logan said, "You forgot to tip me."

She swallowed a bite of pizza, licked her lips and then said, "Don't mess with a chick from Brooklyn."

"Excuse me?"

"That was your tip." She started to close the door,

but Logan stopped her with his hand and entered. "Hey, just whadaya think you're doin'?" Sophia fumed.

Logan came up with the first thing that popped into his head. "Inspecting. I do it monthly. It's in the lease."

"Oh, tryin' to find another reason to toss me out?" She bit hard into the pizza and had to chase the melted cheese with her tongue.

Logan tried not to stare. "Look, my reason for coming over here was to apologize. The pizza and wine were my peace offering. I was rude. I'm sorry, Sophia. Will you accept my apology?"

Sophia hesitated. She wanted to accept his apology because she could see in his eyes that he was sincere, but despite his earlier behavior she remained incredibly attracted to him . . . and not just physically. She just wasn't sure she wanted to put herself in that position. Oh, but damn, he was making resistance difficult. Logan had a warm smile and a quick wit, and even though he had hurt her feelings, the fact that he was looking out for his sister spoke volumes about his character.

"I know what you're thinking," Logan said when she remained silent.

"Oh really?" His comment surprised and rather amused her. *Just who's the psychic here, anyway?* "Tell me."

He took a step closer, invading her space in the small kitchen and putting her already-heightened senses on full alert. "You're thinking that a redneck bartender like me could never comprehend what you do, so why get something started when it's destined to end badly? Am I right?"

Okay, maybe he is psychic. Sophia frowned, not knowing quite what to say. "Well, in a roundabout way you've hit the nail on the head."

"I just might surprise you, though. Why don't we get to know one another and take it a step at a time? I'm not in the market for forever and you're only here for a while. Let's make the best of it."

Sophia's heart started beating faster. She wasn't sure if she liked where this was going or not. "Whadaya suggesting? A summer fling?"

He shrugged those incredibly wide shoulders. "I'm suggesting that we get to know one another and then go from there without any expectations."

Sophia didn't know whether to be flattered or disappointed. *She* wanted forever, so getting something started with someone who was up-front about not wanting to get serious was probably a mistake. Oh, but when had that ever stopped her?

"Hey," he said with a slow smile, "you look like you're carrying the weight of the world on those shoulders of yours. How about just having some pizza, wine and conversation?"

"Deal." Sophia smiled back. Maybe it was time that she lightened up. The last couple of weeks had been rough.

"You've got a killer smile, you know," he said while helping himself to a slice of pizza. "You should smile more often."

While rummaging around for a corkscrew and glasses she asked, "You know what? I think you're right." She poured the wine and handed him a glass.

"To smiling more often," he toasted, and clinked his rim with hers.

Sophia took a sip of the full-bodied Chianti and nodded. "This is delicious. Thanks for your peace offering, Logan. It's hittin' the spot." Sophia had another spot she'd like him to hit but pushed that thought from her mind. She gathered plates and napkins, and sat down next to him at the small table, feeling a bit shy at first, but he carried the conversation for a while, telling her about Nashville, his bar and his sister's singing.

"Am I boring you to tears?"

"Not at all. Actually I'm more relaxed than I've been in a very long time." She dabbed at her mouth with her napkin and realized that it was true. Logan's easygoing demeanor and the wine had her feeling mellow and at ease.

"Now, tell me about yourself," Logan prompted while topping off their glasses.

Sophia toyed with the stem of her wineglass, wishing that her life were normal. *Why the hell can't I be a nurse or waitress or anything else other than what I am?*

"Hey," he said, covering her hand with his, "I know I acted like a jerk earlier, but I'm definitely interested. Tell me about your work, Sophia." He leaned back in his chair and confessed, "I Googled you and there were pages and pages of information. Do you really work with the police, solving cases?"

She nodded slowly, surprised but pleased by his interest. "I mostly work with clients wanting to reach out to loved ones who have crossed over, but I've helped the police solve unsolved crimes on occasion. Believe me, they only call psychics when they've exhausted all other sources, and still remain very skeptical throughout the process."

Logan leaned forward in his chair as if truly interested, encouraging Sophia to continue. "I can't solve the crimes, just give clues that at first glance don't always make any sense . . . maybe a number that ends up being an address or a description of the criminal that no one has seen."

"You come up with the pieces and they have to put them together?"

Sophia nodded. "Yeah, like that."

"And you've really helped solve some cases?"

Nodding, Sophia reached for her wineglass and was horrified to see that her fingers were shaking. Her dream about Jimmy Tucker was still too fresh in her mind. She looked over at Logan, hoping that he didn't notice, but his blue eyes narrowed and he asked, "Hey, what's wrong?"

"Nothin'." She forced a laugh, but it sounded brittle.

"Bull." He took her hands in his and began rubbing her cold fingers. "Tell me."

"It's nothin' . . . really." She wanted to withdraw her hands but then didn't want to alarm him, so she attempted a casual smile.

Squeezing her hands, he said, "I know that you don't know me that well, yet, but anything you say to me stays in this room."

Sophia's brain pounced on the word *yet*. So he wanted to get to know her better? Unloading her crazy problems on this down-to-earth guy would most likely end their relationship, like, five minutes from now. Oh, but how amazing would it be to have someone strong and caring to confide in? Torn, she simply shook her head and remained silent.

"Tell me," he encouraged. When Sophia looked up at him with those fathomless brown eyes, Logan wanted to gather her in his arms and chase away the fear that he saw there. He might not buy into all of this, but he felt the intense need to soothe and protect her.

She inhaled sharply and the fear rolling off her sent a chill down Logan's spine. He rubbed his thumbs over her knuckles and waited.

"There was an unsolved murder that I was called in to help with twelve years ago." She shivered, making Logan wish he had never brought it up, and yet he wanted to know, so he didn't stop her. "I helped put this creep, Jimmy Tucker, in jail for smashing his wife's head in with a shovel. But it was a crime of passion, not premeditated, so he was recently up for parole and this time they let him out."

"So he's *threatened* you?" The thought made Logan see red. "Why haven't the police done anything?"

Sophia looked at him for a long moment and then said, "Because the only real threats have come in the form of dreams."

"Oh." He frowned.

"You think I'm nuts, don't you?"

"Look, I won't pretend to understand all of this. . . ."

"Oh, you dodged that question," she said with a shaky laugh.

"You didn't let me finish," he said, gently putting his index finger to her mouth. "Tell me about this dream."

Lowering her eyes, she shook her head. It hit Logan hard that this self-proclaimed tough chick from Brooklyn needed a shoulder to lean on. He remained silent while he waited for her to open up to him.

Finally, she swallowed and said so softly that he almost couldn't hear her, "Jimmy Tucker was . . . *angry* and chasing me down this dark street. I . . . I tried to run, but I was so afraid and he kept closing in on me . . . ." She paused and shivered. "He grabbed me by my hair. Dragged me into an alley and . . . pushed me against this . . . wall. He . . . *oh, Logan* . . . I struggled, but he was ripping at my clothes and I was powerless to stop him and then, thank God, I woke up."

Logan felt a surge of rage. "If this guy tries to contact you or threatens you in any way, shape or form, even if it's just in your dreams, I want you to call me, okay?" He motioned sideways with his thumb toward his place. "I'm at the bar or in my apartment most of the time, so *don't hesitate.*"

"Thank you, Logan." She gave him a trembling but genuine smile that did funny things to his gut. When she stood up to clear the table, he followed her to the sink with his own dishes.

"I should get over to the bar to check on things."

She nodded, drying her hands on a dish towel. Because she stood in her socks her head came about to the tip of his nose and in her ponytail and sweats she seemed vulnerable, so different from their first encounter. The thought of anyone hurting her had him drawing her into his arms without really thinking, just feeling.

✳ Chapter Four

$\mathcal{S}$ ophia knew that for her own sanity she should push him away, but it felt so damned good to be enveloped in his warm embrace that she sighed and buried her nose in his shirt. God, he smelled good, like laundry detergent, musky cologne and warm man. She knew the hug was meant to comfort her, but a sudden longing had her tilting her face up for a kiss.

Logan didn't disappoint her. He lowered his head and captured her mouth with his. Comfort flew out the window, replaced with heated passion that had Sophia wrapping her arms around his back and pressing herself close. It was as if the pilot light that had gone out long ago was struck by a match and suddenly came roaring back to life. She opened her mouth for him, seeking more. His lips were soft, his mouth was hot, and his tongue was firm and commanding as he kissed her deeply. He came up for air but then kissed her again, cradling her head and slanting his mouth over hers, teasing . . . tugging on her lips with his teeth and then licking softly as if savoring the last taste before pulling his head back.

Sophia placed her hands on Logan's chest and could feel the rapid beat of his heart. His breathing was a bit ragged, telling her that he was as affected as she was. "Do you really havta get back?"

He swallowed and traced her lips with his index finger. "If I don't go, do you know where this will likely lead?"

"I suppose I do." Sophia smoothed her hands over the soft cotton shirt and could feel the heat of his skin. She wondered if a down-to-earth guy like Logan could ever fall for an oddball like her, but then again M. J. was pretty insistent that she should introduce herself to him. Did M. J. think that Logan was her soul mate? *Oh God, what should I do?*

"You've got that weight-of-the-world-on-your-shoulders expression again, Sophia," Logan gently chided.

"Sorry," she said, plucking at a button on his shirt.

"I know what you're thinking."

"Again? Are you sure *you* don't have a sixth sense?" she tried to joke, but she waited for him to elaborate.

"You're thinking again that we're worlds apart."

"We are, Logan. You're down-to-earth and I'm . . ." She shrugged.

"Out there?" His tone was teasing, but they both knew that it was true.

"Admittedly, yes. But there's even more. You mentioned that you're not looking for forever."

"And you are?"

Sophia spread her hands out and nodded. "Eventually . . . *hopefully*, yes. I know that I'm putting the cart way before the horse but"—she shrugged—"I have to know that sleeping with you could at least potentially lead to more."

"I'll be honest with you, Sophia. I'm thirty-five years old and I've never once felt the urge to settle down. I work hard and I play hard, leaving little time for anything or anyone else."

"Oh." Her heart sank. "*Okay* . . . point taken."

"Sophia, I already care too much about you not to be completely honest. But I want you to call me if you need me," he said, handing her a business card from his wallet. "I'm serious."

Sophia nodded, taking the card from him. "I suppose I should be grateful," she said a bit stiffly.

Logan leaned in and kissed her softly. "I wish things could be different."

Oh, wow, *that* was original, Sophia thought, but forced a smile as she walked him over to the door. "Thanks again for the pizza and wine. It hit the spot." *Even if you didn't.* Sophia closed the door and leaned back against the cool wood, fighting tears. She picked up the empty bottle of wine, wishing for another glass, and let out a little screech of frustration. Logan Parks had encouraged her to open up to him . . . *and* to feel the stirring of desire, which she tried to keep carefully tucked away. Then he had the nerve to blow her off! Sophia took a deep breath and exhaled it. She supposed that she had spooked him with her dream. Or maybe it was the psychic-medium thing in general. She put her head in her hands and moaned. God, or maybe the fact that she had just told him that she was looking for forever! "It's a wonder he didn't run outta here!"

"So, you're giving up that danged easily?"

"Who's there?" Sophia whipped around looking for the source of the husky Southern voice but saw only a slight flicker of light. Her heart beat faster and she whispered, "Ohmigawd. Pixie?"

"The one and only. I guess M. J. told you all about me?"

"She did," Sophia answered with a grin. "So what are you doing here with me? Isn't your job done?"

"Not at all. I'm not supposed to tell you this," she began, and flickered closer, "but I have it on good authority that Logan Parks is your one and only."

"M-my soul mate?" Sophia's heart skipped a beat.

"You're darned tootin'. Wasn't supposed to tell ya. M. J. wanted you to figure it out on your own, but I thought these were extenuating circumstances, being that you're mucking it all up."

Sophia put the empty wine bottle down on the kitchen table with a hard plunk. "Well, isn't that just dandy? I'd be more excited if the man hadn't just told me that he never plans on settling down. Soul mate or not, he's a player, not a keeper. At least he was kind enough to tell me."

"Oh, horse pucky. They all say that. Come on, girl. Show me some spunk. March your ass over there to that honky-tonk and make him jealous. Find you a big ol' cowboy stud muffin to flirt with and we'll see just how much Mr. Logan wants to remain footloose and fancy-free. Wear somethin' that shows off your boobies."

Sophia blinked at the shimmering little light. "Show off my boobies? That's not a very angelic suggestion."

"I'm still in training," Pixie replied with a laugh. "Look, I succeeded in getting your sister and that crazy singing cowboy together. Now, don't you go messin' this up for me."

"For you?" Sophia narrowed her eyes. "There's a bigger picture here, isn't there?"

"Maybe."

Sophia folded her arms and began tapping her foot while watching the light flicker around the room.

"Okay, *okay*," Pixie said gruffly. "Boy, oh boy, you're tougher than your sweet little sis."

"Tell me!"

"I can't. This thing has to happen in sequence. But believe me when I say that you and Logan are meant to be together."

"Ohmigawd."

"What?" The light stopped flickering and hovered in front of Sophia's face.

"You're Savannah and Logan's grandma."

"M. J. tell you that? That girl has a big mouth."

"No, she didn't. I'm a psychic medium, remember? Wait a minute. . . . I'm seeing my brother and . . . and *Savannah*?"

"You didn't hear it from me! Keep it under your hat and let nature take its course."

"Wow . . . Luc and Savannah?" Sophia smiled at the thought.

"That's on the horizon. Don't worry 'bout that now. Go put on somethin' tight and low-cut."

"Pixie!"

"Hey, there's nothin' wrong with usin' what the good Lord gave ya. I may be old, but I ain't dead. Oh, yeah, I *am* dead." She laughed at her own joke. "Now, go shake that thing!"

"But Logan made it clear—"

"Pishposh and hogwash. You've found your man, Sophia Barone. Now go get him!"

Sophia would have argued the point further, but Pixie vanished in a swirling cloud of sparkling dust. Sophia took a deep breath and headed into the tiny guest bedroom and opened up the equally tiny closet. After careful consideration, she decided on a pair of low-rise dark blue jeans and a contrasting plain white V-necked T-shirt. At first glance the outfit wasn't very sexy, but the denim clung in all the right places and the shirt was understated but molded to her breasts and showed just a hint of her flat tummy.

Sophia decided to go easy on the makeup, highlighting her eyes with some smoky shadow and eyeliner and a touch of mascara, but generously applied rose-tinted lip gloss. After spraying on a bit of floral perfume, she removed the ponytail and brushed out her long, straight hair, adding a dab of gel for shine.

Music drifted her way, upbeat and energetic. "Maybe this will be fun," Sophia told herself. Although she wasn't much on crowds, she loved live music, and as for flirting, well, she was rusty, but unlike M. J., who had always been shy around guys, Sophia had no trouble finding her inner sexpot when she chose to. After slipping essentials into a tiny purse she was out the door.

Sophia walked around front to Broadway, where the sidewalk was teeming with tourists. The guy at the door gave her a once-over and an appreciative grin, providing Sophia with the boost of confidence that she needed to pull this off . . . well, she hoped, anyway. Since it was early, Logan's was just beginning to fill up and Sophia was lucky to find a seat at a tiny table. An instant later a cute waiter hustled over.

"What can I get for you, beautiful?" he asked with a suggestive smile.

Sophia smiled back, flexing her flirting muscles even though he was way too young and probably was just hoping for a big tip. Deciding to blend in with the crowd, she said, "A Bud Light, please."

"Coming right up." He gave her a wink and hurried off.

While tapping her toes to the music, she scanned the room for Logan. A stab of disappointment hit her when she didn't spot him, so she turned her attention to the small stage, where a hot cowboy revved up the crowd with Toby Keith's hit "I Love This Bar." Unlike M. J., Sophia had converted to country a while ago, loving the humor, the honesty and the stories that the lyrics told.

When the waiter returned with her beer Sophia tried to pay him. "No charge," he responded, and pointed to a muscle-bound cowboy seated at the end of the bar. The cowboy tipped his hat in her direction and lifted his own brown longneck in a silent toast.

"Tell him I said thanks," Sophia said, and handed

the waiter a tip. She gave the cowboy a small smile that was just encouraging enough to have him head her way.

"How y'all doin'?" he asked while resting his elbows on the tall table. "I'm Cody McNeal."

"Just fine," Sophia answered with a grin. "And I'm Sophia Barone." She was getting nice-guy vibes from him but noticed up close that he was way younger than she had thought.

"I haven't seen you around here before," he ventured. "You here on vacation?"

Sophia nodded. "You could say that. So, I gather that you're a regular?"

He pointed his beer bottle in the direction of the stage. "I'm singing later."

Sophia raised her eyebrows. "Really? Cool. So are you hoping to land a recording contract someday?"

He shrugged his shoulders. "What I really love doing is writing songs. I'm not big on performing, but this is how you get your stuff heard."

Sophia took a sip of her beer and nodded. "Interesting." She gestured toward the stool and said, "Have a seat, Cody. Tell me more."

"Don't mind if I do," he answered with a sexy Southern twang, and settled his big frame next to her. His easy smile and shy charm had Sophia actually enjoying his company. She forgot that she was supposed to be flirting and simply listened to the music while chatting with Cody about the hardships of breaking into the competitive music business. Since Logan failed to appear, playing the jealousy card became moot anyway.

Chapter Five

After knocking on Sophia's door for the third time, Logan let it sink in that she wasn't home, cursing himself for not getting her cell phone number. While Nashville wasn't considered a dangerous town, Sophia's comments about that jerk being on parole had Logan a bit nervous. Maybe she had been threatened only in her dreams, but she was a psychic after all, so her nightmares could be a very real warning.

Bracing one hand against the brick wall, he inhaled sharply, mentally acknowledging the fact that he took her psychic powers more seriously than he had let on. He secretly believed in the possibility of connecting with the other side, which made his reasons for Savannah *not* having a reading with Sophia even more valid. Some things were just better left alone, including the dead. With a sigh, he pushed away from the wall, wondering what to do. Nashville wasn't all that big of a city, but unless he was extremely lucky, finding

Sophia on the crowded streets would be next to impossible.

"Well, damn." Feeling a bit grumpy, Logan decided to hole himself up in his office and do some paperwork, hoping to fill his head with numbers instead of images of Sophia.

Thirty minutes later he shut his computer down in sheer frustration. "This is useless," he muttered, and pushed away from his desk. Deciding that a cold beer might mellow his mood, he headed into the bar and motioned for Jack Shea, his head bartender, to toss him a longneck. Although it was early, the bar was already hopping, thanks to Jesse Boone, who was belting out a damned good rendition of Keith Urban's "Who Wouldn't Wanna Be Me."

After this set, next up was Cody McNeal, a kid that Logan was especially fond of and who was quiet and unassuming but chock-full of talent. Logan had been around long enough to realize that the kid had potential. Since Savannah had called in with the excuse of too much schoolwork Logan had given Cody McNeal her spot so that he could showcase his songs. Just last week Toby Keith had stopped into the bar looking for fresh talent for his new record label and Logan would like nothing better than to see Cody make it.

After taking a long pull of his beer Logan scanned the bar, looking to see if Cody had arrived, and almost choked when he spotted Sophia and Cody with their heads bent together in what appeared to be an intimate conversation. Cody said something in Sophia's ear and she angled her head back and laughed.

"Just who are you fixin' to kill?" Jack asked, nudging Logan with his elbow.

"What?" Logan pulled his gaze away from Sophia and Cody.

Jack chuckled. "If looks could kill, somebody's ass would surely be dead as a doornail."

"I don't know what the hell you're talking about."

"Bull. Who is she?" Jack nodded in the direction of Sophia and Cody. He uncapped another beer and handed it to Logan, who was surprised that he had already drained his first one.

Logan grabbed the cold bottle. He took a long swallow and then said, "She's Sophia Barone, M. J.'s sister. She's staying in M. J.'s apartment for the summer."

"Ah, so it's Cody that you want to kill."

Logan slammed the bottle down so hard that foam oozed over the top. "I don't give a rat's ass about who Sophia talks to."

Jack slid a beer down the bar to a customer and then grinned. "Oh, man, *denial*. You've got it bad for that chick. Not that I can blame you. She's damned hot."

Logan shot Jack a glare.

"Hey, man, it's just an observation. I'm not about to step into your territory." He raised his hands in surrender.

"She's not my territory."

"Then she's fair game?"

"Jack, I'm gonna kick your pretty-boy ass."

"I'm not a fucking pretty boy."

"Yeah, well, you won't be after I break your damned nose."

"Whoa, I'm so scared." He looked at Logan in mock horror but took an involuntary step back. Jack had come to Nashville to become a country singer, but there was only one problem. He sucked. Jack was, however, cover-model material and had actually made some decent money doing bit parts for music videos. "So what are you gonna do?" Jack asked, nodding in Sophia's direction.

Logan shrugged. "Nothing."

"Oh, come on. You gonna let that dude get your girl?"

"She's not my girl," Logan insisted, but still felt a stab of jealousy. Trying to shake the feeling, he continued. "And she's not my type." He picked up some empty beer bottles and tossed them in the trash with a loud clank. While Jack filled an order, Logan nursed his beer and brooded. The longer he watched Sophia and Cody, the more jealous he got.

"Want another one?" Jack asked when there was a break in the action.

"No, thanks. I'm heading back to the office to do some paperwork."

"Yeah? Well, Cody just got up and left, so you've got yourself an opening. You'd better hurry before someone else beats you to it. Hey, is she a psychic like M. J.?"

"Sophia is a *psychic medium*."

"Dude, she talks to dead people?"

"If you believe in that sort of thing."

Jack shrugged. "Who knows? I try to keep an open mind about psychic phenomena."

Logan raised his eyebrows.

"Hey, I'm more than just a pretty face."

He seemed serious, so Logan swallowed his laughter. "Give me a Bud Light."

Jack tossed him one. "I thought you were done for the evening."

"Maybe *not*." Logan took the beer and headed over to Sophia's table. She saw him coming and her eyes widened a fraction, but then she looked away. *Okay*, thought Logan, *this isn't going to be easy*. "Hey there," Logan said close to her ear so as to be heard over the crowd and the music. "Brought you a beer."

"Thanks, but I'm fine," she answered with a small smile, and turned her attention back to where Cody was warming up. She smiled at the cowboy and he winked back.

Well, hell. Logan stood there feeling uncertain. Getting snubbed wasn't something he was used to. Clearing his throat, he asked, "Mind if I join you?"

Sophia turned those luminous eyes on him and hesitated. Logan's heart hammered while he waited for her answer, but she remained silent. He watched her fingers caress the neck of her beer bottle and his mouth went dry. Then, as if still in thought, she nibbled on her bottom lip, bringing Logan's attention to her mouth. He realized that he wanted to kiss her, right here, right now, right in front of Cody McNeal.

"I don't think that's a good idea," Sophia finally answered firmly.

"Kissing you?"

"What?" Sophia frowned. "I meant sitting down."

Feeling like an idiot, Logan shook his head but managed an embarrassed grin. "I think I should just walk away." He turned to go, but she surprised him by putting her hand on his arm.

"So you were thinking about kissing me?"

"Yeah, well, *that* and decking Cody."

"Well then, do it."

"Deck Cody?" Logan asked with a grin. He tried to sound cocky, even though his damned heart started pounding like he had just finished a hard run.

Sophia leaned closer so that her mouth was a mere inch from his. "No, kiss me."

"Right here?" Logan glanced around, but no one was paying them one bit of attention.

She arched an eyebrow as if issuing a challenge and it was all Logan needed. He closed the tiny gap separating their mouths and kissed her softly, briefly, but his reaction rocked him hard. Pulling back, he tried for a *See, I did it* grin, but the sight of her mouth moist from his kiss sent him into sexual overload. "Come back to my place with me," he said hotly in her ear.

Sophia swallowed but then replied, "I, um, told Cody that I'd listen to his set."

"Screw Cody," Logan growled.

Sophia grinned.

"I meant figuratively."

Sophia laughed harder than she could remember laughing in a long time and it felt damned good. Wiping a tear from the corner of her eye, she finally got her mirth under control. Logan looked at her uncertainly but with such hope in those incredible blue eyes that there was no way she could refuse. He was irresistible. "Okay."

"Okay . . . what?"

"I'll go back to your place with ya," she answered in his ear just as Cody began playing.

Logan smiled and tugged on her hand.

"Right after this song. I don't wanna be rude."

"Okay," Logan said reluctantly, but eased onto the bar stool next to hers.

Cody began singing a pretty good cover of Kenny Chesney's "No Shoes, No Shirt, No Problems." Sophia began singing along like most of the crowd did, while Logan drummed his fingers on the top of the table impatiently. She acted like she was enjoying the music and in any other circumstances she would have been, but all she could really think about was getting Logan out of his jeans.

"Ready?" Logan asked when the song finally ended.

Was she *ever*, but she pursed her lips and said, "Maybe I should listen to another song. I don't want Cody to think I hated it so much that I left."

"You're kidding," he said in her ear.

"Yeah."

Logan laughed and stood up, pulling her to her feet. "We'll go out the front door and around back."

Sophia smiled, realizing that he was playing the gentleman, not wanting others to speculate as to where he was taking her. They walked out the door, weaving through the thickening crowd. Once outside, however, they picked up the pace and hurried around the brick building to the back. As they ran Sophia laughed, feeling lighthearted and younger than her thirty-four years. She decided not to worry about what tomorrow might bring and to just enjoy the moment.

Logan fumbled with his keys, finally finding the right one, but dropped them to the ground. "Fuck," he growled, bending over to pick the key ring up. "Sorry," he said with the cutest grin Sophia had ever seen on a man.

"I forgive you, buttafingas! Just hurry up."

"I meant the language."

"That does it." Sophia shoved Logan up against the brick wall and kissed him soundly. She heard the clink of the keys hit the concrete and then he wrapped his arms around her, kissing her back so hotly and deeply that her knees threatened to give. When Logan's hands slid to her ass and he pressed her harder to him Sophia moved sensuously, letting her breasts rub against his chest. The delicious hardness of his erection moving over her mound made Sophia moan. She tugged the shirt from his pants and slipped her hands beneath the soft cotton, loving the smooth texture of his skin and the ripple of muscle.

"Let's get inside," Logan pleaded, barely penetrating through the haze of desire clouding Sophia's brain.

"Okay," she rasped, and backed away from where she had him trapped against the wall.

A man on a mission, Logan managed to make quick

work of the lock this time. They tumbled into the house, tripping, stumbling in the dark.

"Turn on a light," Sophia requested, giggling.

"That would take too long."

"A second?" she asked with a laugh.

"Like I said, too damned long."

Chapter Six

Logan pulled Sophia into his bedroom and then into his arms. They attempted to kiss and remove clothing at the same time, hopping, tugging, while keeping their lips locked. Logan reached over and blindly reached for the small lamp on his nightstand and managed to flick it on, casting a soft glow in the dark room. Sounds of the bar drifted in, voices, laughter . . . the thump of the bass guitar, but all Logan could hear was Sophia's soft sigh, a low rumble of laughter and then a long moan when they were finally skin to warm skin.

They tumbled backward onto the bed in a tangle of arms and legs, kissing, caressing and exploring. Logan felt the need to kiss Sophia everywhere . . . her elbow, the palms of her hands and then her navel. When he moved south to the tender insides of her thighs, she moaned and arched her back. With a low chuckle Logan kissed her kneecaps, her calves and then the tip of her big toe.

"Logan!"

He looked up to where Sophia had raised her head. She gazed at him with the fire of frustration in her eyes. Logan knew that he was teasing, hitting every spot on her delectable body except for the erogenous zones where she wanted his mouth the most.

"You're beautiful," he said, smiling when the fire died from her eyes, replaced by deep longing that touched Logan in places where he hadn't been touched before.

"Get your ass up here," she said softly.

"My ass?"

She grinned. "All of you. Although you *do* have a nice ass."

"Really?"

"You know you do. You—*oh!*"

Logan smothered her comment with a kiss. He loved this side of her . . . playful, feisty and so damned sexy. She seemed sensual by nature and Logan would bet the farm that he just recently bought that she would be un-inhibited and wild in bed.

He was damned well going to find out.

"I'm not very good at taking orders," he told her with a wicked grin.

"Oh *really*, because—oh!" she yelped when Logan moved over to the other end of the bed and dragged her toward him by pulling. Kneeling on the floor, he flung her legs over his shoulders.

"What do you think you're do-*ing*, oh God!"

Parting her folds with his fingers, Logan dipped his head and licked her lightly with the tip of his tongue. She was sleek, wet and *warm*, surrounding him with her natural scent that mingled with her floral perfume. Wanting more, Logan licked harder, savoring the taste, and then slipped his tongue inside where she was tight and hot. At that moment nothing existed except for his mouth and her body.

Sophia's breathing became reduced to short pants and she opened her thighs wider for him, uninhibited like Logan somehow knew that she would be. This encouraged him to devour her, knowing she would want it that way. Loving this freedom, Logan licked harder, delved deeper until he found the spot that drove her wild. Even as she came, he didn't let up, pushing her over the edge and then right into another climax that had her arching up from the bed while calling his name.

"Wow," she murmured with her eyes closed. "Amazing."

Logan grinned down at her as he pushed up to his feet. Her cheeks were flushed a rosy red and she suddenly shuddered as if feeling a little aftershock. While she was recovering, Logan located a condom and rolled it on. With a low moan that had her opening her eyes halfway, he scooted her up to the pillows.

Sophia gave Logan a slow smile as he joined her on the bed. Her dark hair fanned out in stark contrast with the white sheet. Unable to resist, he leaned in and ran his fingers through the soft tresses and then down the long column of her throat. With a sigh, he cupped her creamy white breasts and then circled her dusky nipples with his thumbs. She shivered and arched up, filling his hands with beauty.

"Ahh, Sophia . . ." When her gaze locked with his, Logan felt something warm and tender open inside him . . . something like love? Shaken by his thoughts, he leaned in and kissed her while bracing himself above her with his arms. Surely this was simply lust . . . intense desire stemming from the fact that he hadn't been with a woman for such a long time. Oh, but as he eased himself inside her slick heat, Logan wondered if sex had ever felt this good, this right.

Logan moved with a slow and easy rhythm at first, wanting to get Sophia revved up all over again, but that didn't take long. She wrapped her endless legs around his waist, urging him deeper, harder. Arching her back, she met him thrust for thrust while digging her fingers into his shoulders. Logan gritted his teeth, trying to keep from climaxing until she was ready. When she cried out he buried himself deep and exploded with a long surge of intense pleasure that seemed to come all the way from his toes.

He rode the moment out, then kissed her long and deep to express how he felt because words would be useless.

"Mmmm." Sophia ran her hands down his sweat-slick back, loving the ripple of muscle when he shifted his weight. He was still hard and thick and buried deep, filling her up and making her want to keep him there for a moment longer, so she kept her legs wrapped around him. As if sensing this, he kissed her again with such lingering passion that it took her breath away.

Finally when Logan's arms started to tremble, Sophia released her legs and he eased out, rolled to the side, but then propped himself up on one elbow. With a soft smile he traced her bottom lip with his fingertip. "You were amazing. I know that's an overused word, but it fits."

Sophia licked the tip of his finger and said, "What do you mean . . . *were*? We're not nearly done, ya know."

His finger paused and his blue eyes widened.

"You mean you're not up for more?" She was really teasing since she felt pretty damned satisfied but arched an eyebrow in challenge.

"No, but I can get there damned quick. Give me a little breather, okay?"

Sophia pursed her lips and tried not to grin. "Okay . . . ," she said slowly, "I suppose I can wait."

"I'll be right back." He kissed her lightly and then scooted from the bed. Grinning, she openly admired his naked backside as he walked across the bedroom.

After he disappeared into the bathroom, Sophia smiled and then stretched like a contented cat. Curious, she glanced around the room. It was impeccably clean and sparsely furnished with sturdy oak pieces but nary a knickknack in sight except for a framed photograph of Savannah on his dresser and another one of an older couple that she guessed was of his parents. A digital alarm clock and a Tom Clancy novel on the nightstand were the only other clues into his world.

Sophia was processing all of this when the bathroom door opened and Logan walked back in stark naked and proudly erect. Sheathed in a condom and armed with a killer grin, he appeared ready for action. Sophia thought she was sated until she took one long look at him and realized with a hot shiver that she could *never* get enough.

"What are ya doing?" Sophia asked when he stood there perfectly still.

"Letting you look," he teased. "Do you like what you see?"

Sophia angled her head and let her gaze travel over his body from head to toe, pausing in a few places to linger. "Hmmm . . . maybe. Come a little closa."

He took two steps nearer, just out of her reach.

"Closa, please, so I can do more than look. I need ta touch ya, Logan." She rose up to a kneeling position when he came to the edge of the bed.

"Show me what you like."

Sophia placed her hands on his shoulders and squeezed and then ran her hands down his arms. "Mmm, strong . . . smooth. I like that." She let her fingertips trail over the contours of his chest, lightly scraping her nails over his nipples before trailing downward over his abs. She tickled him, smiling when his muscles quivered in response to her light touch. When she caressed his dick and cupped his sac he inhaled sharply. "Nice. Very nice."

With a groan Logan started to push her back onto the mattress, but Sophia stopped him with a hand on his chest. "No, you lie down. I'd like for you to be my boy toy for a while," she teased. But when she looked up at him there was something inscrutable in his eyes that made her pause. "If that's okay?"

Logan suddenly had the strange urge to tell her that he didn't want this to be just a game, but then again she was having so much fun that he decided to play along. There would always be later to tell her that he hoped that this was the beginning of something much more than a summer fling. For all of his bullshit about being a player, the thought of Sophia with anyone else set his teeth on edge. He had just purchased a small farm outside of town with the intention of building a retirement cabin someday, but the sudden image of Sophia standing on a big wraparound porch welcoming him home was very enticing. "Wow," he murmured, amazed at his sudden train of thought.

"What?" Sophia asked, angling her head so that her long hair slipped over her shoulder. "Afraid ta give me full control here?"

Logan laughed. "Not at all. Have a go at me. Turn me every way but loose." With that, he flopped down onto the bed and grinned. "I'm all yours."

"Yeah, well, don't ya *fuget* it," she said with a chuckle.

"I'm not about to." Although his tone was joking, beneath the humor he realized that she was damned serious.

"Sit up heah and rest against the pillows," Sophia requested.

"Your wish is my command."

"Mmmm, now we're talkin'."

Sophia straddled him at his thighs and then leaned in to kiss his chin, letting her tongue linger on the bristled stubble. Then, instead of moving up to his mouth like he, *oh, so* wanted, she dipped her head and began a trail of hot wet kisses down his chest. The soft tickle of her hair skimming over his skin felt deliciously erotic.

Sophia kissed, nibbled and caressed Logan into an

absolute frenzy. He remained pretty much still even though he wanted to thrash and buck and make wild and crazy love to her. She had him laughing and groaning while she kept her promise of turning him every which way but loose. Just when Logan thought he would have to flip her over and pound into her like a damned jackhammer she rose up to her knees and sank down onto his dick.

"God," she said with a shudder. "Ya feel so good insida me." She put her hands on his cheeks and kissed him long and deep while she rocked against him. Logan put his hands around her waist and guided her while gently thrusting upward in a sensual dance, a slow climb peaking with a long, lazy climax.

"Logan . . ." Sophia said his name in a sort of breathless wonder, causing him to open his eyes and hold her gaze for a silent moment. He felt a connection . . . an emotional thread that went way beyond sex. Wrapping his arms around her, Logan held her close and wondered if he was finally falling in love.

✦ *Chapter Seven*

"The past two weeks have been friggin' amazing," Sophia gushed to M. J. over the phone while sitting cross-legged in the middle of her bed. She twirled her hair around her finger, feeling like a love-struck teenager.

"I'm so happy for you, Sophia. I knew this day would come."

"M. J., if my life were a movie, right now this would be the part where the guy and the girl fall hopelessly in love."

"Oh, that's *so* sweet. So you mean like taking you in a rowboat while you sit there with a parasol while he does all the work, and then you have a romantic picnic on a red-checkered blanket?" M. J. sighed. "And to quaint little restaurants where he talks you into dessert and you share, feeding him?"

Sophia laughed. "Well, yes, but not exactly. Logan took me on a lake, but it was on a Jet Ski, where I hung on for dear life, since he proceeded to scare the living shit outta me. The man has a serious need for speed. Last night he took me to the Hard Rock Cafe here in Nashville and bought me a souvenir T-shirt because he said that when he's in the same room as me he gets as hard as a rock. Romantic, huh?" Sophia scoffed.

"Yeah, it is . . . as far as guys think, anyway. Well, tell me, are ya wearin' the shirt right now?"

"Of course."

"Oh, Sophia, you're in love!" M. J. shouted so loud that Sophia pulled the phone away from her ear. "Brody, did you hear that? My sista is in love with Logan."

"Don't tell everyone, M. J. What if it doesn't work out?"

"Why wouldn't it?"

"Well, there is this issue of my profession."

"Hey, I'm a psychic too, Sis. Brody is dealing with it. Freaks him out sometimes, though."

Sophia tugged on the hair twirled around her finger. "Yeah, but my gift is a bit weirder."

"Hey, speaking of weird, that jerk Jimmy Tucker hasn't tried to contact you, has he?"

Sophia's heart beat faster at the thought. "No, and I haven't had the dream in a while either."

"Well, don't let your guard down, Sophia. That dude is nuts. I don't know why in the hell they would let a guy like him back out on the streets," she said with the vehemence of a worried sister.

Sophia inhaled sharply and then pointedly changed the subject. "So, just where are ya?"

"Um, I'm not sure. Brody, where are we?"

"Somewhere near Reno," Sophia heard him answer in the background.

"Brody, stop. I'm on the phone!"

"Holy shit, is he feeling you up?"

"Yes."

Sophia laughed. "I'll let you go. I've been keeping your place clean and tidy by the way."

M. J. giggled. "Brody . . . I said *stop*! Sorry, Sis."

"You don't really want him to stop, do you?"

"Not on your life. Love you, Sophia."

"You too. Now go take care of your man."

"You too!"

Sophia flipped her cell phone shut and then sat there for a long moment with a smile plastered on her face. Giddy . . . she felt positively giddy. For a person who was used to talking to the dead, this was a very different and welcome feeling. In fact, she felt like bursting into song or dancing in a circle and maybe she'd just do both. After all there wasn't anyone around to see her.

With a hearty laugh, Sophia stood up in the middle of the bed and spun around while singing the first song that popped into her head, which just happened to be Gretchen Wilson's "Redneck Woman." It wasn't related to anything she was feeling, but it was the kind of song that you could belt out for no good reason.

"I said hell yeah," she shouted while pointing her fist toward the ceiling.

"Girl, you are two kinds of crazy?"

"Pixie?" Sophia stopped singing and bouncing and looked around the room for the elusive little flicker of light.

"What in the Sam hell are you doing?"

"Acting like a love-struck teenager."

"You're almost thirty-five."

"Yep, I'm well overdue. Hey, where have ya been lately?"

Pixie flitted closer to the bed. "You haven't needed me, so I've just been busy polishing my halo."

"You have a halo?"

"Ha! Not likely."

Sophia chuckled. "So then why are you here now? . . . Oh, am I going to need you? Is something bad gonna happen?"

Pixie flitted around in silence for a minute, making Sophia's heart race.

"Pixie? Come on. *Spill.*"

"Dang it, I'm not supposed to. . . . I'm breaking the rules."

"Rules? Pixie, what? Does it have to do with Jimmy Tucker?"

Pixie's light flickered and got dimmer.

"Pixie!"

"Be strong. . . ."

"Be strong? What the hell does that mean? Come back here!" Sophia waited, but it seemed as if Pixie was gone. "Be strong?" she muttered, shaking her head. "That could mean anything or nothin'." With a sigh, she thought that maybe she should get to work on her book, something that she hadn't been doing much of lately, and she wanted a distraction from Pixie's cryptic message. Logan had informed her that he was going four-wheeling out on his farm with a few guys and would spend the night, so she had a bit of quiet time to actually get some work done. Since she did have a looming deadline, Sophia hopped down from the bed and went to get her laptop.

Deep in concentration, she was reading through her notes when there was a sharp knock at the kitchen door. Sophia jumped in surprise but then smiled when Logan's handsome face appeared on the other side of the window. Laughing at his comical expression, she hurried over to the door.

"I thought you were already gone."

Logan sighed. "I was in my truck and ready to roll when I thought about being away from you all night."

Sophia angled her head in question. "So you're not going?"

He gave her a sheepish grin. "Well, yeah. I just wanted"— he pulled her to him—"a little send-off."

Sophia arched one eyebrow. "Ya mean a quickie?"

He nodded eagerly.

"Ya gotta be kiddin'." Sophia's head was full of notes, and sex was the last thing on her mind.

He guided her hand to the bulge in his worn jeans. "All I had to do was think of you and *wham* . . . I'm hard."

"That you are," she said, and ran a hand over his fly.

He groaned. "So what do you say?"

"Logan . . . I'm busy . . . ," she sighed, but he smothered her protest with a kiss. "I'm not in the mood," she complained a little less forcefully.

"I'll get you there," he promised while nuzzling her neck.

"I'm working." This time her protest was feeble and punctuated with a breathy sigh.

"Time for a little sex break." Ignoring her next protest, he slid his big hands beneath her T-shirt and cupped her bare breasts. Sophia inhaled sharply and tried to swallow a moan.

"You're not wearing a bra." He said this with a sense of male wonder. "Sweet."

"I wasn't expecting company."

"Lucky for me." He tweaked her nipples hard, the way he knew she liked it, sending a hot flash of desire throbbing between her thighs. With a flick of his wrist he untied the bow on her sweatpants waistband and slipped his hand downward. "God, no panties *either*. Don't ever wear them again. Underwear is highly over-rated." With a low chuckle he pushed her up against the wall and kissed her while massaging his middle finger over her clitoris.

"Logan . . . stop!"

"Really?"

"No . . . are you kiddin'?" Sophia moaned deep in her throat and spread her legs for him. He worked his magic, slipping his finger into her where she was hot, wet and wanting him.

"God, Sophia." Logan tugged her pants past her hips. Sophia helped by wiggling the loose cotton to the floor and stepped out of the legs. Then, she reached out to impatiently unzip Logan's jeans. Digging into his pocket, he pulled out a condom and rolled it on, lifted her up and then plunged inside of her.

Sophia cried out and then clung to Logan, wrapping

her legs around his waist. Her back was pinned against the smooth, cool wall while Logan made wild love to her, hard and deep, frenzied and fast. He cupped her ass and pounded into her. Fully clothed except for his cock, he was raw masculinity and Sophia loved it. Digging her fingers into his shoulders, she climaxed just moments later with a sharp intense orgasm. His ragged cry next to her ear had her pulling his head back for a deep, delicious kiss.

"Wow," Logan said with a weak laugh. He leaned his forehead against hers. "Now I'm not sure if I want to go at all."

Sophia ran her fingers through his damp hair. "Oh, I'll miss ya, Logan, but I really do need to get going on this book. I have a deadline and I don't wanna be late." She ran a fingertip over his mouth. "You've been quite a distraction."

"Are you complaining?"

She answered him with a steamy kiss.

"I guess that's a no."

"You got that right. But if you stay, you will be a major distraction. Plus, I know ya wanna hang out with your guy friends." She kissed him hard and then said, "Go! Quick before I beg ya ta stay."

"Go ahead . . . *beg*."

Sophia laughed and almost told him right there and then that she loved him. Instead, she pushed at his shoulders. "Go play with your man toys. Just be ready for action when ya get back."

"Not to worry." He kissed her once more before easing her to the floor and for a moment Sophia actually thought about begging him to stay. Two days without a Logan fix was going to be hard. It was a good thing she was going to be busy.

After waving good-bye, Sophia went back to her work. For a few minutes she found it difficult to concentrate, but she finally knuckled down and outlined an entire chapter before a knock at the door forced her into a break.

"Savannah! Hey!" Sophia opened the door for her to enter. "What brings you here?" The serious look on Savannah's face had Sophia putting a hand over her mouth. "Ohmigawd, is Logan okay? Is he hurt?"

Savannah grabbed Sophia's shoulders. "He's fine."

"Thank God."

Savannah gave her a quick hug and then stepped back. "You're in love with him, aren't you?"

Sophia looked at Logan's sister, not knowing whether to confess her feelings or not.

Savannah waved a hand at her. "Oh, don't even try to deny it. It's written all over your pretty face."

Sophia sat down in a kitchen chair and leaned her elbows on the table. "Do ya think your brother will evva settle down?" She swallowed and continued. "Especially with someone like me?"

Savannah plopped down in the chair opposite of Sophia's. "What do you mean, someone like you?"

Sophia gave Savannah a *Come on, get real* look.

Savannah waved her hand again. "Okay, so you're not exactly normal. I think it will take someone *extraordinary* to snag Logan."

"You made that last part up."

"Guilty."

Sophia sighed and rested her chin in her hands.

"Hey, he's falling for you."

Sophia sat up straighter. "Ya think so?"

"I know so. Women throw themselves at Logan all the time, and Sophia, he hasn't even so much as flirted since you came along."

Sophia reached over and patted Savannah's hand with a knowing smile. "Someone special will come your way."

"Yeah, that's what M. J. said, but I'm not so certain. When she comes back I'm going to have her do a reading for me." Savannah licked her lips and said, "Um, speaking of *that* . . . the real reason I came over was because I was wondering if you would try to contact my granny for me."

Sophia felt a little nervous tingle. "Logan might not approve."

"I'm twenty-three. Logan doesn't have to approve."

"True . . ." Sophia felt torn.

"Oh, Sophia, I'm sorry. I don't want to mess things up between you and Logan. I shouldn't have asked." She sighed and then went on. "It's just that I've *felt* Granny's presence for a while now. I worry that she's trying to tell me something." She swallowed obvious emotion and that was all it took for Sophia to agree.

"I'll do it." How could she not?

Savannah brightened but then frowned. "Yes, but what about Logan?"

Sophia shrugged. "He's had a real interest in what I do lately. I think he's being more open-minded. Besides, if things are gonna move forward in our relationship, he's gonna havta accept and hopefully believe in what I do. This will be his first test."

"Oh, I don't want that on my shoulders!"

"He'll be fine with it," Sophia said firmly, hoping to convince herself.

"But what if he isn't?" Savannah asked softly.

"Then he isn't the one for me after all." God, it hurt even saying that, but Sophia knew that this was true. Love didn't really conquer all. She needed Logan to believe in her, not just to love her. "So," she said with a bit of a forced smile, "are ya ready?"

Savannah's blue eyes rounded, but she nodded quickly. "Yes, I'm ready."

Chapter Eight

"Let's go into M. J.'s office. It's more comfortable there."

"Okay." Savannah nodded and then followed Sophia down the short hallway. "I'm a little bit nervous," she admitted while Sophia lit some scented candles and lowered the shade so that the room was in semidarkness.

"That's normal," Sophia assured her, and gestured to an overstuffed chair in the corner of the room. "Have a seat and try to relax. The calmer we have things, the more likely that we can make a link. It's up ta your granny to show up, though, Savannah."

"I understand." She folded her hands primly in her lap and looked over at Sophia. "I can ask questions, right?"

Sophia came around to the edge of the desk and propped her hips against the smooth wood. "Yes, but sometimes the answers are kinda cryptic. They might only make sense to you. My readings are mostly clairaudient, meaning that I hear the reading in my head . . . but sometimes I'm clairvoyant, meaning I see images or colors too."

"How long will I have?"

"It varies. If we do make a link, your granny might not let ya get a word in edgewise."

Savannah chuckled. "Sounds almost like you know her."

"I feel as if I do," Sophia said with a little guilty twinge. That was as close to the truth as she was willing to get, for Granny Parks's aka Pixie's sake. As a matter of fact Sophia wasn't at all sure that Pixie would make an appearance. But taking a deep breath, she closed her eyes and silently called to Pixie to appear.

A good five minutes or so went by, making Sophia fear that Pixie had her reasons for staying away, but then she suddenly felt a surge of energy that made her whole body tingle. "Okay, I've made a link." Sophia opened her eyes and looked over at Savannah, who was now gripping the armrests and leaning forward.

"Tell her that I miss her."

"She says that she misses you too but that you shouldn't feel bad about not being with her when she died. She says that she felt you were there with her anyway."

"Oh . . ." Savannah clutched her hands to her chest and then waited with big eyes for Sophia to go on.

"Um, she says that she is proud of you for staying in school."

"Sophia, tell her that I'm sorry that we argued about that. Oh, and that I'm carrying a three-point-eight grade point average," she said, swiping at tears, "and about to graduate."

"She's saying something about red cowboy boots? That you should wear them?"

"Ohmigawd. Her favorite boots . . . snakeskin. . . . I—I was afraid to scuff them." Savannah inhaled sharply and gave her the amazed look that Sophia was used to getting the moment that she said something that no one else could have possibly known.

"She said to wear them when you're singing at the Ryman, because someday you *will* be."

"Oh . . ." Savannah was crying openly now. "Tell her that I l-love her so much. I'll make it for you, Granny Parks. You wait and see," she said with tearful determination.

Sophia smiled as she said, "Your granny says that you need to find yourself a good man and make some grandbabies for your mama."

Savannah sniffled. "Yeah, well, that might be harder than having a hit record."

"She's fading, but she says *not* to give up and she wants you to know that she is safe and happy, so not to worry about her anymore." Sophia felt herself blush when she started to repeat the last comment from Pixie, "And she says to tell Logan . . ."

"What? Tell Logan what?"

"To quit pussyfootin' around and to make her some fine grandbabies too."

"Tell her that it will be my pleasure to tell Logan that."

Sophia nodded, since she didn't trust her voice.

"Is she gone?" Savannah whispered.

Sophia nodded again.

"My God, she was really here with us, wasn't she? I mean, you couldn't have known something as weird as the red cowboy boots. Oh, not that this was a test or anything, but still . . . *wow*." She shook her head and swiped at another tear. "Thank you, Sophia. You don't know what this means to me. What a wonderful gift you have." Savannah got up and they hugged and cried and then hugged some more.

"I've got to get over to the bar," Savannah finally said. "You want to come over for a beer?"

"No, I'd better get back to work. Maybe I'll head on over later."

Savannah nodded and then gave Sophia another fierce hug. "Thank you again." She pushed open the front door but then paused. "You think I'm going to fall in love? Granny seemed like she *knew* something. Think she did?"

"Could be," Sophia answered, thinking that that was as good an answer as any. She thought of her brother, Luc, hooking up with sweet Savannah and smiled.

"When M. J. comes back I'm going to have her do a reading for me." Then she wiggled her eyebrows. "You gonna make some babies with Logan?"

Sophia felt the heat of another blush and shrugged. "We'll see."

"I hope so!" Savannah closed the door and hurried off, leaving Sophia a bit nervous about the reading. She wondered if Logan would be okay with the whole thing.

Not that she needed his permission, and she *had* warned him that if Savannah came to her, she wouldn't turn her away. But still . . . she wondered how he was going to react. Sophia took a deep breath, telling herself that Logan had seemed really interested and supportive lately and that he would be cool with this . . . but her psychic intuition was giving her a very bad vibe.

Trying to shake off her sudden insecurity, Sophia worked for the rest of the afternoon and then ate a light supper of canned tomato soup. After putting on her jammies, she tried to get into a Lifetime movie but kept dozing off. Finally, she gave in and snuggled beneath the covers, hoping to fall fast asleep so that she could get an early start working in the morning. Since giving an emotional reading always left her exhausted, she didn't anticipate that this would be a problem tonight.

Sophia fell asleep almost immediately and was swept into a delicious dream where she was swimming naked with Logan. They frolicked and played in warm, deep blue water and then made love beneath a misty waterfall. The dream was so vivid that Sophia could almost feel the water pelting on her back while Logan wrapped his sleek, wet body around her. Threading his long fingers into her hair, he angled her head to the side and then kissed her over and over while pumping slow and easy until an orgasm washed over Sophia like warm waves lapping against the hot sand.

The shrill sound of the phone ringing startled Sophia awake. Blinking, she fumbled for the receiver on the nightstand, almost knocking the lamp off in the process. "Hello?"

"Oh, babe, did I wake you?" The deep, sexy sound of Logan's voice transformed Sophia's scowl into a smile.

"Yes."

"Oh, sorry . . . go back to sleep."

"No," Sophia protested while scooting up to a sitting position, "it's okay. I need to get up and get working anyway." She yawned and blinked in the early morning light.

"I miss you."

Sophia grinned. "Yeah, well, I miss *you* so much that I had a very steamy dream about you."

"Aw, man, you're killing me."

Sophia chuckled.

"Tell me about it."

"*Mmmm* . . . well, we were skinny-dipping in the ocean."

"Oh, I like the sound of that," he said with a low moan. "Tell me more."

"We swam in the warm water, pausing now and then to kiss. . . ."

"And then?"

"We made slow and easy love beneath the soft spray of a waterfall."

"Uh-oh."

"What?"

He chuckled. "You just gave me the mother of all boners. Now, just how am I going to ride a four-wheeler like this?"

"Very carefully. Put a little helmet on the little guy."

"Hey, who are you calling little?"

Sophia laughed.

"Seriously, I miss you."

"I seriously miss you too."

"I'll get out of here early so we can have dinner together, okay?"

"You bet. I'll cook."

"You can cook?"

Sophia laughed. "I haven't shown ya all of my talents yet. Of course I can cook. . . . I'm Italian. Now go have some fun, but be careful and protect the little guy too, ya hear me?"

"Loud and clear. See you soon."

Sophia hung up the phone and sat there with a silly smile on her face before getting up and springing into action. If she was going to cook, she was damned well going to impress him. She wasn't lying—she was a good cook—but it had been a while since she had prepared a meal from scratch.

"Hmmm, chicken cannelloni, a fresh Caesar salad and something rich and decadent for dessert . . . maybe chocolate mousse?" She mulled the possibilities over in her head while in the shower.

Tonight couldn't come soon enough.

✳ Chapter Nine

"Okay, the cannelloni is baking in the oven, the salad is tossed, and the chocolate mousse is in the fridge. Oh . . . the whipped cream!" Sophia snapped her fingers and then retrieved the bowl and beaters from chilling in the freezer like her mother had taught her. She proceeded to whip the cream into soft peaks while adding the sugar until she achieved the perfect sweetness before popping the bowl into the fridge.

Dusting her hands off, she checked on the cannelloni, which was just beginning to bubble around the edges, and then hurried to change into something sexy. Logan should be arriving soon. He had called a while ago to say that he was about an hour away and after checking on the bar, he would be over. Sophia clasped her hands and smiled in anticipation.

Sophia slipped on a flesh-toned satin demibra that clasped in the middle and made her breasts look as if they were spilling out of the lace-edged cups. Her barely-there thong was more of a tease than actual underwear and made her feel just a bit naughty. After slathering on some skin-softening lotion, she changed into silky black gaucho pants slung low on her hips and a red sleeveless shell that showed an inch or so of her tummy. She pulled her hair back with a simple gold clip and touched up her makeup before spraying on vanilla spice perfume. After a last glance in the mirror Sophia hurried back into the kitchen, turned the oven down and then lit the fat candle on the small table.

"There." She stepped back to survey her work and then decided to reward her efforts with a glass of Chianti. She sipped her wine and then glanced at her slim gold watch, wondering what could be keeping Logan. After a few more minutes she decided to give him a call on his cell phone.

"Hey, where are ya?" Sophia asked brightly when Logan answered. "Still on the road?"

"Uh, no, I'm back. I've just been talking to Savannah."

"Oh." A little spark of alarm ignited in her brain. "So, will ya be ova soon?" She forced the brightness to remain in her tone.

He hesitated just long enough for the alarm to spread like wildfire. "In a few minutes. Let me just finish up here." While his statement wasn't exactly harsh it certainly wasn't teasing or playful. Oddly, anger might have been easier to take than his stiff, impersonal tone.

"Okay . . ." She downed the rest of the wine and swished more into her glass. Savannah must have told him about the reading and he didn't seem happy. "Alrighty, then," she muttered calmly, but the whole flight-or-fight thing sizzled through her blood. Sophia wasn't one to back down from a fight, but the urge to run and hide from Logan's disapproval was incredibly strong. In fact, she was about to do just that when he rapped sharply on the door. She hesitated, saying a little prayer that she was for once dead wrong. Maybe Logan was going to sweep her into his arms and thank her for bringing closure to Savannah.

Taking a deep breath and then squaring her shoulders, she slowly walked over and swung the door open. "Hi there," she said with a smile that by some miracle didn't tremble. "Hope you're hungry."

He didn't say anything but ran his fingers through his hair. Sophia noticed with disappointment that he was dressed in faded jeans and a plain white T-shirt . . . not that he didn't look sexy, but he obviously hadn't dressed for an intimate dinner. He glanced over at the decked-out table and had the grace to appear sad.

"Would you like a glass of wine?"

Logan shook his head.

"Are ya gonna speak to me?"

He looked at her, swallowed and then began, "Sophia, I talked to Savannah and she told me that you did a reading for her."

"That's right."

"I thought we had an understanding about that." He pinned her with a look that had flight turning into fight.

"I told ya that I wouldn't seek Savannah out but that I wouldn't turn her down if she came to me."

He frowned. "But so much has happened between

us since then. I thought that you would have respected my wishes on this."

"It brought her such joy and closure, Logan. Why wouldn't ya want your sista to have that?" When her damned voice shook he took a step closer.

"Look, Sophia, I know that you meant well but . . ."

Sophia raised her eyebrows. "But what? Oh, let me finish. You think I'm a fake, a *phony*, and you don't want your sista subjected to the likes of me."

"I didn't say that. I know that you believe in what you do and maybe—"

"Did ya even ask her about the reading?" Sophia interrupted.

"We argued and didn't get that far. Sophia, listen. I'm just looking out for my sister."

"Oh, protecting her from evil *me*?" She shook her head. "Just go, Logan." She wanted to shout it, but her voice came out a shaky whisper.

"Aw, damn, I'm not handling this very well. I shouldn't have barged on over here before thinking this through."

When he took another step closer Sophia backed up. "Get out."

"Look, let's talk about this. . . ."

"I can be packed and outta heah by tomorrow night."

He looked stricken. "No! Sophia, I don't want you to leave. Where would you go? What about that crazy guy out on parole?"

"Well, that's not your problem or your concern, now, is it? Please go, Logan. I'm about to cry and you can at least allow me the dignity to blubber without ya watchin'. I'll be fine, really."

"God . . ." He ran his fingers through his hair. "No, I'm not going to leave you like this."

"Get. Out." She pointed at the door.

"Sophia, I'm sorry. . . ."

"Now!" She shoved his chest as hard as she could. "I mean it. *Go!*"

He looked ready to argue, so she shoved harder and harder until he was at the door. When he finally turned and left, Sophia locked it behind him and then let the tears flow.

She didn't just cry; she sobbed, she cursed, and she seriously considered throwing things but didn't want to deal with the cleanup, and well, she didn't think she had the energy anyway. In the end she just felt sad and weary. So instead, she turned off the oven and removed the homemade chicken cannelloni that had taken her hours to prepare. She wished it looked even remotely appetizing. But not one to let things go to waste, she wrapped the dish in aluminum foil and put it on the counter to cool. Later she would freeze it so that M. J. would have a treat when she and Brody came back.

Then she blew out the candle and decided to dress for bed. Maybe sleep would come quickly so she could rise early and begin packing.

"Well, hell," she muttered, and punched the pillow. "This really, *really* sucks." Finally, she fell into a fitful sleep, tossing and turning well into the night.

And then the nightmare began. . . .

Jimmy Joe Tucker was chasing her while shouting,

"Git back here, you little bitch! I'll show you what happens to girls who do Jimmy wrong. You're gonna pay!"

Sophia ran faster and faster, but she could feel the heat of Jimmy Joe's body as he bore down on her. She could smell his fetid breath and the stench of body odor made her gag and stumble. She fell and screamed when he pounced upon her and leaned in for a slimy kiss. Sophia kicked and screamed, trying to shake him off, but he held her hands above her head with one hand while he ripped at her clothes with the other. "Stop!" She bucked and tried to bite him and then screamed again, praying for someone to rescue her.

Logan flipped over to his back and flung an arm over his head, knowing that sleep was wishful thinking. Savannah wasn't speaking to him and now Sophia was leaving and he didn't know how to make things right. He pondered this for the millionth time and it suddenly hit him that he was being narrow-minded and all around jackass to the two people in the world who meant the most to him. "Damn!" He *had* to think of a way to make Sophia stay and in the back of his mind, the knowledge that she could be in danger from some sleazy ex-con made his blood run cold. Now, if he could just think of a way to make it right . . .

The sound of a scream from the other side of the wall had Logan jackknifing into a sitting position. His heart pounded as he threw back the covers, grabbed his huge set of master keys from his nightstand and rushed out the back door. Without bothering to knock, he unlocked Sophia's door and rushed in.

"Stop!" Sophia's shout made his heart race even faster as he ran to her bedroom, fully expecting the worst.

"Sophia!" Logan approached the bed, relieved beyond belief that she appeared to be only having a bad dream. He looked around the room, but there was no evidence that anyone was there. "Baby, wake up. It's only a dream," he said softly, only to be smacked in the shoulder when she continued to thrash and kick.

"No," Sophia whimpered, making Logan attempt to wrap his arms around her, but she struggled against him.

"Sophia, it's Logan. Wake up." He held her arms still and gently pinned her to the bed. Her eyes opened and she blinked up at him in fright. "It's okay," he said softly. "You were having a nightmare."

When she closed her eyes and shuddered Logan slid his hands beneath her shoulders and gathered her into his arms. "You're safe, Sophia," he murmured, and kissed the top of her head. *Thank God*, he thought while trying to get his own heartbeat under control. "Are you okay?"

She nodded but remained silent except for her uneven breathing.

"You can relax now," he encouraged her, and was relieved when he felt some of the tension leave her body. When she shivered again, he wrapped his arms more tightly around her while rubbing her back. "You want to tell me about it?"

"No," she said, resting her cheek against his bare chest. "Just hold me."

"It was about that guy, wasn't it?" Logan persisted. "Was he chasing you again?"

"Yes," she admitted gruffly. "He was chasing me . . . and I fell and he was ripping at my clothes. . . . *God* . . ." Instead of going on, she inhaled a shaky breath and snuggled closer.

"It's okay, now, hush." He continued to stroke her back until her breathing became less erratic and the shivering subsided. Logan was relieved that she remained in his arms instead of pushing him away the way he feared that she would. Not that he would have left her, anyway. . . . Wild horses couldn't have dragged him away from her side. "I love you, Sophia." He said the words without thinking, just feeling. "And I don't want you to leave."

Sophia sighed and pushed back so that she could look up at him. "Logan . . ." She shook her head. "Don't you see that this will never work? Love isn't everything." She cupped his cheeks in her hands. "The very thought of never being in your arms again, of never touching you, kissing you . . . seeing you again, is almost too much to handle. But having you not believe in me . . . maybe even be embarrassed or, heaven forbid, want to keep me away from Savannah? That's so much worse, don't you see?"

"I didn't want to keep you away from her, Sophia."

"Yes, ya did. Sure, it was okay to be friendly or to have lunch but to not be able to be myself around her?" Sophia shook her head.

"I was wrong."

"No, you weren't. One of the things that I love about you is that you wanted to protect your sista from hurt or harm even if that includes me."

"I didn't think you were going to hurt or *harm* her."

"On a certain level, you did."

"Give me a chance to get used to this, to learn more."

"We're worlds apart, Logan. This isn't going to work no matter how much I . . ." She faltered and had to swallow the emotion clogging her throat.

"You what?" This was torture, but he needed her to say it.

"No matter how much I love you."

"God, Sophia . . ."

"Go, Logan. I'm fine now. It was just a dream, nothing more."

"But this guy—"

She put a finger to his lips. "It was a *dream*."

"Let me stay with you until morning. At least give me that."

"I *can't*. I don't wanna make this any harder than it already is."

Logan would have argued, but the stubborn set of her chin and the determination in her eyes led him to believe that it would be pointless. Although Logan wasn't the type to give up without a fight, he realized that the middle of the night wasn't the time to argue, so he reluctantly scooted from the bed and stood up. But seeing her huddled in the middle of the mattress hugging her knees to her chest was almost his undoing.

"Sophia, if there is anything that you need or if you decide that you want me to come back, I'm a phone call away, you hear me?"

She nodded and looked up at him with such sadness in her brown eyes that Logan's gut clenched. He stood there and waited, hoping that she might hold her arms out to him and ask him to stay. But after a long moment she lowered her gaze and Logan left the room. He was careful to lock her door, but he stood there in the darkness for a few minutes daring himself to go back in. But with a low curse he finally headed back inside his apartment.

Once inside he grabbed a bottle of water and paced, wishing he had handled things differently. He wondered, though, if Sophia was right. Maybe they *were* worlds apart and no matter how much they loved each other it might never be enough.

*S*ophia rolled over into a little ball of despair, hugging the squishy pillow that was a poor substitute for Logan. She cried silent tears until her eyes felt hot and gritty. But then she got pissed and punched the pillow several times until feathers were flying. Finally, she slipped into an exhausted slumber and didn't move until the sun came streaming in her window.

Sophia blinked and groaned, wanting the world to just go away and leave her alone. She rolled over and tugged the covers up over her head, trying to ward off the light of day, but then sat up straight when she heard someone banging on the back door.

God, she did *not* want to face Logan again. She sat there frowning, hoping that he would leave, but then again hoping that he would come barging in and insist that she stay. "I'm a mess," she moaned while holding her head in her hands.

"Well . . . *shit*." When the banging got louder Sophia

threw back the covers and stomped into the kitchen fully prepared for battle. . . . What she was fighting she wasn't quite sure, but she clenched her fists and hurried over to the door.

"Lucio?" Sophia swung open the door in surprise.

"It's 'bout time you answered the door," he growled as he stepped into the kitchen.

"Well, hello to ya too, little brother." Of course there was nothing little about all six feet two of him. He gave her the patented Lucio Barone scowl and flopped his muscular frame into a chair.

"You got any coffee?"

"No, but I'll make some."

"Good, I've been driving all night."

"So what brings ya here?"

"I needed a change of pace, I guess." He ran his fingers through his shoulder-length black hair and shrugged. Although Luc always vehemently denied any kind of psychic power, he somehow always managed to show up when someone in the family needed him.

Sophia arched an eyebrow at him. "Oh, so you drove all night for a change of pace?"

"Yeah, you gotta problem with dat?" he asked in a thick Brooklyn tough-guy tone.

"No, I'm glad you're here." Sophia busied herself with making coffee so he couldn't see the emotion that she knew was written all over her face.

"You okay, Sophia? You look like hell."

"Gee, *thanks*. I didn't sleep well."

"Well, I've got some news that will make you sleep better. You remember my buddy Josh Dunkin?"

"The cop?"

"Yeah, he's a detective in the Sixth Precinct and he's been keepin' tabs on Jimmy Tucker for me. I got a call a little while ago from Josh and it seems that Jimmy Tucker is back in jail."

Sophia's heart started pounding. "Why?"

"He chased some chick down last night and assaulted her, so it's back to the slammer for Jimbo."

"Ahhhhh!" Sophia shrieked, and spun around in a circle. "Whoooohoooo!"

"Great news, huh?" When Luc stood up to give Sophia a hug the back door suddenly opened and Luc was grabbed from behind and yanked backward by his shirt.

Sophia screamed, "No!"

But Logan was on a mission. "You son of a bitch!" He pulled Luc out the open door and put him in a head-lock.

Luc, however, was no pushover and elbowed Logan in the gut. Logan grunted and released his hold but took an uppercut swing and clipped Luc in the jaw, sending him staggering backward with a trickle of blood running from the corner of his mouth. Sophia yelled, "Stop, he's my brother!" but neither of them was listening. Luc had barely regained his balance when Logan took a roundhouse swing, narrowly missing when Luc dodged left.

"Logan . . . *no!*" Sophia shouted, making him glance her way. Luc took the advantage and punched Logan in the gut, knocking the wind out of him and sending him to the ground. Logan staggered to his feet, but Luc was right there ready to take another swing when a loud scream had all three of them turning toward the sound.

"Leave my brother alone!" Savannah yelled, and came running at Luc with a broom held high over her head. Luc blinked and tried to dodge the broom-wielding crazy woman, but she swung the thing like Ken Griffey Jr. and caught him in the arm with a loud *thwap*.

"Ouch, shit!" Luc grabbed his arm and staggered sideways, grunting when she hit him again.

Sophia rushed forward and tried to yank the broom from Savannah. "Stop! He's my brother!"

Savannah yelped and dropped her weapon. "Your brother?" She glared at Luc, who was clutching his arm. "Why were you attacking Logan?"

"He didn't," Logan said with a grunt, and then pushed up to his feet. "I came after him. Damn, I'm sorry. I though you were hurting Sophia. I heard her scream and obviously came to the wrong conclusion." He held his hand out to Luc, who glared at him and pushed up to his feet on his own.

"Who is this guy, Sophia?" Luc asked.

"He owns the building and he knew about Jimmy Tucker, so, Luc, he did have a legit reason for coming to the wrong conclusion."

"Sorry," Logan said again.

"Ohmigawd!" Savannah said, and rushed forward. "Your arm is bleeding!"

Luc looked down at blood trickling down his bicep. "Yeah, well, that tends to happen when you smash shards of glass into a person's arm."

"Glass?" Savannah put a hand to her mouth. "Oh no, I was sweeping up a broken beer bottle." She hurried over to Luc, who backed away. "Come on inside and let me . . . *help*."

"You've done enough, thanks." He gave her his best bad-boy glare, but to Sophia's surprise, little bitty Savannah refused to back down.

"I insist," Savannah said firmly, standing up a little straighter to her full five feet two inches. She gave her dark blond hair a little flip over her shoulder and stood her ground.

Sophia watched Luc closely and for a split second she thought he might actually smile . . . a rare but dazzling thing.

"We can go inside the kitchen," Sophia offered. "You really need to get that cleaned up, Luc."

He glanced down at his arm and shrugged. *"What-evva."*

"I'm so sorry, Sophia," Savannah said, putting a hand on her arm. "I didn't know he was your brother."

"I understand." She flicked a glance at Logan. "This was just a big misunderstanding all the way around, but it's over now."

Savannah gave her a small smile, but Logan gave her an *It's not nearly over* look.

"Yo, ya gonna shoot the breeze all day? I'm bleedin' here," Luc asked, and stomped in the kitchen ahead of them.

"He sure is a grump," Savannah mumbled as she entered the kitchen, but Sophia noticed that she couldn't take her eyes off her broody brother.

Luc flopped down into a chair and stretched his long legs out in front of him. "You'd be a grump-ass too if you were tired, hungry, and had glass protruding from your arm."

"Hey, easy there." Logan gave Luc a narrow-eyed look. "Back off."

Luc raised his dark eyebrows. "Back off? Man, after you yanked me from my sista's kitchen and tried to beat the crap outta me?" He pointed at Savannah. "And that little dynamo tried to kill me with a glass-filled broom."

"He's right, Logan," Savannah pointed out. "We owe him an apology."

Logan ran a hand down his face. "Point taken. Sorry, Luc. I thought I was protecting Sophia from that jerk out on parole. I heard her scream and feared for the worst."

Luc's expression softened a bit. "I hear ya. I woulda done the same thing."

Sophia smiled as she entered the room with a pan of warm water, tweezers and hydrogen peroxide. "My shout was one of joy. Luc was just telling me before all of that went down that Jimmy Tucker is back behind bars."

"Really? Sophia, that's great news. What did he do this time?" Logan asked. Relief was written all over his features, making Sophia want to hug him, but she kept her distance.

When Sophia remained silent, Luc answered for her. "He chased some woman down last night who had supposedly refused his advances in a bar. He tried to rape her."

With a frown Logan turned to Sophia. "That sounds like your dream."

Sophia avoided his gaze but said, "Sometimes I see things in my dreams that come true. I assumed that this was about *me* since there was a connection there, but as it turns out he was attacking someone else. Had I known, maybe I could have warned the police."

"Would the police have believed you?" Savannah asked while gently putting a bath towel beneath Luc's injured arm.

Sophia shook her head. "Not very likely but I woulda felt better at least tryin' to do somethin'."

"The woman is okay and Jimmy Tucker is behind bars, so don't go beatin' yourself up over this, Sis." Luc shot her a *Don't make this your fault* look.

Logan's frown remained, as if he was mulling this over.

"Sophia, your psychic powers are amazing," Savannah said. "I can't thank you enough for contacting my granny. By the way, I'm wearing the red boots tonight when I sing, just like Granny said." She gave Logan a glare before turning her attention to Luc's arm.

"The snakeskin boots that she treasured?" Logan asked.

Savannah nodded.

His eyes widened and he turned to Sophia. "How could you have known that?"

"She's a *psychic* medium, Logan," Savannah muttered, and rolled her eyes at him. "Granny Parks told her."

Logan jammed his hands in his jeans pockets and rocked back on his heels. "I've been an ass, haven't I?"

Sophia shook her head. "This is all pretty hard to swallow, Logan."

"Oh, phooey," Savannah said, and waved a hand at Logan. "Yeah, you've been an ass. A big one." She turned back to Luc and plucked a small shard of glass from his arm. "Sorry if that hurt."

He shrugged. "Don't worry 'bout it."

"I'm really sorry and I just want you to know that I'm not usually so . . . violent."

Luc chuckled.

"What?" Savannah asked.

"I'm just remembering you coming at me, hell on wheels with that big broom."

Savannah blushed. "Don't you dare make any references to witches." She carefully removed another sliver of glass and asked, "Are you psychic like your sisters?"

"No!" he quickly responded, drawing a chuckle from Sophia.

"So he claims," Sophia said, and was rewarded with a Lucio Barone scowl. "Sometimes I wonder."

"Hey, don't you two have somethin' to talk about?" Luc asked.

Savannah shooed her hands at Sophia and Logan. "Yeah, y'all go kiss and make up."

✳ Chapter Eleven

*S*ophia glanced over at Logan, who motioned toward the door with a nod of his head. "If only it were that easy," she said when they were outside.

"It is," Logan said as he pulled her into his arms and kissed her soundly. "See?" he asked, still holding her around the waist.

"Logan . . ." She shook her head.

"Logan, *nothing*. I'm making this way too difficult when it's pretty simple. I love you, Sophia. Really *love* you and your damned psychic powers too."

"Yes, but I need—"

"For me to believe in you," he finished for her. "I think I pretty much have from the very beginning. I've been hell-bent on trying *not* to believe."

Sophia frowned. "But why would you do that?"

"Because believing in you meant that there wasn't any reason not to settle down."

Her eyes widened and she swallowed. "Settle down?"

"Yes, Sophia, I think you just might have tamed my wild ways."

She inhaled sharply.

Logan chuckled as he tugged her inside his apartment. "Don't worry, I'm not proposing . . . *yet.*" He hugged her closer. "When I do I want it to be special . . . to knock your socks off . . . hmmm, even better, maybe knock your pants off," he said with a chuckle.

Sophia gave him a shove. "Don't forget about a big rock." She wiggled her ring finger at him. "I like a little bling, ya know?" She laughed, but her eyes were filled with emotion.

Logan laughed. "You are a piece of work, you know that?"

"So what took ya so long?"

"I had this crazy notion that I didn't want a woman to interfere with my free time . . . you know, fishing, hiking, four-wheeling. . . . The list is pretty much endless."

Sophia angled her head and asked, "So what changed your mind about that? Surely you still want to do that stuff."

Logan grinned as he snagged her around the waist again. "Yeah . . . but I've got a plan. I'll just take you with me."

Sophia wrinkled her nose. "Ya mean, like, camping? Outdoorsy stuff?"

"Yep. You game?"

"I'll go anywhere with you, Logan," she bravely proclaimed.

"Spelunking?"

"Spl-*what*-ing?"

"Exploring caves."

She swallowed. "Uh . . . sure."

"I was kidding about that one."

"You!" Sophia punched him in the shoulder, but then suddenly they were kissing. Logan tugged her into his bedroom and they tumbled onto the bed. He started to pull her blouse out of her pants.

"What are you doing?"

"I think it's obvious. I want to make love to you."

"But what about Luc and Savannah?"

Logan chuckled. "Are you kidding? If your brother as much as touches her, she'll melt into a puddle at his feet. She was making goo-goo eyes at him. They'll never miss us."

"Did you just say 'goo-goo eyes'?" Sophia fell back onto the bed in a fit of laughter. "You mean like this?" She batted her eyes at him.

"Yeah, and don't you go batting those beautiful brown eyes at anyone but me."

"Not a problem," she teased, but then suddenly turned serious. "I love you, Logan. I'll warn you, though: Life with me won't be easy. I have nightmares; I get moody . . . tired. I keep odd hours sometimes—up all night and sleep all day."

Logan shrugged. "I run a bar, Sophia. My hours are pretty odd too. I'm not worried about any of that."

"Some people will give you a hard time about what I do."

"Screw them."

Sophia laughed and traced her finger over his mouth. "You are such a guy."

"That's good, right?"

"Oh, *yeah*." She ran her hand up the bulge beneath his fly and then unbuttoned his jeans. "Oh my, going commando?"

"I was in a hurry to be your hero," he explained with a laugh.

"I'm not complaining," she said, and then swirled her tongue over the smooth head of his dick. She curled her hand around his shaft, loving the feel of him growing hard and hot in her hand. She peeled his jeans over his lean hips and tugged them off. "Take off your shirt. . . . I love your chest."

While Logan complied Sophia tugged her Yankees sleep shirt over her head, tossed it to the floor and wiggled out of her panties. She quickly straddled him and rubbed her wet heat over his hard length, teasing while she leaned in for a long kiss. With a groan, Logan reached up and cupped her breasts, tweaking and rolling her nipples until she came up to her knees and sank back down with a long sigh.

"Mmmm . . ." But when she started to move Logan held on to her hips, stilling her movements.

"Wait a minute and let me calm down." He gave her a weak chuckle. "You got me too worked up already. That's how damned crazy I am about you."

"I'm still not complaining." Sophia leaned in for a hot kiss. "But I'm not about to wait a minute longer." She rose up slowly and then sank all the way back down while watching the play of emotion on his face. Threading her fingers through his, she moved slow and easy, coming up to her knees again, but then she did the same motion a bit faster, a bit harder. "Oh . . ." Sophia gripped his hands tighter, and then letting her emotions take over, she loved him with a wild intensity that sent her flying over the edge, taking him along with her. With a half laugh, half moan, Logan rolled her to the side, still buried deep, while kissing her over and over.

Finally, Sophia said, "We'd better get back before Luc and Savannah come searching for us."

"Mmmmm, do we have to? I just wanna sleep. You wore me out and I didn't sleep well last night worrying about you."

Sophia was touched at his confession. She kissed him tenderly but then said, "I would love to stay here all day, but we can't."

"Okay, I guess somebody has to be the voice of reason." Logan took a deep breath while rubbing his finger over her bottom lip. "I'm glad that Savannah is going to wear the red boots tonight."

Sophia bent her elbow and then propped her head up. "Why? You know something, don't you?"

He grinned but remained silent.

"Tell me!"

"Well, keep this under your hat because if Savannah finds out, she'll be a basket case."

"What? Spill, Logan."

"Brody called me late last night. He had given Savannah's demo to someone at his record label and tonight one of the executives is coming to listen to her sing live at the bar."

"Shut up!"

"Yep. Brody seemed pretty excited. Wouldn't it be

fitting if they approached her tonight while she's wearing Granny's boots?"

Sophia nodded, moved by the emotion in Logan's voice.

"She wouldn't have thought to wear them without you."

Sophia shrugged. "I was just the messenger."

Logan cleared his throat. "Um, by the way, did Granny mention anything about me?"

"Well . . ." Sophia felt the heat of a blush warm her cheeks while she plucked at the bedsheet.

"What?" Logan asked, tipping her face up with his index finger.

"She said that you should stop pussyfooting around and make her some great-grandbabies."

Logan went so still and silent that Sophia was suddenly afraid that the player in him was rearing its ugly head. She waited for him to jump up and run for the hills. Finally he chuckled.

"What?" Sophia asked, trying but unable to keep the trepidation out of her voice.

"You know the farmland I bought?"

Sophia nodded.

"My grand plan was to stock the pond, build a weekend cabin so I could fish and hunt and maybe retire there down the road. Well, that plan has been blown all to hell."

"Whadya mean?"

He gazed down at her with a warm smile. "Maybe I'm turning psychic because I see a future with a rambling farmhouse with a wraparound porch instead of a cabin." He frowned with the tips of his fingers against his forehead as if concentrating. "Oh, and is that *you* standing on that porch with a baby on your hip?"

"Are you makin' funna me?"

Logan shook his head. "Look, seriously, I wouldn't want you to give up your work. There are studios here in Nashville where you could tape your talk show. . . ."

Sophia squeezed her eyes shut trying to keep the tears from flowing, but she could feel the hot moisture trickle out of the corners and slide down her face.

"Sophia? What's wrong?"

"Nothin'!" She laughed and it came out gurgled. "Oh, Logan, I know that we'll have things to work out, but if livin' on a farm with chickens or *whatevva* means being with you, then by God I'll give it a try."

"Chickens?" Logan laughed.

"And a cow named Bess."

"Huh?"

"We havta have a cow. What's a farm without a cow, right?"

Logan chuckled. "So let me make sure I've got this right. You'll milk the cow and muck out the barn?"

"Damned straight! Wait a minute. . . . What does muck mean?"

Logan kissed her lightly on the nose and said, "Oh, my little psychic city girl. You have much to learn."

"I just might surprise you," she said with a determined lift of her chin.

"Oh, I have no doubt about that. That's one of the things that I love the most about you."

"Say it again, Logan."

"What?"

"The *l* word."

"Love?"

She nodded.

"I love you, Sophia."

She swiped at a tear.

"Oh man, you're not going to cry, are you?"

Sophia punched him in the shoulder. "No way. I'm a tough Brooklyn chick. We nevva cry."

"Yeah, well, you're gonna be crying when you're mucking out that barn. . . ."

Sophia narrowed her eyes. "Aha, that means shoveling out the poo, doesn't it?"

"Yep, it does. You might break a nail."

She tried to punch him again, but he pulled her into his arms and kissed her tenderly.

"We're an unlikely pair, aren't we?" Logan asked while nuzzling her behind her ear.

"Yeah, you're a little bit country . . ."

"And *you're* a little bit out of this world."

Sophia gave him a saucy grin. "Really? Well, speaking of worlds, how about rocking mine one more time? . . . Think you got it in you, cowboy?"

"Oh . . . *yeah*."

Walkin' After Midnight

Savannah's fingers trembled as she opened the shoe box and unwrapped the tissue paper from her granny's treasured snakeskin cowboy boots. While sitting on her bed, she slipped them on and then stuck her legs out straight so that she could admire the deep red color and the pointed toes.

After a moment, Savannah stood up and walked around the room, smiling at the sharp click of the heels on the hardwood floor. The boots were snug but surprisingly comfortable and she felt like a honky-tonk princess wearing them. "Wow," she breathed as she gazed at her reflection in the floor-length mirror, glad that she had chosen the denim skirt that flared out slightly at the hem and showed off the boots.

Sure, her outfit was a little old-school country with the Western-cut white blouse and the denim vest embroidered with a red swirling pattern, but Savannah didn't care. So what if she looked more like Patsy Cline than

Shania Twain? The outfit suited her mood and show-cased the boots. After all, she was only singing the early set at Logan's, so there was no need to worry about looking young country hip.

Sometimes Savannah thought she was an old soul trapped in a young body. While she loved the new wave of country music she usually felt more in tune with the old songs from when it was all about the music and not sexed-up videos. With a sigh, Savannah acknowledged that she might be having a case of sour grapes, since she couldn't see herself singing in a sexy music video.

With that thought in mind Savannah turned around and looked in the mirror at her butt and groaned. "I will work out!" she adamantly promised herself . . . again. Between her job at the bar, studying and singing, her free time was limited. But now she finally had her degree in business, thank God . . . boring, boring, *boring*, but landing a recording contract was such a long shot that she had felt compelled to have something to fall back on. Plus, knowing the business side of things was just plain smart, or so her granny had insisted. As a matter of fact, she would soon be moving out of her shared apartment near the Vanderbilt campus and relocating to her parents' farmhouse just outside of Nashville. While she would still work at Logan's, Savannah would also devote endless hours to perfecting her songs and strengthening her voice.

"Oh no, it's almost seven o'clock!" Savannah groaned after glancing at her digital alarm clock. Logan would be ticked if she was late again. "Doggone it," she muttered, wondering where the time had gone. No matter

how hard she tried she always managed to be a few minutes late for just about everything. This drove Logan nuts
since he was always on time, *damn him.*

Savannah couldn't help it if her mind tended to wan-
der. Today, for example, when she was soaking in the
bathtub she daydreamed a little . . . okay, *a lot*, about
Sophia's very hot brother, Lucio Barone. Sophia referred
to her brother as Luc, but Savannah thought that he
looked much more like a Lucio with his swarthy Italian
good looks. Not that a stud muffin like him would be interested in a country bumpkin like her, but a girl could
dream, couldn't she? Lucio had said that he would be in
town for a while when she had patched up his arm
(God, how embarrassing that she'd attacked him with a
broom of all things), so Savannah knew she would likely
see him again if just on a casual basis. "Oh!" Her heart
did a little skitter in her chest at the thought.

She paused to picture him in her head while wondering what his shoulder-length midnight hair would
feel like sifting through her fingers . . . and, God, that
mouth! The man had a full-lipped mouth that just
begged to be kissed. And then there were his heavy-
lidded bedroom eyes the color of dark Godiva chocolate, which made Savannah absolutely melt like gooey
caramel. His nose was a tad long, saving his face from
being too perfect, but as far as Savannah was concerned,
this just gave him a bad-boy edge that made him even
hotter.

The shrill *bing-bong* of her doorbell startled Savannah out of her delicious fantasy. "Who in the world
could that be?" she mused out loud, a little irritated to

be interrupted when she was in a hurry. When she swung the door open, her breath caught and she gaped in total surprise when her little daydream was standing there in the oh-so-sexy flesh. Savannah felt a blush creep up her neck to her cheeks and swallowed. Her heart started thumping as she wondered about the reason for his visit. *Is he feeling the same attraction as I am?* Had he been thinking about her as well?

"Hey," Lucio said in his low rumble of a voice. His eyes were hidden behind aviator sunglasses, but Savannah could feel the heat of his gaze.

"Hey there, yourself." Savannah had to tilt her head back to look up at him. Even with her wearing her granny's amazing boots, he towered over her. Damn, she wished she were taller. And skinnier. And had bigger boobs. Oh, yeah, and a smaller butt. "So, what's up?"

"Whaddyamean?" He gave her a slow grin that turned her insides to warm jelly. "Aren't you ready?"

"R-ready? For what?"

"For *me*, Savannah."

"Well . . . well, I . . ." *Holy crap. What am I supposed to say?*

"Listen, I've got to get you there quick. You *are* ready, right? Sophia said you would be."

"She . . . she did?"

"Yeah." He frowned. "Come on. This is your big night. The one you've been waiting for, right?" He put the heel of his hand to his head. "Oh, damn, I'm such a putz. Fugetabout what I just said, okay? I don't want you to be nervous or anything. Just give it your best performance is all I'm sayin'. Come on. Whadaya waitin' for?"

"Well . . . ?" What *was* she waiting for? Damn, he was so sexy and Savannah couldn't remember ever being as drawn to a guy as she was to Lucio.

"We've gotta hurry, Savannah."

Savannah gave him what she hoped was a sultry smile and decided to stall. "But why hurry? We do things a bit slower here in the South, Lucio." She considered batting her eyes but refrained. God, she wished that she were better at this sort of thing. "Would you like a drink first?"

"Savannah, I don't think you're grasping the urgency of this situation. Plus, Logan is gonna be pissed."

Savannah blew out a breath. "I'm tired of Logan telling me what to do. I'm twenty-three years old, for goodness' sake."

"Whatevva. You got a beef with your brother, that's your business." He shrugged his wide shoulders and then raised one arm to lean against the door frame, looking all bad-boy sexy in a solid white T-shirt and worn jeans. "I think my car might be illegally parked, so can we get a move on it?" His voice was both silky smooth and Brooklyn tough but had just enough impatience in it to make Savannah bristle.

Get a move on it? Well. Lucio Barone might be as sexy as sin, but Savannah wasn't about to be impatiently ordered around even by a hottie like him. She really was getting tired of people telling her what to do. "Thanks for the offer, Mr. Barone, but I'm not quite *ready*. Sorry to disappoint you."

Lucio slowly removed his glasses and brushed past her into the apartment. With a sideways once-over he disarmed her a bit with a lazy smile. "What's not ready about you?"

"I'm not about to be rushed," she replied coolly, even though the lingering gaze from his warm brown eyes made her feel hot all over. "Some other time, maybe."

"Some other time? Are you crazy? This could be your big chance! Oh, shit, there I go almost giving it away again."

"You want me to *pay* you?" she sputtered.

"Pay me? Of course not." Lucio gave her a confused frown. "Did I say somethin' to piss you off? I am doin' you a favor here, ya know."

"*A favor?*" So this was a favor, was it? Otherwise Mr. Hot Stuff wouldn't dare darken her doorstep. *Well.* Savannah squared her shoulders. "Oh, of course you didn't piss me off, as you so eloquently put it. I'm simply not ready," she replied stiffly. Lucio pursed his lips, bringing her attention to his mouth, and she felt her anger begin to fade a smidge. One kiss from that mouth and she would be ready and willing, big-time.

"Look, Sophia was pretty insistent that I get your sweet little tush there, pronto. She even promised me homemade chicken cannelloni as a reward." He leaned closer . . . so close that Savannah could smell the spice of his cologne. "And Savannah, chicken cannelloni is my favorite, so please, will you come with me right now?" He totally flustered her again with a smile that flashed straight white teeth in his tanned face. When he pulled back, a lock of his hair brushed against her cheek. His gaze lingered on her face, making her feel a bit breathless. Lucio Barone's approach might be a bit fast, but it was working, nonetheless.

"Okay, since you said the magic word."

"*Please?*"

Savannah shook her head. "No, *little*."

"Little?"

"Anyone who describes my butt as *little* will win me over," Savannah joked, but wished she hadn't because he angled his head and was checking out her backside. *Great.*

"Why? Your butt isn't that big."

That big?

"Why are you suddenly looking at me like you wish you had that glass-studded broom in your hand again?"

"I'm *not*!" Savannah felt the heat of a blush begin at her neck and creep upward. She glanced at his bandaged bicep and felt her face grow even hotter.

"Yes, you are. I'm having trouble figuring out how I've managed to tick you off by coming here to give you a ride. Are you always this b—difficult?"

"A ride? So is that what they call it in Brooklyn?" Savannah sucked in a breath. She put her hands on her hips and shot a glare at him. "Oh, so I'm a bitch if I refuse your kind offer?"

He shrugged and gave her a confused grin that was so damned sexy that Savannah was torn between kissing him and slapping him . . . not that she would have the nerve to do either one. This was crazy. She never acted like this! But she found herself stepping forward and poking a finger in his chest. *Wow . . . hard as a rock* registered in her female brain and sank lower. Oh, and she could see his pecs nicely outlined beneath the soft white cotton shirt. Ignoring her traitorous body's reaction, she ground out, "And FYI, I am not a bitch!"

"I said *difficult*," he reminded her smoothly.

"But you wanted to say *bitchy*!"

While shaking his head, he raised one hand up and said, "You're right. Happy now?"

Savannah flipped her hair over her shoulder and said, "Look, I'll admit that there *is* something going on here, but I don't know you that well. So my answer is no. My big chance, as you so arrogantly put it, will just have to wait."

"I can't let that happen," he informed her calmly but firmly. "I can't believe that you're acting this way. Now, come on, let's go."

"You can't make me do this."

"Oh, I think I could." Lucio took a step closer to her, invading her space. His tone was teasing, but *still* it was really hard for Savannah not to back away from him. Not that she was afraid, because there was a bit of a twinkle in his dark eyes and his mouth twitched a tiny bit like he was suppressing a smile. The fact that he was laughing at her increased her ire, but there was also something else smoldering between them that left her a bit shaken and really needing to take a step back. . . .

But she stood her ground, and glared up at him. "Yeah, you and what army?"

Lucio blinked at her for a moment and then burst into a low rumble of laughter. "You're kiddin', right? I can't believe that you're being so childish about riding with me."

"Yeah, well, maybe that's because you're being such a big bully!" Savannah actually took a step closer to prove that he didn't intimidate her, even though on so many levels he did.

"Yeah, well, maybe *you* need a time-out, or better yet . . . a spanking. . . ."

Whatever Savannah was about to retort was smothered by the image of herself bent over his knee with her ass perched up in the air for him to . . . *spank. Good Lord.* Not that she was into that or anything, but her gaze strayed to his hand and she had to suppress a hot shiver. "You wouldn't dare," she said, but instead of her voice having a hard edge, she almost sounded like she was issuing a breathy invitation. . . .

"*I* wouldn't bet on it." In a split second Luc went from being mildly amused to being totally turned on. Sophia had described Savannah as being sweet-natured bordering on shy. *Yeah, right.* She was a little hellcat spitting fire and oozing sex even in that hokey getup she was wearing. That was fine with him; he liked his women wild and willing. Ignoring the fact that he was supposed to whisk her back to the bar and that his car was indeed illegally parked, he put her guitar case down, reached out and pulled her against him.

Her baby blue eyes widened and she gasped, but she didn't protest when he slipped his hands around her waist and then leaned his head down for a kiss. "I think I'd rather do *this* instead." She was curvy but a little bitty thing with her dark blond head barely reaching his chin even though she was wearing boots.

Luc wasn't prepared, though, for the sizzle of pure heat at the mere touch of his mouth to hers. When she yielded to him Luc deepened the connection, sinking into her soft, sweet warmth. When he coaxed her mouth open wider she leaned against him, slid her hands up his back and pressed him even closer. Encouraged, Luc reached up with one hand to thread his fingers through her golden hair and cradle the back of her head. He slanted his mouth, trailing his tongue over her wet, silky bottom lip, and then still not satisfied, he dipped inside again for another long, hot kiss.

Somewhere in the back of his brain Luc knew that he should end this before it went too far, but he couldn't quite bring himself to break the delicious contact with Savannah's hungry little mouth. But still, he was going to be a gentleman and pull back in another minute or two . . . or three—really he *was*—but then she moved her hands from his back to his butt and squeezed. And if that weren't enough . . . *and it was*, she did this sultry little shimmy against him that screamed that she wanted him . . . bad. How he went from giving her a ride to the bar to this, Luc wasn't quite sure, but he wasn't going to argue, Luc thought to himself as he backed Savannah up to the sofa, which was conveniently close.

He lowered her to the plump cushions, still kissing her like there was no tomorrow, and then leaned his weight against the back of the sofa so that he could begin to unbutton her crisp cotton blouse. After lingering on her bottom lip, he moved his mouth to nuzzle her neck and slowly worked his way to the soft swell of her breasts exposed above the white lace of her bra. With a quick flick of his wrist he unhooked the front clasp and sucked in a breath when her breasts tumbled free.

"God, *Savannah*," Luc murmured just before taking a dusky nipple into his mouth. The delicate scent of her vanilla perfume filled his head while he lightly circled her nipple with his tongue. Cupping her breast, he licked harder and then tugged with his teeth when with a low moan she arched her back, offering him more.

Spurred on by her obvious enthusiasm, he slid his hand beneath her skirt and caressed the smooth skin of her thigh. When he reached the lacy edge of her panties she inhaled sharply and let out a breathy sigh. Luc leaned in for another deep kiss while toying with the edge of her panties. The moist heat on the tip of his finger made him want to sink inside, but he teased back and forth instead, driving them both wild.

When Savannah eased her thighs apart for him, he pushed past the lace and slid his middle finger inside of her slick heat. "God, you feel so good," Luc said in her ear while easing his finger slowly in and out. "So hot . . . so tight. I want to make love to you, Savannah. Right here, right now."

"Mmmm, *yes*," Savannah said low and throaty with closed eyes and parted lips. A hot shiver trembled through her body when Lucio rubbed the pad of his finger over her clitoris. She had never in her life been this out-of-control sexually charged . . . and she was somehow shameless with need for this man. Shoving her fingers in his silky soft hair, she arched her back, offering him her breasts once again. His mouth was so hot and his tongue was deliciously abrasive against her sensitive skin. She could feel the heat of his body and the ripple of muscle through the soft cotton T-shirt, making her want to see some skin.

"Take off your shirt," she whispered in his ear.

"Anything you want." He tugged it off in one fluid motion and tossed it over his head.

"Wow," Savannah breathed as she took in miles of tanned skin. Reaching up, she trailed her fingers over smooth sculpted pecs and downward over his washboard abs. Lucio was sheer male perfection . . . and that suddenly reminded Savannah that she was *not* . . . which led her to the question, what in the hell was she doing? Her fingers stilled and she pulled back her hands as if his skin were too hot to touch.

"Savannah, what's wrong?" he asked gently.

She felt her cheeks flame. "Y-you need to get up."

"Mission accomplished," he teased with a grin.

Savannah's gaze landed on the bulge in his jeans and she felt her face grow even warmer. "I—I mean get . . . off. Of me." The teasing light went out of his brown eyes and he looked so disappointed that Savannah felt guilty.

"Gotcha." Luc eased off of the sofa and stood up. "Okay, this is awkward." Locating his shirt, he shrugged into it, but his erection was clearly visible in his tight jeans. "Uh, give me a minute and I'll hightail it out of here."

Savannah hooked her bra and then tried to button her shirt, but her damned fingers were shaking. "You don't have to get so ticked."

He folded his arms across his chest and took a deep breath. "What game are we playing here, Savannah?"

"I don't play games," she said hotly.

"Coulda fooled me," he responded, but there wasn't much heat behind his statement.

Oh, *why* couldn't she push the buttons through the holes?

"Here," he said gruffly, and knelt down beside the sofa. He proceeded to quickly close up her shirt. God, he smelled so good and the mere brush of his fingers against her skin sent a tingle to her toes. When he was finished he looked at her with those deep, dark eyes. "I shouldn't have said that. Things just got outta hand."

Savannah swallowed the sudden emotion clogging her throat. She lowered her eyes and nodded. "Yeah, they did."

Luc tucked a finger beneath her chin and gently tilted her face up. "I'm sorry."

"Why?"

"Because I'm the kind of guy your mama warned you about, Savannah. I'm rough around the edges, while you're all sugar and spice. You should stay the hell away from me."

Savannah didn't think he was as big and bad as he pretended to be. After all, he was kneeling on the floor next to her speaking in gentle tones after she had just been about the biggest dick tease ever. He might be a little Brooklyn-bred rough-and-tumble, but he didn't have her fooled for a minute. Beneath his tough-guy exterior Lucio Barone was a softy, but for some reason he didn't want the world to know it.

Savannah also knew from Sophia that Lucio was a smart and successful businessman, having transformed an abandoned YMCA in Brooklyn into a state-of-the-art workout facility where he filmed a couple of popular exercise videos. Sophia also said that Lucio had recently worked with few celebrities as a personal trainer and was now writing a book on fitness and nutrition. Not exactly a slacker, but she decided to play along and nodded. "Thanks for the warning." Besides, they might have shared a hot and heavy moment, but the fact remained that Lucio didn't seem the type who would be attracted to a country girl like her for the long run. Not that she should even be thinking in those terms! Now that she was finally finished with school she could concentrate on her career, so just *what* was she doing mooning over some hot Brooklyn bad boy anyway?

"I'd better go," Luc said, but couldn't help but be a little disappointed that Savannah had given up so easily. Granted, she wasn't his usual type, but she was such a heady mix of sex and innocence that he found himself wanting to lean in and kiss her senseless all over again.

"Stop," Savannah protested when he leaned a tad closer and focused on her mouth. She placed her hands on his chest, but then with a groan instead of pushing him away, she fisted her fingers in his shirt and pulled him closer. "What the hell are we doing, Lucio?" she asked, her voice dripping with her sexy Southern comfort.

"Damned if I know," he answered with his mouth almost touching hers. "But I can't seem to stop myself. There is just something about you. . . ."

And then they were kissing again . . . hot, open-mouthed and deep. Luc's heart pounded in his chest and he was instantly rock hard. He rose from his knees to sit on the sofa and pulled Savannah onto his lap to straddle him. His erection pushed against his jeans, begging for release.

"Come up to your knees," Luc said in her ear. When she did he quickly unzipped his fly and sighed. The hard ridge of his dick strained against his boxer briefs with the head almost poking out of the waistband. When Savannah sank back down and rubbed the silky heat of her panties over the soft cotton, Luc closed his eyes and moaned. He was wondering if he had a condom in his wallet when his cell phone rang and vibrated in his pocket. He ignored it, but then it immediately rang again.

"You'd better answer it," Savannah said while nuzzling his neck.

"It's probably Sophia wondering where we are." He fished into his pocket and answered the phone. "Calm down, Sophia. I'm here with her now. I know we're late, but Savannah said it's no big deal. Oh. *Oh shit*. Okay! I said okay!"

"What?" Savannah pulled back to look at him. "Is something wrong?"

Luc nibbled on his lip for a second, wondering what the best way to put this to her was.

"Spill, Lucio!" She gave his shoulders a little shake.

"You know how I was supposed to give you a ride over to the bar?"

"Oh . . ." She frowned and then her eyes widened a fraction. "A ride *to the bar* . . ."

Luc swallowed and ran his fingers through his hair. "Yeah, well, let's just say that your big chance is about to walk out the door."

"Lucio, tell me what's going on here. I'm confused."

"Sophia said not to. Just hurry, okay?"

"I'm not going anywhere until you tell me what in the world is going on."

Luc had lived with two sisters long enough to know that Savannah wasn't going to give up, but she was also going to panic if he told her, so in a very calm and even voice he said, "Now, keep your cool, okay? I'm not supposed to tell you for a good reason."

"Tell me," she said in a low and urgent voice. "Tell me and I'll make you the doggone chicken cannelloni."

"You know how?"

"Yes!"

"You're lying."

"Of course I'm lying. I don't even know what the hell it is. Just tell me, Lucio! Whatever it is, I promise I won't panic."

✳ Chapter Three

"*R*emember your promise," Luc said. "Stay calm."

Savannah shook his shoulders and shouted, "For the love of God, tell me what's going on."

"That wasn't calm."

"I'm going to kill you."

Clearing his throat, Luc finally said, "It seems that there is a record producer at Logan's waiting to hear you sing. Brody Baker sent him your demo and he wants to hear you perform live."

Savannah blinked at him while her brain tried to process this information. "You . . . you mean while we were tangling tongues here on the sofa, there has been someone from Heart Records waiting for me?"

"It appears so, yes. Look, I let it slip a couple of times earlier that someone was gonna listen to you sing tonight, but you were so insistent that you weren't ready and then, well . . . I got sidetracked."

"For the love of God!" Savannah scrambled off his lap so fast that she tumbled to the floor in a heap of panic.

"Stay calm, Savannah."

"Easy for you to say! Your career isn't on the line." She glared at him. "Don't just sit there! Zip up your pants and hurry!"

Savannah pushed up to her feet and grabbed her purse. "Come on, Lucio."

"I'm trying," he said, tugging his zipper over his erection.

Savannah felt heat creep into her cheeks. Good God, just what in the world had gotten into her? She had almost just had sex with a virtual stranger. True, he was Sophia and M. J.'s brother and hotter than a firecracker, but still . . . *what had she been thinking*? And to top it off, he was there to give her a *ride* . . . in a *car*, not to . . . oh, she couldn't even think about it. He could never know her crazy mistake.

"Oh, I'm a wrinkled mess," she said as she slung her purse over her shoulder. "Hurry! What if he leaves?"

Luc picked up the guitar case and held it in front of his obvious discomfort and headed toward the door. "Sophia and Logan won't let that happen," he said calmly.

"Quit being so danged calm!"

"Someone hasta be."

Savannah followed him out the door and down the sidewalk, blinking in the waning sunlight while trying to keep up with his long-legged stride. This whole day was beginning to have a surreal feel to it. First, she attacked Lucio with a broom, then she almost had sex with him, and now he was taking her to what could be one of the most important moments in her life. For someone who was usually a low-key kind of person, this aggressive behavior and excitement was almost too much.

Savannah stopped in the middle of the sidewalk and put a hand to her stomach. The sandwich that she had for dinner was doing cartwheels. Whenever she got nervous her stomach did crazy flip-floppy things that she couldn't control.

"Savannah?" Luc stopped in front of a black Lexus SUV parked on the street and opened the rear door. "What's wrong?" He put her guitar in the backseat and walked over to her. "You okay? You don't look so good."

She swallowed. "Yeah, well, I don't feel so good. Oh God, I can't do this." She turned around and started heading back to her apartment, but Luc snagged her around the waist from behind.

"You *can* do this, Savannah," he said low in her ear, and she shivered in spite of the summer heat. There was something about Lucio Barone that turned her inside out.

"Uh-uh . . . can't."

"Listen, you gotta do this for my sake now."

"Why is that?"

"Because I was supposed to come here and pick you up. Instead I let you seduce me."

She gasped. "I didn't seduce you! I thought you were . . ."

"What?"

"Nothing."

"I get it. You thought I was coming here for a booty call."

"I did *not*!"

He chuckled but then shrugged. "Maybe in the back of my mind, I was. But anyway, fugetabout all that. I let the friggin' secret out of the bag, making you a nervous wreck. This is all my fault."

Savannah inhaled a shaky breath and put her hand to her stomach again as she turned around to face him. "Oh, Lucio, I don't know. . . ."

He reached inside of his pocket. "Here, chew this peppermint. It will help settle your stomach."

Savannah took the small disk of candy from him and tugged on the plastic edges to unwrap it. It was warm from being next to his body.

"Don't bite it. Suck it slowly," he advised so seriously that Savannah had to chuckle.

"That's what they all say," she said, searching for humor to relieve her anxiety.

"I didn't mean to sound suggestive."

Savannah shook her head. "Lucio, you sound suggestive just breathing."

"Are you saying that I'm sexy?"

"You know that you're gorgeous. Why do you think I melted all over you?"

Lucio gave her an odd look that she couldn't quite fathom . . . *disappointment*? How could that be? She had just told him that he was gorgeous.

"Do me a favor and get in the car." He smiled then, making Savannah's heart beat a bit faster. He was gorgeous when he was being the broody bad boy, but his smile was something to be reckoned with. It lit up his face and went straight to her heart. How could she possibly refuse? "Okay."

"Hurry up." Lucio held the door open for her and then rushed over to the driver's side and hopped in. While he sped down Broadway Savannah brushed her hair and then applied a thin coat of pink lip gloss. She rubbed her lips together and then inhaled a deep breath when he stopped in front of Logan's.

"You have to get out, Savannah," Lucio said gently. When she just sat there, he reached across, unhooked her seat belt and then tugged on the door handle. "Don't forget your guitar in the backseat."

"Are you coming in?"

"Do you want me to?"

Savannah nodded, realizing that she did. "Of course."

"Okay, then, I will. I'll park and be right there. Now go in there and knock 'em dead."

Savannah gave him a smile that shook a bit around the corners. "This is it, huh?"

Lucio leaned over and gave her a tender kiss on the mouth. "You can do this," he said with such conviction that Savannah almost believed him. "Go!"

"Okay!" Savannah slid from the soft leather seat and retrieved her guitar. With a last wave at Lucio she hurried inside.

Logan spotted her and pointed to the stage in the

front corner of the bar. "You're on," he mouthed, trying to look so casual that Savannah almost laughed except that she was having another case of nerves.

Savannah sucked on the sliver of peppermint that was left on her tongue, took her guitar out of the case and turned toward the stage. Although she had walked up the two steps onto the small platform countless times, tonight she felt as if she were walking into her future and her knees suddenly wobbled.

God, how am I going to do this?

Savannah swallowed and then blew out a mint-scented breath as she put one foot onto the first step. She looked down at Granny Parks's kick-ass snakeskin boots and smiled. "You can do this, Savannah," Granny's gruff voice seemed to whisper in her ear. Then, Lucio's voice filtered into her brain . . . low and sexy, saying, "You gotta do this for me."

So with her knees knocking and her heart pounding, Savannah walked up onto the stage. She sat down on the stool, adjusted the microphone and then gave the audience her biggest smile. "Hi, y'all." Okay, her voice shook only a tiny bit. "Welcome to Logan's. I'm Savannah Parks and I'd like to get things started off with a song that I wrote myself called "Wake-up Call."

Savannah belted out the crowd-pleasing tune, knowing that some of the locals who had heard the lyrics many times before would sing the refrain along with her. Feisty and fun but without much vocal range, the easy melody gave her a chance to warm up her voice before she went into her next song, a popular Martina McBride cover that showcased Savannah's talent. The crowd roared their approval, making Savannah wonder if Logan and Sophia had given their friends a heads-up that some record execs were watching her.

Savannah wrapped up her set with one of her own songs, a soulful country ballad. Knowing that this was her chance, she poured her heart into the music and was rewarded with thundering applause and whistles. Savannah thanked the crowd and stepped down from the stage. While she was slipping her guitar in the case Logan approached her.

"You sounded great tonight, Savannah."

"Thanks, Logan. Sorry I was late."

He waved her apology off. "No problem. Listen, there are a couple of guys from Heart Records who want to talk to you. They're waiting in my office."

Savannah gulped and her pulse started to race. Okay, she knew this was coming, but the reality of it was another thing altogether. "Will you go back there with me?"

Logan gave her a kiss on the forehead. "I could, but I think you can handle this one on your own. Now, don't sign anything . . . but listen closely to what they have to say, okay?"

Savannah nodded and put a hand to her tummy. "Okay." She headed to Logan's office at the back of the bar, pausing to grab a bottle of water along the way. Out of the corner of her eye she spotted Lucio and lifted her hand to wave, but a tall shapely blonde in painted-on jeans approached him. When Lucio laughed at something the blonde said, Savannah told herself that it didn't matter. The leggy blonde was certainly more his type than Savannah could ever hope to be. Telling herself that she had more important things to tend to, she pulled her gaze from Lucio and hurried to Logan's office.

Chapter Four

Lucio tried to disentangle himself from the annoying woman who was hanging all over him, but by the time he blew her off Savannah was gone. "Damn," he muttered, and took a long pull off his beer. He saw his sister Sophia weaving her way toward him through the smoky, crowded bar and waved.

"Hey there, little brother," his sister said with a smile. "I didn't know that you were here."

"I dropped Savannah off at the door and came in after I finally found a place to park. All eyes were on Savannah, so I guess you didn't notice me coming in."

"Savannah was amazing, wasn't she?"

"Yes, she was," Luc said, and realized that he meant it. "She has a hellava voice. Hey, sorry about getting her here late. I didn't know how important it was to be here on time until you explained things."

"Well, all's well that ends well, I suppose, even though I was ready to wring your neck." Sophia angled her head and asked, "What was keeping you two anyway?"

While Luc wasn't prone to blushing he felt a bit of heat creep up his neck.

"Lucio Barone . . . you naughty little boy."

"What are you gettin' at?" Luc scoffed. "Savannah wasn't ready when I arrived, that's all."

Sophia arched a delicate eyebrow. "Liar. Something happened between you two. Tell me."

"I don't kiss and tell."

"Ah, so you *were* kissing."

Luc sat his beer bottle down on the small table with a thump. "Oh, come on, Sophia. Sweet little Savannah Parks is hardly my type."

Sophia rolled her eyes. "Right. You go for slinky air-heads. . . . Sorry, I forgot. For a moment there I thought you might actually be attracted to someone with sub-stance."

"Wow, that was a little harsh."

"If the shoe fits . . ." Sophia flipped her long hair over her shoulder, making her bracelets jingle, but Luc also noticed that she was wearing cowboy boots and jeans, which he found rather amusing.

"Do I have to remind you that until recently that shoe fit *you* pretty friggin' good?"

"I was just waiting for the right guy." Sophia glanced over at Logan, who was serving up drinks be-hind the bar, and smiled softly.

Luc groaned. "Don't go shovelin' M. J.'s soul mate garbage at me, Sophia."

"It's not garbage, Luc." Sophia poked him in the chest.

"Yeah, yeah." He reached up and ran his fingers through his hair, drawing attention from a tableful of women. Normally he would stroll over there and flirt, but all he could seem to think about was Savannah, who had failed to reappear. Confused at his intense reaction to a woman he barely knew, he said, "Listen, I'm tired. I'm going to head next door to shower this cigarette smoke offa me and hit the sack."

Sophia frowned. "Aren't you going to wait for Savannah to come out? She might sing another set."

"Why are you pushin' this girl on me?"

"I'm not!"

Luc narrowed his eyes at his sister. "You're not trying to tell me that Savannah Parks is *the one* for me, are ya, Sophia? I mean, that would be ludicrous. The last thing that sweet girl needs is someone like me."

"Someone like you? Hmmm." She tapped her cheek with a red-tipped fingernail. "Let's see, you're handsome, successful and available. What's not to like?" Sophia shook her head and reached up to pinch his cheeks. "You can quit with the badass act, Luc. This isn't high school, where you have to prove you're all big and tough Lucio Barone embarrassed of his crazy psychic sistas."

"I was never embarrassed, Sophia," he said quietly. "I just never could stand jackasses making fun of my family. If I got into a scuffle or two—"

"Or twenty."

"It was to defend you and M. J."

Sophia gave him a look indicating she wasn't entirely buying his story but leaned over and hugged him.

"Just open your heart to the possibility of finding your true love. That's all I'm sayin'." Her New York accent was at odds with her cowboy boots, making Luc smile. *You can take the girl outta Brooklyn. . . .*

"So, how are things in good old Williamsburg, Brooklyn, Luc?"

" 'Bout the same. Mom and Pop's shop is doin' good."

Sophia laughed. "Yeah, it's finally hip to be psychic. So we're not weirdos anymore?"

"Wouldn't go *that* far."

"God, I'd kill for some curly fries at Teddy's Bar and Grill."

"Yeah, well, I'd settle for some homemade chicken cannelloni. Do I still get it even though I got Savannah here late?"

"Yeah, I got some in the freeza."

"In the freeza? Why's that?"

"Long story, but it's there with your name on it."

"Sounds good, Sis. Okay," Luc said with a nod. "Now I'm gonna shower and hit the sack."

"Can't you stay a little longa?"

"Nah, I'm dead on my feet, Sophia."

"Oh, all right," she said with a disappointed little pout. "Um, I'll likely be late, so don't worry about me."

"In other words, I'll see ya at breakfast," Luc said with a chuckle. "I get it."

When Sophia put her hands to her cheeks and laughed Luc admitted to himself that he was glad to see his sister so happy. Luc would never have guessed that both Sophia and M. J. would have ended up falling for smooth-talkin' cowboys. Leaning over, he kissed her on the cheek and then wove his way to the front door. Once outside, Luc took gulps of fresh air. Being a fitness guru, secondhand smoke was one of his pet peeves.

After letting himself in Sophia's apartment, he quickly shed his clothes and jumped into the shower before the water was even hot. He scrunched up his face at all of the peach-scented body wash and shampoos displayed but lathered up anyway. Smelling like a peach would mess with his tough-guy image, which Sophia claimed he cultivated to counteract his New Age family, but the truth was, he had gotten over that long ago.

True, back in Brooklyn Luc had tried hard, especially as a teenager, to be the opposite of his sensitive sisters and hippie parents, but deep down he had always believed in their psychic abilities. The problem was that he had always felt a little like odd man out in his family. He supposed this was rather ironic, given what they did for a living. While he didn't have the talents that they possessed, he did seem to sense when something was wrong or when he was needed, but Luc had always chalked it up to instinct rather than something supernatural. He dearly loved his family, though, quirkiness and all.

Luc was toweling dry in the peach-scented steam when he heard someone knocking at the back door. Wrapping the damp towel around his waist, he padded on bare feet down the short hallway and through the kitchen. With his fingers he slicked his wet hair out of his eyes while opening the door, thinking it must be his sister. "Forget your keys or somethin'?"

"Uh, that's my line," Savannah said while holding up his sunglasses. "You left these in the bar. Sophia said that they were expensive and that you'd want them. She asked me to drop them off on my way home."

"Thanks." Luc accepted his Oakleys and set them on the countertop. He noticed how her gaze lingered on his chest and while he was proud of the shape that he worked so hard to stay in, he found himself wanting to be more to Savannah than beefcake. "By the way, you were amazing tonight. You have a beautiful voice. If they don't sign you to a record deal, those guys are nuts."

"Thank you. Oh, and your peppermint helped. I'll have to keep some on hand. I was so nervous at first."

"Didn't seem like it. You were a real pro up there. Had the crowd eatin' outta your hand."

Pleased but embarrassed, Savannah managed to smile. "Think so?"

"You bet," he said, but then frowned. "Hey, you aren't thinkin' of walkin' home, are you?"

"I do it all the time, Lucio. It's only ten o'clock and the streets are well lit. I'll be fine."

"No way, I'll walk you."

"Um, you're a little underdressed."

Luc glanced down at his towel and grinned. "Come on in. I'll grab my pants." He chuckled, "Okay, that didn't sound right."

"Well . . ." Savannah paused and swallowed. The sight of his bare chest beaded up with water was a reminder that she easily lost her head where Lucio was concerned. "I appreciate the offer, but I'm fine, really."

"Don't be silly. You've got that guitar to lug too," Luc protested. He grabbed her hand trying to gently tug her in the doorway, but the tip of her boot snagged on the metal toe strip, and her guitar thumped to the floor when she lurched forward.

"Whoa!" Savannah stumbled and caught her balance by grabbing on to Luc's shoulders while she kind of head-butted into his chest. He grunted and backpedaled into the kitchen until he came up against the small table and landed in a sitting position with Savannah falling, breasts first, into his face. "Sorry!" Savannah tried to push back while still unbalanced, causing her to rub his face in her cleavage.

Luc steadied her with his hands around her waist and grinned. "No problem."

Savannah winced. "Sorry, I'm a bit clumsy at times. That was an accident."

"I tugged on your hand. It was my fault."

"I meant the boobs-in-your-face thing."

"Oh, no need to be sorry for that." He grinned. "In fact if you want to do it again . . ."

Savannah had to laugh. She would have backed up, but he held her firmly. Her own hands remained on his wide shoulders and she suddenly wasn't in any hurry to remove them either. His skin felt warm and slightly damp from his recent shower and reminded Savannah that he was almost naked. "You smell like peaches," she observed, a bit embarrassed that instead of teasing like she intended, her voice sounded husky and a bit suggestive.

"I know. . . . I used some fruity shower gel stuff that belongs to Sophia."

"Yeah, right."

Luc chuckled. "Caught me. I was going to go try on her underwear next. Wanna watch?"

The thought of sexy Lucio in frilly underwear had Savannah laughing.

"You think I'm kiddin'?"

"Yeah."

"You're right. I'm the only sane member of the Barone clan."

Savannah laughed again, glad to have some of the nervous tension ease from her body. "You know you love your sisters."

"Guilty."

"No need to feel guilty. You obviously have a strong sense of family and loyalty. I like that in a guy." Savannah meant to be teasing again, but Lucio looked at her with such seriousness in his eyes that she was taken off guard. "What?" she prompted when he remained silent.

"Nothin'."

"Come on." Savannah shook his shoulders. "Tell me what's on your mind, Lucio. Did I say something wrong?"

He looked at her for a long moment and then said, "You're gonna think that I'm such a girl for admitting this. . . ."

"Uh, not hardly," she joked, but waited expectantly for him to elaborate.

He opened his mouth but then hesitated. "Nah, fugetaboutit."

"I'll let you walk me home if you tell me what's on your mind."

Luc smiled then, that bone-melting flash of white teeth that had Savannah clinging to his shoulders for support. He licked his bottom lip as if in thought and finally said, "Add a kiss to that deal and we're on."

Knowing that she shouldn't, Savannah nodded. "Deal, but tell me first."

"Ya know how you just asked what's on my mind?"

Savannah frowned. "Yeah."

"Women don't usually care what I'm thinkin' or that I'm loyal or that I care about my family." Lowering his gaze, he licked his bottom lip again as if trying to put what he wanted to say into words.

"I get it," Savannah said softly and he quickly looked up to meet her gaze. "You're eye candy."

"Well . . . yeah. I mean, I don't wanna sound like I'm bragging, but at the age of twenty-eight I own a successful fitness business that I built from the ground up. I'm also a licensed nutritionist and yet in social situations I get treated like I don't have a brain in my head, ya know? Sure, I could cut my hair, wear a suit and tie and take the Brooklyn from my accent. . . ."

"But that wouldn't be you."

With a shrug he said, "I am what I am."

"Nothing wrong with that, Lucio."

"God, it must be the peach-smelling body wash getting to me. I can't believe I'm telling you this stuff," he said with a grin. "And I guess it's hard to be credible sitting here half-naked. Am I impressing you yet?"

More than you know. "A tiny bit," she teased.

"So, do I get my kiss now?" While his tone was teasing, the air suddenly became sexually charged.

"Okay, but just a little one," Savannah warned, and then leaned in for a fleeting touch, but the moment her lips brushed his her resistance melted like a snowflake on her tongue. She opened her mouth for more and Luc delivered with a long delicious kiss.

"Wow, that was knee popping," Savannah said with a sigh.

"Knee popping?"

"Yeah," Savannah said, and demonstrated by bending her knee and kicking her booted foot backward. "Like in the movies."

"You're kiddin', right?"

"A little. But you're a damned good kisser, Lucio Barone."

"You can call me Luc."

"Oh no, you're *Lucio*," she said, making him laugh when she tried to roll his name off her tongue but bumped into her Southern accent. "Okay, you can walk me home now."

"Um, well, your knee wasn't the only thing popping. "You'll have to give me a minute."

Savannah glanced down and then placed her palms on her cheeks.

"You weren't supposed to look."

"I *didn't*," she protested, and backed away so that he could get up from the table.

"Did so," Luc called over his shoulder as he hurried from the kitchen.

Savannah put her hand over her mouth and giggled while watching him walk from the room. So bad-boy Lucio had a fun side to him as well. He was so different from her, but she could feel herself falling for him hard and fast. Savannah knew she should take it easy and back way off, since her career looked like it was ready to take flight and Lucio was in town only for a while anyway. She groaned. Getting involved with him would be a mistake on so many levels and yet she couldn't remember a guy ever making her feel like he did in nothing flat.

Savannah smiled when she thought of his confession that he wanted to be taken seriously. This was something women fretted over and she never really gave much thought to a guy's feeling the same way. Now she regretted her comment about melting because he was gorgeous. She already knew that there was so much more to Lucio than his good looks. He *was* smokin' hot, but although Savannah was physically attracted to him, he wasn't the type of guy she ever imagined herself being with.

"Oh, stop thinking in those terms," she whispered to herself. This was *not* the time in her life to get tangled up with a guy. Savannah smoothed her skirt and took a deep breath, promising herself that she would tell him as much on their walk to her apartment.

"Ready?" Luc asked, startling Savannah from the speech that she was practicing in her head. But when she turned to look at him his warm smile already began chipping away at her resolve. He was dressed in low-slung faded jeans and a black T-shirt just tight enough to make her gaze linger.

"Sure."

"Let's go, then." He picked up her guitar case and held the door open for her.

The night was still warm and a bit sultry, but the sidewalk was crowded with people hitting the strip of honky-tonk bars and various restaurants. A few of the gift shops remained open, catering to the tourists who frequented Nashville year-round. Neon lights blinked, lighting up the street with color. Music and laughter drifted out of the bars, mingling with the horns honking on busy streets. Once they got past the congestion Luc began asking her about her music.

"Is it okay for me to ask how things went with the record people?"

Savannah nodded. "Of course. Brody Baker's agent has agreed to represent me, so the business end of things will be up to him to iron out. It's hard for me to wrap my brain around the thought that I might have a recording contract soon. Of course it sure helps that Brody is pulling for me."

Luc shook his head. "Don't kid yourself. Brody might have gotten you in the door, but you have to have talent to get beyond that. And baby, you've got it out the wazoo."

Savannah put her hand to her stomach. "I get butterflies just thinking about it. There's so much competition and I know that I have a decent voice, but nowadays you need a stage presence that I don't think I have," she said as they stopped at her front door.

Luc shook his head. "You gotta be kidding. Savannah, the crowd at Logan's loved you."

"Yeah, but a lot of them were friends. Beyond Logan's I don't have much experience. And I'm not slinky and sexy like the new wave of country stars."

"I think you're sexy as hell, Savannah." When he sat her guitar case down and gazed down at her she started to melt all over again.

"Oh, you're a smooth talker, Lucio," she teased, searching her brain files for her good-bye speech but coming up blank. If he smiled, she was a goner.

Luc would never describe himself as being jovial, but there was something about Savannah that kept a silly smile plastered on his face. Like now, for instance, he knew that he should leave and yet he couldn't get his body to obey and instead stood there grinning like a fool. He probably could have done it, but then she put one small hand in the middle of his chest and although there wasn't anything sexual about this gesture, her touch made him suck in a breath.

"You okay?"

"Sure," he lied. "Were you gonna ask me somethin'?" *Something like "Do you want to come in and spend the night?"*

"Yes. It's still so warm out that I thought you might want to pop inside and grab a bottle of water for the walk home."

"Oh." Disappointment sank all the way to his toes. Realistically, he knew that he could seduce Savannah, but he already cared too much about her for it to go down that way. It hit him hard that he wanted much more from her than sex, but then the knockout blow came with another thought.

Maybe this girl is the one.

Sure, he had told Sophia and M. J. that the whole soul mate thing was a crock, but he didn't really believe that deep down . . . *way deep down*, but still it was there and was now bubbling to the surface like a damned volcano.

"You okay?" Savannah asked once more with a frown. "I think you could use a cold drink." Without waiting for an answer, she quickly unlocked her door and entered.

Luc hesitated for a fraction. While he never considered himself psychic he acknowledged that there must be some recessive genes floating around inside of him because he had a strong premonition that stepping into her apartment again would somehow change his life forever. "Aw, bullshit," he muttered, trying to shake the feeling.

Savannah came back to the door clutching a plastic bottle. "Are you a vampire and I need to invite you in?"

"What?" Luc asked when she interrupted the crazy argument he was having with himself.

"Never mind. Come in, Lucio. It's nice and cool in here." She gave him an odd look and stood back for him to enter.

Before he could answer, a bright flicker of light just behind Savannah's head caught his attention. Then, a gruff voice crooned in his ear, "What the hell you

waitin' for, boy? Get your tight little tushie in there."
Tight little tushie?

Luc blinked at the light, but in a sparkling flash it disappeared making him wonder if he had imagined the whole thing.

"Lucio?"

"D-did you just see a bright light . . . hear a voice?" he asked weakly.

"No, I didn't," Savannah answered, and grabbed his hand. "You must have low blood sugar or something. When was the last time y'all had somethin' to eat?"

"Um, not for a while, come to think of it," Luc answered with some relief, thinking that she had to be right. "Yeah, must be low blood sugar."

Tugging him into the small kitchen, Savannah said, "Don't know what we can muster up, but let's see." She opened the refrigerator and bent over, humming while she looked around. "Oh, here we go. Chicken fried rice." She pulled out a carton and showed it to him triumphantly.

Luc angled his head and read the bold writing on the side of the carton. "It says 'belongs to Lindsay, eat this and I will kill you' on it."

Savannah chuckled. "Yeah, right. Like she didn't eat my leftover veggie pizza last night."

"So this is payback?"

"You got it." She dumped the rice into a skillet and turned on the gas burner.

"You're not going to microwave it?"

Savannah wrinkled her nose. "No, it becomes mush. This will taste much better, trust me."

Luc grinned. "You're preaching to the choir. I love to cook. Microwaves should be outlawed."

She gave him a high five, but then her eyebrows rose. "Really? You don't seem like the type."

"Oh, so you think I'm the 'Hey, baby, fix me some grub' kinda guy, huh?" he asked, deliberately making his Brooklyn accent more pronounced.

"I didn't mean that, Lucio," she protested while stirring the rice, which was popping and sizzling in the skillet. "Guys I know around here don't do more than barbeque or maybe scramble some eggs. I'm impressed."

"Thank you. You should be," he joked, but he was pleased. His stomach rumbled at the tantalizing aroma. He usually stayed away from carbs, so this was a rare treat.

"Well, I expect you to put your money where your mouth is," she said while scooping the rice onto plates.

"And cook for you?"

"Yep," she said, and handed him a steaming plate of food.

"You're on." Cooking a meal for her was something that he found appealing. Of course he was finding that doing *anything* with her was appealing. He accepted the fried rice and took a hot bite. "This is hitting the spot."

They ate their food in companionable silence and Luc acknowledged how completely at ease he felt with Savannah. He didn't feel the need for mindless chatter or pretense and for the first time in a long time he felt as if he could just be himself. When they were finished Luc knew it was getting late and although he didn't want to leave, he couldn't think of a reason to stay. . . . Well, he *could*, but that was dangerous territory that he was trying rather unsuccessfully to ignore. After draining his bottle of water, he said, "I suppose I should get going. Wouldn't want to be here when your roomie finds out that we ate her fried rice." He held his breath when Savannah hesitated and looked as if she might ask him to stay.

"Lindsay went home for the weekend."

"Oh?"

Savannah looked at him expectantly.

"Is that right?" He arched one eyebrow. *Okay, that was smooth*. He supposed it was because he didn't want to mess things up with her that he was suddenly a cheese ball. When her eyes widened and she put her hands to her cheeks Luc thought he had screwed things up royally.

"Oh . . . Lucio you're bleeding."

"What?"

"Your arm. Where I smacked you with the doggone broom." She grabbed a napkin and pressed it to his biceps. "I'm so sorry. Does it hurt? What if there is still glass in there? God, why did I attack you with that damned broom?" She stomped her foot and then looked up at him with such cute concern that Luc just wanted to grab her and kiss her.

Aha. He had his reason to stay at least for a while. "Savannah, don't worry. It's just a scratch." He glanced down at his arm. "But maybe you should take a quick look for glass. Just to be on the safe side, ya know?"

"Oh, of course. Follow me to the bathroom. I've got some bandages and salve in there."

The bathroom was surprisingly spacious with a huge claw-foot tub and a pedestal sink. Old-fashioned tiny squares of pink and white tile covered the floor and rose halfway up the wall. Savannah opened a large linen closet and located bandages and a tube of antiseptic lotion.

"This is nice," Luc said as he rolled up his T-shirt sleeve.

Savannah nodded. "Yes, I'm going to miss that big bathtub."

He glanced at the tub and suddenly pictured Savannah soaking in a fragrant bubble bath with rosy cheeks, her hair piled on top of her head, and her breasts—oh shit, he was getting hard. "You goin' somewhere?" he asked, trying to change his train of thought without a whole lot of success.

"Not far," she explained as she gently dabbed at his arm with a warm washcloth. "Since I'm finished with school I'm moving to my parents' farmhouse not too far from here. They're retired to Florida and they lease the acreage out, but the house is empty. It's so peaceful and quiet."

"You plan on workin' on your music there, I suppose."

"Yeah. I'll still help Logan out at the bar but not as often." She gently prodded his arm. "I don't see any glass. I'll just rub this salve on and bandage you back up."

Luc leaned his hips against the sink and watched Savannah. She concentrated with her bottom lip caught between her teeth, giving him the chance to study the details of her face. She was a natural beauty in an understated way and Luc could easily picture her barefoot in cutoff jeans on a farm. That being said, Savannah also possessed a sensuality that she was unaware of, making her all the more alluring, in Luc's opinion.

"There. All done."

"Hmm?" His brain was elsewhere.

"You're all patched up."

Luc glanced down at his arm and then back at Savannah. "Oh, thanks."

There was a sexually charged silence that sizzled with unspoken words.

"Well, I guess I should go."

Savannah nodded and said softly, "I suppose," but then she surprised him and continued. "But I don't want you to."

Luc's heart thudded.

"There's something simmering between us, Lucio."

"I sense a big 'but,' though, Savannah."

She angled her head and said, "I'm not a one-nighter kind of girl."

"That's not what I want from you, Savannah. One night with you would never be enough."

She licked her lips and continued. "But you don't live here and you're Sophia's brother and that complicates things. If we got something started, then where would it go?"

"All true." He reached over and tucked a lock of hair behind her ear.

She placed a hand in the middle of his chest. "But

none of that seems to matter right now. All I can think of is how much I want to be with you, Lucio."

Luc gazed down at her pretty face. He wanted so much to lean in and kiss her and she was giving him the opportunity that he had been hoping for, but it suddenly hit him that he wanted her to want *him* and not just his damned hard body. *I must be fucking crazy*, he thought, but forced the words past his lips, "I think it's best that I go—"

"Oh . . . ," she interrupted, and her eyes widened. "You're turning me down?" She backed away from him. "Oh, of course, God, I feel so stupid."

"Why in the world would you feel stupid?"

"Well, for starters I've been throwing myself at you all day and it's painfully obvious now that you . . . you don't want me." Savannah pushed past him and quickly headed out of the bathroom.

"Wait a minute," Luc said, following her. "Of course I want you, Savannah."

She stopped and whirled around so suddenly that Luc almost plowed into her. "Really?"

"Just not . . . yet."

Her eyebrows rose and she sputtered, "So you want a *rain check*? Oh, here, let me go fill one out for you. Let me warn you that there will be an expiration date, though."

Before he could stop her she rushed into a bedroom and over to a small cluttered desk and scribbled something on a sticky note. "Here." She thrust it at him.

Curious, Luc looked down at the pink slip of paper

and then glanced at his watch. "Savannah, this expired five minutes ago."

"Exactly. You can go now."

Luc crumbled the paper. "Savannah . . ." Damn, he was royally screwing this up. When she looked at him with luminous eyes ready to spill tears, he ran his fingers through his hair trying to think of a way to explain something he didn't quite understand himself.

"Do you know how hard it was for me to ask you to stay with me, Lucio?"

Luc shook his head. "Yeah, well, not nearly as hard as it was for me to turn you down."

"Then why? Why did you?"

Luc inhaled a deep breath and then blew it out. "Savannah, I've had women eating out of my hand since I was a teenager. I was the tough guy with the long hair in the leather jacket that girls wanted to do in the back of their Mustang." He hesitated and then said, "But they didn't want to take me home to meet their parents." He shook his head. "I even had a motorcycle. I was pretty much the clichéd rebel and my cause was to be as different than my New Age family as I could possibly be. So, in answer to your question? Savannah, I don't want to be your leather jacket. I want to slow things down and do this right."

A tear slid down her cheek.

"Aw, man, don't cry." Luc took a step closer and wiped the tear away with his thumb.

"I'm such a *bitch*," Savannah said so vehemently that Luc almost chuckled, but she was so serious that he couldn't.

"You're not a bitch."

She looked up at him while blinking back tears. "Really?"

"Look, it's been a crazy, emotional day for you. Let's just take a giant step back and take things slow. I plan on being in Nashville for a few weeks workin' on some business-related stuff. I'll call you, okay?"

" 'Kay." She sniffed and brushed at a tear, making Luc want to gather her in his arms.

"Oh, and Savannah, for the record, I've never wanted a woman more than I want you. Make no mistake."

"Lucio Barone, you had better hightail it out of here before I throw myself at you again."

"Yeah, I should because my resistance isn't that strong."

"Run! Go!"

Luc hesitated. He was already having second thoughts about leaving. "Savannah . . ."

"Go! Call me tomorrow and we'll start this going-slow thing."

✶ *Chapter Six*

The next two weeks for Savannah, however, were a whirlwind of activity mostly centered on the move to her parents' farmhouse and the contract negotiations with Heart Records. Brody Baker was still on tour on the West Coast but took the time to answer a million questions that Savannah tossed his way. Brody's agent agreed to represent Savannah, but she still had so many decisions to make that her head was spinning. Near the end of the second week she was working with a singing coach in preparation for some studio time that was already scheduled.

Studio time! Savannah put her hand to her stomach and groaned. As if that weren't exciting enough, the powers that be at Heart Records wanted her first single to be her very own song "Wake-up Call," which they thought was a little reminiscent of Miranda Lambert's hard-hitting megahit "Kerosene." A music video was in the works. *A very sexy music video!* "I'm never going to be able to pull this off," Savannah wailed, and went to search for a peppermint in her purse . . . but first she had to locate her purse in the last pile of stuff from her apartment.

After finding it, she dug around for the candy. "Aha!" She slipped the disk in her mouth and then immediately thought of Lucio. Savannah sighed. Peppermints would forever make her think of him. They had played phone tag, but Savannah had been so busy that she had seen him only in passing at Logan's. This was taking it slow to a new level and it was killing her, but there wasn't a solution in sight, since *busy* was her new middle name. While Lucio had made it clear that he understood, Savannah worried that he would lose patience.

The sound of her cell phone ringing in her purse interrupted her thoughts and made her jump about a foot in the air. Digging past the junk, she grabbed it and answered, "Hello!"

"Hey, I actually got you." The sound of Lucio's voice made Savannah smile and sent a little sexual shiver down her spine. "Think we can have dinner tonight?"

"That sounds heavenly."

"Any suggestions?"

Savannah twirled her hair around her finger. "Hmm, I seem to remember—oh damn, I've got a call coming in. Can you hold on?"

"Sure," he said, but she detected a bit of frustration in his voice.

Savannah took the call from her agent, thinking that she would cut it short. "Good news," he informed her. "They've found a director for the video."

"Cool." Savannah's heart beat faster at the thought.

"Uh, but Savannah, don't take this the wrong way because you are a beautiful girl, but I've been told that you need to sex it up a bit. Start an exercise regime and slim down. The camera packs on pounds, you know."

"Gotcha. No problem on the exercise, but sex it up? What exactly does that mean?"

"Well, we're talking cute like Carrie Underwood but with a hot, sexy edge like Miranda Lambert . . . sort of a combination, if you will."

"Okay . . ." Savannah asked a few more questions but suddenly remembered Lucio on the other line. *Crap!* "Thanks, Jay. I'll get right on it." But when she clicked over, Lucio wasn't on the line. She dialed his number and breathed a sigh of relief when he picked up. "Sorry I kept you waiting, Lucio."

There was a bit of a pause and then he said, "Listen, Savannah . . ."

"Yes?" Her heart plummeted. This tone of voice didn't sound good. She sank down cross-legged on the kitchen floor and leaned against the wall.

"I don't know how we can start a relationship when I can't ever seem to get in touch with you. I'm not blaming you for being swamped, but then again I don't see how we'll ever get this off the ground."

"But I have tonight free."

He paused again but then said, "I'm sorry, Savannah. I'm not blaming you. The timing for us is just wrong."

Savannah closed her eyes and swallowed. All of the stress and pressure seemed to be crashing down on her, so she snapped, "Whatever. If that's the way you want it."

"It's not the way I want it."

"I think it is."

"Savannah, don't be angry. Try to understand where I'm coming from."

"Listen, I've got to run. Have a nice life, Lucio." Savannah ended the call and tossed the phone in her purse. Determined not to have a meltdown, she scrambled to her feet. "Damn him. Damn him, damn him, *damn him*!" Of course realistically she couldn't blame him, but still . . . *Damn him!* It wasn't like she didn't want to be with him or hadn't thought about him all the doggone time. Last night she even had a sexy dream about him!

Savannah decided that she'd forget all about Lucio Barone and get all—how did her agent say it? Oh yeah, sexed up. Yep, she thought, she was going to get sexed up, and jacked up, find her a cowboy or two and dance the night away at Logan's. She wouldn't give Lucio a second thought.

Mumbling under her breath, Savannah stomped across the big country kitchen and up the narrow staircase that led to her bedroom. She pushed through her closetful of clothes and realized that she didn't have very sexy clothing and made a mental note to change that immediately. Finally, she settled on a tight pair of Wranglers and a red Western-cut shirt and defiantly left the first three buttons undone. She searched for her boots with the highest heels because she was so damned short. Not knowing what to do with her hair, she decided to put it up in a sloppy bun, letting tendrils of hair frame her face. After freshening her makeup, adding a generous amount of lip gloss and an extra splash of perfume, she was out the door and behind the wheel of her beat-up Blazer.

Savannah rolled down the windows, cranked up the radio and sang along with Gretchen Wilson in an attempt to lighten her mood. She should be on top of the darned world anyway because, by God, she had a record deal!

"A record deal!" she shouted while bouncing down the bumpy gravel path leading to the main road. "The first thing I'm gonna get is a new car," she said, and her Blazer backfired as if in protest. "Oh, I'll still keep ya around, old girl," she said, and patted the dash.

When the Big & Rich song "Save a Horse (Ride a Cowboy)" came on the radio, Savannah belted it out along with the crazy duo, thinking that it was going to be her theme song for the night. Yeah, she was going to find herself a sexy cowboy and hold on tight all night long.

Luc wasn't much of a drinker, but he tossed back a shot of Wild Turkey just for the hell of it. Yeow, it burned all the way down, but he was in one pissed-off mood and he hoped the whiskey would take the edge off.

"Need a chaser?" Logan asked, and thumped a bottle of beer down on the bar in front of him.

"Yeah, thanks." He reached in his pocket for money, but Logan shook his head.

"It's on the house."

Luc nodded his appreciation and took a swig of the cold brew. His mood had gone downhill with each passing day that he had been unable to connect with Savannah, but his decision to end what had never been given a chance sent him into a really bummed state. Over the years he had perfected the bad-boy broody-guy attitude and tonight he wore it like armor. His scowl, however, only seemed to attract women, making him decide to retreat to a small table at the back of the bar where he could brood in relative peace.

And then Savannah walked in.

With her shoulders back and her lips in a pout she had a don't-mess-with-me attitude in her step that had every guy looking her way. Luc was a little stunned at his own reaction at seeing her for the first time in several days. His groin tightened and his heart kicked it up a notch. If he thought he could get over her easily, he was dead-ass wrong. When she looked his way his hand curled around his beer, but she changed her direction and headed to the far end of the bar, where she scooped some ice into a glass and then splashed some bourbon into it. Logan raised his eyebrows at her, but she shrugged her shoulders and took a sip.

With one elbow propped against the table Luc casually sipped his beer and tried to appear indifferent. Out of the corner of his eye, he watched Logan approach Savannah. Logan nodded Luc's way as if telling Savannah that he was here, but she shrugged her shoulders and didn't even glance his way. *Well,* he thought as he took a long swig of beer, *two can play this game.*

Oh hell, no, I can't.

Try as he might, he couldn't keep his gaze from seeking out Savannah. *This is stupid.* Luc needed to touch her, to inhale her perfume, to hear her husky Southern voice. He had needed her for two weeks and now that she was standing not twenty feet away it was crazy not to approach her. Ending a relationship that he wanted so badly was the dumbest damn thing he had ever done and deep down he knew why he had done it.

He was afraid. Having lived in the shadow of his psychic sisters, Luc was afraid of loving someone who was destined to become a star. He didn't want to live his life in the background once again. *Oh well, screw that.* He was no longer an insecure teenager who had to prove to the world how big and bad he was. So what if Savannah became a superstar? He was falling for her and that's all that he needed to know.

A sudden flash of light caught Luc's attention. At first he thought the cowboy sitting next to him was lighting up a damned cigarette, but the light hovered in front of Luc's face. Luc blinked, wondering why no one else seemed to notice.

"What ya waitin' for, hot stuff?" said the same gruff voice that Luc had heard at Savannah's apartment. "You gonna go after Savannah or what?"

Luc opened his mouth, not sure if he should reply to a flickering light, when it disappeared as quickly as it had appeared. *What the hell?* He looked down at his beer bottle and pushed it away. "Must be the alcohol," he muttered to himself, remembering the shot of whiskey he had tossed back.

"Hey, little brother," Sophia said as she slid onto the

bar stool next to his. "You okay? You look like you've seen a ghost."

"Uh, that would be your territory," Luc replied.

"Very funny. Hey, what's up with you and Savannah? I thought the two of you had it going on."

Luc sighed. "I was supposed to have dinner with her tonight after almost two weeks of trying to chase her down, and like an idiot, I backed out."

"Why?"

Luc shrugged. "I decided it was stupid to start a relationship with someone who is never available."

"But now you're rethinking that whole theory."

"Wow, how'd you know? You psychic or somethin'?"

"You're getting funnier by the minute."

"I try."

Sophia nudged him on the shoulder. "So, you gonna approach Savannah or not?"

"She's so pissed that she won't even look at me, Sophia."

"You gonna let that stop you, Brooklyn boy?" She nudged him harder.

"I don't know. I've messed this up from the get-go."

"She's the *one*. You know that, right?"

"You know I don't believe in that bullshit, Sophia."

"Liar."

"I'm not lying!"

"Are too. You're a closet believer." She nudged him again.

"You nudge me one more time and I swear I'll kick your butt."

"Yeah? You and what army?"

Luc laughed. "Savannah said the same thing to me the other day. Okay . . . *okay*. I believe. You happy now?"

"No. I won't be happy until the two of you are together, where you belong."

"Yeah, but I've blown that all to hell."

Sophia arched a dark eyebrow. "Oh, but baby brother, I have a plan."

Luc gave her a skeptical look.

"No, no, it's brilliant." She nibbled on her bottom lip. "As long as I can get Brody and Logan on board . . ."

"Brody and Logan? Why am I getting the feeling that I'm not gonna like this?"

Sophia smiled and rubbed her hands together. "Trust me, baby brother. This is the perfect plan."

✳ *Chapter Seven*

Savannah was sipping her morning coffee while jotting down lyrics to yet another sad country song when she heard the crunch of tires on gravel. Thinking it might be Logan coming out for a visit, she sat her mug on the oak table and hurried to the back door. Her heart began to hammer when she spotted Lucio's black Lexus coming to a halt next to the detached garage.

"What the . . . ?" Her heart hammered even harder when Lucio got out of the SUV and then pulled a huge leather duffel bag from his backseat. He hefted it over his shoulder and headed her way, looking suspiciously like he was coming . . . to stay? The morning breeze ruffled his shoulder-length hair and Savannah tried to ignore how sexy he looked in low-slung, frayed jeans, a wide black belt and a tank-style white shirt. The bright sunlight glinted off of his aviator shades as he looked around the yard as if taking it all in. "City boy," Savannah muttered, and couldn't suppress a grin. When he looked in the direction of the house, Savannah backed away from the window and let the curtain drop, but it was too late to pretend not to be home.

"Damn," Savannah grumbled when she realized that she was still in her sleepwear, consisting of hip-hugging sweatpants that said BEACH BABE on the butt and a worn tank top sporting a shark's head that read, BITE ME. Since her parents had moved to Florida she had found herself with an abundance of beach-themed clothing. To make matters worse, she was braless. Thinking that she should run and grab a robe, Savannah then decided the hell with it and opened the door after the first knock.

"Hello, Savannah," Lucio said with a smile.

"Hello . . . ," she returned the greeting with less enthusiasm. His Adam's apple bobbed and she wondered if he was checking out her braless boobs, but he had on those damned sunglasses that hid his eyes. She barely refrained from crossing her arms over her chest. "At the risk of sounding rude, what are you doing here and why do you have that duffel bag?"

"I'm here to work out with you."

"Come again?" she asked, and then felt the heat of a blush warm her cheeks.

"I've been hired as your personal trainer to get you in shape for your music video."

Savannah narrowed her eyes, smelling a rat. "How come I haven't been told about this?"

"I was just hired."

"Hired by whom?"

"Heart Records."

Savannah's eyes remained narrowed. "Aren't you pretty expensive? Sophia said that you've worked with some movie stars. I can't believe that Heart Records would pay for this. . . ."

Lucio shrugged and gave her a slow grin. "I guess you just got lucky." He brushed past her and entered the kitchen.

"What are you doing?"

"I'm movin' in."

"Moving *in*?" Savannah sputtered. "What do you mean, *moving in*?"

"Oh, you have the *deluxe package*."

"Deluxe p-package?"

He removed his sunglasses and gave her a look that could be described only as hot. "Yes. Not only will we be exercising together, but I'll be cooking all of your meals and I'll also be available at a moment's notice for personal massages."

"M-massages?"

"Full body. I'm certified, if that's a concern."

"Yes . . . I mean *no*. I won't be needing any massages."

He rubbed his hands together. "Oh, you will after I get through with you. We've got four weeks before the video begins shooting. Admittedly not a lot of time but we'll just have to work hard."

She could only blink at him.

"Now, where is the guest room? I wanna get settled in before we get to work."

Savannah swallowed. "Uh, up the stairs and to the . . .

wait a minute. No. I'm not doing this. You are not living here. No way." She wagged a finger at him.

Luc shrugged. "Okay, if ya say so. I'll just call Dan Heart and let him know that you've refused his generous offer to get in shape."

"Dan Heart?"

Luc whipped out his cell phone. "The CEO of Heart Records. Let's see, I have him here on speed dial." He started pushing buttons with his thumb. "Ah, there he is."

"No! Stop!" Savannah closed her eyes and took a deep breath. "The guest bedroom is up the staircase and on the left past the bathroom."

Luc nodded his head. "Thanks."

Savannah felt her nipples tighten when he gave her outfit a once-over.

"Uh, you need to change into shorts and a sports bra."

Savannah willed herself not to blush. "Okay."

"I'll see you in"—he glanced down at his watch—"about fifteen minutes."

"I don't have time to work out. I have to be at the recording studio at ten o'clock."

"I'll be finished with you by then. I have some grocery shopping to do this afternoon anyway."

She nodded, feeling a little dazed. While following his progress out of the kitchen she angled her head to check out his butt but then caught herself and straightened up. "Just what in the hell is going on here?" she whispered, and then hurried to her room to change.

Fifteen minutes later on the dot, Savannah returned

to the kitchen dressed in a pair of black Nike shorts and a matching sports bra purchased in one of her I'm-going-to-work-out moments and then never worn. "We don't have much time," she protested when Luc entered the kitchen. "Hey, how come you aren't dressed to work out?" She eyed the clipboard in his hand, not liking this one bit.

He fished in the pocket of his jeans and pulled out a small disk. "I'm just going to take some measurements and weigh you in."

"Measurements? W-weigh me in?" Savannah took a step backward, coming up against the wall, and waved a finger at him again. "No way."

Luc sighed. "Okay, we'll skip the weighing-in part. But I want to keep track of how many inches you lose. It will be a motivator, Savannah."

"I'm plenty motivated already."

"Come here."

"No."

"Fine. I'll come over there."

Since she was already against the wall, Savannah had no choice.

"Just relax," Luc said as he pulled the measuring tape out. "This is painless, I promise. Now, please take a step away from the wall." Kneeling down, he started with her calves and began working his way up.

Now, although there was nothing remotely sexual about this, and it was slightly humiliating, Savannah began to get a little worked up at the touch of his fingers grazing her skin and he seemed to be taking his sweet time. Seeing his dark head positioned between her thighs was enough to get her heart thumping and when he measured her there, he leaned in so damned close that she could feel the heat of his breath and imagine the touch of his mouth. After recording those measurements, he remained on his knees and slipped the measuring tape around her waist, and damn it all to hell, her stomach quivered at his touch.

"You okay?"

"It tickles a bit," she said through her teeth.

"Sorry."

"No problem." But she had to fist her hands.

He seemed to take his ever-loving time kneeling there while measuring her hips. Savannah dearly wanted to thread her fingers through his hair and press his face to her body, but suddenly he was on his feet.

"Spread 'em."

"Excuse me?"

"Hold your arms out so I can measure your bust."

"I'm a thirty-four C. That's all you need to know." God, did he have to stand so close? Did he have to smell good enough to eat?

"I'm not buying you a bra, Savannah. I need to know your exact measurements. Now, spread 'em," he ordered sternly, but for a moment Savannah thought he might laugh.

"This is not funny." Savannah glared up at him but dutifully held her arms akimbo. She tried but failed not to suck in a breath when he wrapped the tape around her breasts and held the ends together directly over her left nipple. Of course, even though she kept a *This is no big deal having you feel me up* expression on her face, her traitorous nipples stood at attention. The saving grace, though, was that she caught him staring and he swallowed. Feeling a bit of power, Savannah inhaled a deep breath, making her breasts push against his fingers, and he dropped the tape measure.

"Want to do it again?" she asked innocently.

"No, uh, you're good. . . . I mean, I'm good."

"I guess it's *all* good."

Luc jotted the numbers down on his sheet and hid a smile, wondering if Savannah was on to the little live-in scheme that Sophia had cooked up. Luc had turned down the idea at first, but he hated that he had managed to blow this relationship with Savannah and he wanted another chance with her. This time he was going to make it work . . . no fear, no excuses.

Luc had to admit that Sophia's plan was genius. Heart Records knew that he was training Savannah, but they weren't willing to pay his normal hefty fee, not that he cared about the money. So that he had a cover, so to speak, he got around the money issue by telling Heart Records that this was research for the book that he was writing. This really was the truth to a degree and while Savannah was off in the recording studio he would have the peace and quiet of the country setting to research, to write and to develop some new healthy recipes that he planned on trying out on her.

Savannah was right. It was all good. And although he thought she was damned beautiful the way she was, if helping her drop a few pounds and tone up for her video shoot helped her career, then this little act was a bonus for them both. Of course the hard part was going to be not blowing the whole thing by grabbing her and kissing her like he had almost done a moment ago.

"Finished," Luc said after recording all of her measurements.

"You mean I can go?"

"Yes. I'll see you for dinner and then we'll talk about your workout schedule."

"I'll warn you that I'm not much of an athlete. Logan got all of those Parks genes. I was sorely short-changed in that particular area."

"I'm up for the challenge, Savannah. *Whatevva* it takes."

She looked at him as if trying to read between the lines but then turned around and left the kitchen.

For the next thirty minutes or so Luc checked out the contents of her kitchen cabinets and her refrigerator, shaking his head at all of the unhealthy foods that he found. "Junk food should be outlawed," he muttered as he tossed a bag of pork rinds in the trash. What the hell were pork rinds, anyway? Except for a lonely apple in the otherwise empty produce bin in her refrigerator, there wasn't anything that represented *real* food to Luc. He shook his head. Everything was packaged and processed . . . and now in the overflowing trash can. He chuckled when he thought of what her reaction would be when she came home and found all of her crappy food gone.

The good news was that her diet appeared to be so poor that with some healthy changes and an exercise regime Savannah would see rapid results. If nothing else, she was going to love him for the hard body she would have at the end of four weeks. The problem was that his body *got* hard every time he was within ten feet of her. Taking a deep breath, Luc wondered if he would be able to pull off the badass-personal-trainer act for any real length of time.

Chapter Eight

*S*avannah arrived at the farm tired, stressed and hungry, having dutifully passed by all of the fast-food restaurants that had shouted her name the whole way home. She tossed her purse on the kitchen table and made a beeline for the fridge in search of a Mountain Dew to perk her up.

"What?" Savannah stood back and surveyed the neat rows of bottled water and fruit juices. There was nary a soft drink or beer in sight. As a matter of fact, there wasn't a can or package of anything . . . just fresh stuff. And just where was her dinner? Then she spotted a lump of something wrapped in butcher paper. Picking it up, she wrinkled her nose and read, "Salmon? Ew."

"Hungry?"

Savannah shrieked as she spun around, still clutching the package. "Do you have to sneak up on a person?" She tried unsuccessfully to ignore the fact that he was dressed in running shorts and was shirtless with a fine sheen of sweat covering his very fine torso. *Goody, maybe I missed workout time.*

He shrugged. "Sorry, since I live here now, I didn't think I was sneaking up." He reached up to swipe at some sweat trickling down his cheek, causing a ripple of muscle that had Savannah squeezing the package of salmon.

"So, where is all of my stuff?" she asked stiffly, hopefully disguising her desire with anger.

"You mean your junk food? Gone."

"Great, so after a grueling day you've left me with nothing in this house that tastes good."

With a lazy smile he said, "Oh, I wouldn't say that."

Savannah's heart pounded when he started moving in her direction.

"Excuse me," he said, and reached past her for a bottle of water in the open fridge. She watched him unscrew the cap, tilt the bottle back and guzzle half of it, and her own mouth went dry. "You want some?" he asked, raising his eyebrows. She sure did.

"Want wh-what?"

"You were looking at . . . me like you wanted some. There's plenty. All you need to do is ask." He thrust the bottle of water at her. "Um, Savannah, you had better be careful with my package."

"Package?" Savannah glanced down at the forgotten salmon that she was squeezing. "Oh, this package." Her laugh was high-pitched. "I don't do fish."

He took the salmon and handed her the water. "Ah, I'll bet you prefer red meat."

"Well, yes."

"We'll have that too in due time. But tonight we're having fish. Salmon is especially heart healthy."

"You don't understand. I hate fish."

Luc sighed. "Well, just give me a chance, okay? I won't disappoint you, Savannah." His dark eyes locked with hers and she had to wonder if it was still fish that they were talking about. "Are you willing?"

She hesitated but then relented. "I suppose."

"That's good enough for starters." He grinned and then polished off the last of the water. "I'm going to shower. Change into something comfortable and you can help me prepare dinner. You do cook, right?"

"Of course." Just not all of that fresh stuff. She might have been raised on a farm, but she cooked with a city-bred out-of-a-box or reheating-takeout mentality.

"Great. It'll be fun," he said over his shoulder as he left the room.

Savannah watched him walk away, determined not to ogle his ass this time, but she did anyway. "My, my, *my*. There's not a better butt on the planet." Shaking her head, she was still trying to make sense of this whole personal-trainer thing and was coming up confused. Was he here to try and win her back or just to do a job? Savannah didn't like dealing with mixed messages. Damn, if only she knew . . .

"I am so stupid!" Savannah slapped her hand to her forehead and grabbed her cell phone, knowing who could give her some answers. She bounded up the stairs and hurried to her bedroom. The sound of the shower let Savannah know that she could make a call without Lucio overhearing her conversation. After shutting the door, she flipped open her phone and dialed M. J.'s number. While tapping her foot on the hardwood floor, Savannah stared unseeing out the window, wondering why she hadn't thought to call on M. J.'s psychic intuition sooner. M. J. finally picked up and Savannah didn't beat around the bush. "Is Lucio my soul mate?"

"Well, hello to you too, sweet Savannah."

"Oh, M. J., please do your psychic thing and answer me!"

"Yes."

"Yes?"

"I said yes."

"*Yes?*" She put her hand to her chest.

"*Y-E-S.* Lucio Barone is your soul mate."

"Ohmigawd." Savannah sat down on the bed. "I should have guessed. I mean, he makes me melt and we can't keep our hands off of each other." She bounced up and down on the bed.

"Hello . . . Luc is my brother, Savannah. Too much information," M. J. said with a chuckle. "So I guess things are going well for you two, huh?"

Savannah stopped bouncing. "Well, no. Actually, they are kind of a mess."

"Have you been seeing him?"

"He's living here at the farm with me."

"*Living* with you and things aren't going well?"

"Not living . . . *living* with me. He's my personal trainer. I need to get in shape for the music video."

"Oh!" M. J. screamed so loud that Savannah feared ear damage. "How cool! Brody, you didn't tell me about the video."

"Brody is with you right now? Are you two joined at the hip?"

"Well . . . not at the hip . . ."

"Ew!"

"Just kidding! We're on a bus in the middle of wine country."

"So you and Sophia have known this soul mate information for a while, I'll bet."

M. J. groaned. "Yes, but Savannah, I wanted things to take a natural course."

"Does Lucio know?" Her heart pounded at the thought.

M. J. hesitated just long enough to make Savannah gasp. "He does. So is he here to win me back? Or maybe he doesn't believe?"

"Should I just hang up and let you have this conversation with yourself?"

"Sorry."

M. J. chuckled. "Luc might not act like a believer, but deep down he is . . . always has been, so don't let him fool ya."

Savannah smiled. "I'm on to him now. Personal trainer, my butt . . . so, M. J., what do I do now?"

"Sweetie, that's up to you. Luc is a hard guy to figure out sometimes, but I *can* tell you this. He's there with you now because he wants to be. But I'll warn you the same way that I do all of my clients. Finding your soul mate is only half the battle. You still have to make it work. Brody and I had some major obstacles to overcome, but if you really love someone, it sure is worth giving it your best shot. So that's my advice. Give it your best shot."

"That's it?"

"Straight up, girl. Think about it, Savannah. If more people would give it their *best shot*, we'd have a lot more love connections that stick. Look at it this way: You're going to give your career your best shot, right?"

"Sure."

"Then Luc deserves the same. Don't give up on him. He might be my brother, but he truly is a great guy. He'll be there for you when you need him, Savannah."

"Are you crying?" Savannah asked softly.

"No, I'm a tough chick. I never cry," M. J. said, and then sniffed loudly. "Okay, damn it, I'm crying happy tears. I cry when Brody sings. I cry when Travis sings. . . . I'm turnin' into a friggin' softy. Good luck, Savannah, with everything. Your life is pretty darned exciting right now." She sniffed loudly and blew her nose. "Don't screw it up!"

"Thanks for the vote of confidence," Savannah said with a chuckle.

"Oh, you know what I mean. Now, quit wasting time and go get my brother!"

Savannah flipped her phone shut and sat in the middle of the bed for a long moment and wondered if she had the courage to do what she wanted to do.

She wanted to make love to Lucio.

Enough of this going-slow baloney. M. J. had just confirmed what Savannah already knew. Lucio Barone was *the one* and she wanted to show in a very physical way just how much she cared about him. She sat there for a moment longer, nibbling on her bottom lip, trying to think if she had ever consciously seduced a guy before, and came up with a great big *no*. Savannah took a deep breath and blew it out before scrambling from the bed. "I'll just do what M. J. said and hit him with my best shot. . . ."

Okay, what exactly is my best shot? Damned if she knew, but Lucio Barone was about to get hit hard with both barrels!

When he heard Savannah approach, Luc glanced up from his task of tearing romaine lettuce into pieces . . . and then did a double take. *Holy shit.* Savannah was dressed in cutoff jeans slung low on her hips and frayed in interesting places. A light blue cotton top sported lacy shoulder straps and hugged her 34Cs like a lover's hands. For a moment he wondered if she was dressed like this to entice him, but a closer look showed very little makeup except for some shiny pink stuff on her lips that made him swallow. Her hair was pulled up into a casual ponytail and he noticed that she was barefoot, so maybe this was her version of dressing comfortably.

While her record company might want her to drop a few pounds, Luc found her abundant curves a total turn-on. Pencil-thin women were not what most guys fantasized about. And in his opinion this was an unhealthy lifestyle that he planned to address in his new book.

"Hey there," she greeted him with her sexy-as-sin Southern drawl and a slow smile. "Whatcha cookin' up?"

Luc glanced down to see that he was totally tearing the lettuce to shreds. "Oh, uh, a tossed salad."

She came closer and leaned her elbows on the center island, giving him a nice view of her cleavage. "So, what can I do for you?"

Several suggestions popped into his head and none of them had a thing to do with food. "Uh . . ." His brain was still on the things she could do for him. "You could get started by chopping some vegetables." He pointed to a pile of fresh veggies on the counter near him.

"Sure." She pushed away from the island and walked around to the other side of him. Luc tried to concentrate on the lettuce but found himself watching her progress. When she turned around and bent over to get something from a cabinet, Luc just about swallowed his tongue. A small hole about the size of a dime revealed the bare skin of her ass and he could see the very top of a red thong peeking out from her shorts.

When she straightened up with a cutting board in her clutches, Luc did his best to appear casual, but then she picked up a zucchini and said, "What do you want me to do with this?" He almost lost his tightly reined composure.

"Uh . . . slice it into disks. We're going to have a . . . ," he began, but when she sat the zucchini on its end and grasped it at the base and raised her eyebrows, waiting, he lost his train of thought.

"Steamed vegetable medley?"

"Yeah . . . uh, that."

She smiled and began slicing. "Sounds good. I'm not into the fish, but I do love my veggies. Speaking of which, are you going to tell me the rules of what I can and can't eat?"

Luc nodded, glad to have something other than how much she was turning him on to think about. "People tend to make dieting complicated when all it really amounts to is healthy eating. We'll cut down but not eliminate carbs and refined sugar. But what I really hate are processed foods."

"Processed?"

"Boxed, canned and even most frozen items. I like to stick to fresh and organic foods whenever I can get my hands on them. I'm a firm believer that additives are the cause of certain diseases and in some cases hyperactivity in both kids and adults." He glanced up from where he was slicing a tomato and was glad to see that she seemed attentive and interested. He might not consider Savannah overweight, but from the stuff that he'd tossed in the trash, her diet could use a total makeover.

"So what if I have cravings?"

"Like what?"

Savannah shrugged. "Things I just can't resist."

Luc raised one eyebrow and wondered if she was serious or flirting with him. "Name one thing that ya can't live without and maybe I'll let ya have it."

*S*avannah made a show of licking her lips while pretending to consider the possibilities. Finally, she said, "Chocolate. Dark, *decadent* chocolate. Just a little square to melt on my tongue and savor."

Luc smiled. "Excellent choice. Dark chocolate is actually good for ya in small doses. It's rich in flavonols, which lower both high blood pressure and LDL cholesterol. I'll pick some up for ya at the store."

"Why, thank you," she said, and reached for a yellow squash. "So what's yours?"

He stopped slicing the tomato and looked at her. "My what?"

"Your one thing you can't live without." She stopped chopping and gave him her full attention.

Luc paused and swallowed while looking at her. Something hot and potent sizzled between them. "Ya mean something that ya eat?"

"Yeah . . . what is so delicious that you just *crave*

and can't stop thinking about until it is in your mouth?"

"I can't seem to pass up something sweet and lus-cious."

"Mmmm, like what?"

"Crème brûlée. I like how it's creamy on my tongue and so smooth going down."

"Oh, God, that sounds so amazing."

"You've never had it?"

Savannah shook her head. "I grew up here on this farm, Lucio. Mom made apple pie, not crème brûlée."

"I'll make some for you."

"Isn't it about a million calories?"

He shrugged. "We can always find a way to work it off."

Savannah was getting about as hot and bothered as a girl could get. Her little game was backfiring in her face. It didn't help that there was something so very sexy about a man who knew his way around a kitchen. She decided to bring her seduction of Lucio Barone down a notch . . . at least until after dinner, when she planned on heating up things big-time.

Luc worked swiftly and efficiently in the kitchen and before she knew it Savannah was sitting at the big oak table with a crisp tossed salad with raspberry vinaigrette dressing that Lucio had whipped up himself. The vegeta-bles were cooked to perfection and the salmon was sur-prisingly tasty with a delicate flavor that Savannah liked.

"So how is it?"

"Delicious. I could get used to this," she said with-out thinking. She met his eyes across the table. "I mean that you're an amazing cook."

"You'll find that I have many hidden talents."

"Well, you'll just have to show me," she said.

After dinner they cleaned up the dishes together and chatted about her diet and exercise program, which they would work around her recording schedule.

"I'll mix things up to keep it interesting," Luc promised. "We'll do cardio and weights, but I'll also introduce ya to Pilates and maybe some fun stuff like kickboxing."

Savannah groaned. "Sounds tiring."

Luc shook his head. "Another exercise myth. You'll actually find yourself with energy to burn."

"You really know your stuff," Savannah quipped, but her compliment seemed to please him. She dried the bowl in her hand and went on her tiptoes to put it in the cabinet.

"Let me help," Luc offered, coming up behind her. He leaned in and took the bowl from her, placing it on the shelf above her head. She could feel the heat from his nearness and smell his cologne, and it was all she could do not to lean back against him. Just when she was ready to give in to her impulse, he backed away.

They were both silent for a long, hot moment and then Luc said, "I'm going to get on my laptop and put together a schedule. You're off the hook for the rest of the evening."

Savannah felt a pull of disappointment. She didn't want to be off the hook but didn't know what to say. "Okay." She guessed her skimpy outfit wasn't as enticing as she wanted it to be. "I'll see you at breakfast, then?"

"Yes, bright and early." He nodded and walked out of the room.

"Thanks for a delicious . . . and *healthy* dinner," she called out to him, hoping to strike up another conversation.

He paused and turned to give her one of his smiles. "My pleasure."

Not knowing how to keep him there any longer, Savannah merely smiled back. Feeling a bit of a letdown, she headed up to her room to either go over some songs or maybe write some lyrics for a while before turning in.

Savannah tossed and turned until the sheet was a tangled mess around her legs. The old farmhouse didn't have air-conditioning and although the paddle fan above her bed helped, Savannah felt too warm to sleep. With a groan she kicked off the covers and turned her pillow over to the cool side. Of course she knew the real reason for her insomnia . . . her awareness that Lucio was sleeping right across the hall.

Finally, unable to stand it any longer, she rolled from the bed and padded over to the window hoping for the cool night breeze to soothe her agitation. "Oh, the hell with it," she grumbled, and pulled on her jean shorts beneath her sleep shirt. The moon was full and so she decided to take a walk down to the lake like she had done so many times on sultry summer nights such as this. Savannah had written many a song by the light of the moon while sitting on the wooden dock that Logan had built.

She opened her bedroom door, wincing when it creaked. After a glance over at Lucio's closed door she wondered briefly what he would do if she let herself in and crawled into bed with him. . . . Shaking off that thought, she stepped into the hallway and tiptoed toward the staircase.

"Savannah?"

With a little squeal she jumped about a foot into the air and whipped around. Lucio stood there sleep rumpled and sexy, clad in his boxers and nothing else. He folded his arms across his chest and gazed at her. "Goin' somewhere?"

"For a walk."

"It's after midnight."

"I know. I like walking in the moonlight. It's peaceful and quiets my soul."

"Quiets your soul? Is your soul usually restless?" he teased.

Savannah giggled softly. "I don't know. . . . Sounded poetic, though, didn't it?" She was going to tell him that she'd be fine, but made a sudden decision that had her heart racing. "Okay, you can come with me."

"Give me a second," he requested, and turned back into his bedroom. A moment later he was back in jeans and flip-flops but remained shirtless. "Okay, I'm ready," he said.

I hope so, Savannah thought to herself as she headed down the staircase.

"Don't we need a flashlight?" Luc asked when they stepped out onto the back porch.

"We'll use the light of the silvery moon," she said with a grin. "Besides, it's a well-worn path to the lake. I could find my way blindfolded."

When an owl hooted Luc jammed his hands in his jeans pockets and looked skeptical. "If ya say so."

"City boy . . . ," Savannah teased, and started walking. "Follow me." With Luc by her side she circled around past the barn to a tractor path near the cornfields and headed toward the woods. The moon was indeed bright in the inky black sky glittering with stars.

"Wow," Luc commented, "without the city lights you can really see the stars."

Savannah glanced up at him. "It's beautiful, isn't it?"

"Yeah," he said gruffly. "Very." His gaze lingered on Savannah long enough for her to wonder if he was talking about her and not the night sky. She shivered at the thought. "Cold?" he asked.

"Oh no, the breeze feels wonderful."

They were silent after that, but when they reached the edge of the woods Savannah was touched when Luc reached for her hand. "I'll protect you from the lions, tigers and bears," he said, leaning in, but just then a long, whinny call made him jump.

"What the hell was *that*?" he asked, and stopped walking.

"An Eastern screech owl. That was a male."

"And you know this how?"

"It's lower than a female's, usually a mellow, muted trill with about thirty-five notes."

"That wasn't muted or mellow."

Savannah grinned. "That was his mating call."

"Oh, come on, how do ya know *that*?"

Savannah started walking but explained, "I wrote a paper on screech owls in high school. It's called song B and is a descending whinny call usually only given during courtship."

"You sound like a Discovery Channel segment," he laughed. "So, screech owls actually court?"

"Oh yeah. They have an elaborate mating ritual. The male approaches the female, calling from different branches of a tree while swiveling his head and bobbing his body to get noticed. He even slowly winks one eye at the female."

"I might be a city boy, but you're pullin' my leg."

"I kid you not. If she ignores him, he gets crazier with the bobbing-and-weaving thing. If she accepts him, they touch bills and preen each other. They mate for life and the male is even politically correct and helps during the incubation period."

"You mean sits on the eggs?"

Savannah nodded. "Yep. Now you know more than you ever wanted to know about the screech owl."

"It's interesting, but truth is, I just love listening to your Southern drawl."

"Are you making fun of my accent?"

"No, I love it. Talk to me some more."

Savannah wasn't sure if he was teasing or flirting, but they had reached the clearing and she no longer had talking on her mind. Savannah wanted to make love to Lucio beneath the stars by the light of the full moon. She only hoped that she had the nerve to make a move. "Isn't this nice?" Savannah asked, waving her hand in an arc.

"Yeah, it is."

They stood there hand in hand for a few moments

drinking in the pristine beauty. The light of the moon sent silvery ripples on the surface of the lake while the breeze whispered through the trees. Bullfrogs croaked and crickets chirped, and when they heard the whinny call of a screech owl Luc gave Savannah a sidelong look and then gave his head a swivel and a bob.

When Savannah giggled and moved away, pretending to ignore him, Luc bobbed his head and then turned in a circle, dipping his shoulders, and then winked. Savannah laughed harder as he bobbed and weaved closer. Finally, when he was standing directly in front of her, he slowly leaned and touched his mouth to hers.

"Have I won ya over? Please say yes because I feel ridiculous."

"Yes!"

Luc leaned his forehead against hers. "Good, because I don't think I could pull off preening or the mating call."

"So . . . are you wanting to . . . *mate*?"

Luc groaned. "More than ya know. Do ya know how hard it was trying to get to sleep knowing you were right across the hallway from me?"

"Why do you think I wanted to go for a midnight walk? I couldn't sleep thinking about you."

"Then what the hell are we waiting for?"

Savannah laughed. "Now, that was almost as romantic as your screech owl mating dance."

"Damn. Am I blowing this?"

Savannah slid her hands up his chest and said softly, "Not a chance."

"God, Savannah . . ." He lowered his head and captured her mouth in a deep, searing kiss. "I want you," he whispered in her ear, "so much." With a sigh, Luc lowered her to the cool, tender grass and then kissed her again and again. He slid his hand beneath her shirt and cupped her breast while kissing her neck. When he sucked on her earlobe she gasped, gripping his shoulders tightly. Knowing he had found an erogenous zone, he sucked and nibbled until she went wild beneath him.

"I want you naked," he said hotly in her ear and then rolled to the side to shuck his jeans and roll on protection.

Savannah tugged her sleep shirt over her head, but when her fingers were fumbling with her jean shorts he gently brushed her fingers away. "Let me," he said, undoing her pants. When she lifted her hips to help, Luc tugged her shorts off and tossed them aside.

"My God," he said, taking in the sight of her naked save for a red, lacy thong. With her golden hair fanned out against the green grass she looked like an earth goddess waiting to be loved. "Savannah, you are gorgeous."

She looked up at him with blue eyes that said *I need you.* "So are *you,* all of you, Lucio, not just your looks. You know that, right?"

"Yes, what we have goes deeper than that," Luc

agreed, wetting his finger and then tracing one nipple and then the other. "But right now, I want *this*. . . ." When she shivered, he slipped his finger in his mouth again and then trailed it over her rib cage, her belly and then over her thong. He moved his finger up and down over the soft lace and warm satin, adding a bit more pressure until the heat became moist and her breath came in shallow gasps. Knowing he was pushing her too close too soon, he stopped and leaned in for another deep kiss.

Luc moved his mouth from hers and licked one breast while playing with the nipple of the other. He sucked and then nipped sharply before soothing her nipple with a long slow lick.

"Lucio . . . ," Savannah said, and arched her back, threading her fingers through his hair. "God . . . ," she breathed while he feasted a few more minutes before beginning a light trail of kisses down her torso. Spreading her legs, he ripped the flimsy thong off and put the heat of his mouth where she was soft, slick and sweet. Luc kissed, licked and teased, but when she arched her hips upward, he slipped his hands beneath her ass and sank his tongue in deep. He plunged in and out, licking, lapping and devouring her until her clitoris was a hard, distended bud. He licked her ever so lightly and she shivered, saying, "God, *Lucio*." Luc looked up, smiling at the sight. Her eyes were closed, her cheeks flushed a rosy pink, and her lips wet and parted.

The scent of her sex filled his head, mingling with the rich scent of the earth. The sounds of the night surrounded them while they made love beneath the inky black sky studded with glittering stars and moonbeams. When Luc circled her clit with his tongue and then sucked, Savannah cried out, arching her hips upward while Luc sent her over the edge.

Crazy with the need to be inside of her, Luc eased her hips back down to the cool grass and slipped his dick in her wet heat and sighed. She felt so slick but tight and hot, but he forced himself to move slowly until she recovered from her climax. When she started to move in rhythm with him, Luc said, "Wrap your legs around me, Savannah."

With a little cry, she did and encouraged him to go faster, deeper. Savannah encircled her arms around his neck, holding on tight while Luc made wild, passionate love to her. Unable to hold back, he loved her with long hard strokes, but she urged him on with throaty little cries of encouragement. When he climaxed, the intense pleasure seemed to go on forever and he knew he connected with her on both a physical and spiritual level. Lovemaking had never been so emotionally intense like this for Luc, confirming what he already knew.

He was falling in love with Savannah Parks.

Luc pulled back while continuing to rock his hips, wanting to see her face while she came. He eased all the way out and teased her clit with the head of his dick, moving in slow circles until she bit her bottom lip between her teeth. When she arched her back Luc plunged in deep and let her milk him dry while another sweetly exquisite orgasm drained him. Never so sated, so satisfied, Luc laughed weakly and rolled over, taking her with him.

"Earth-shattering, huh?" Savannah asked, nuzzling her face in the crook of his neck.

"Uh . . . *yeah*. Without a doubt." He wrapped his arms more securely around her and then kissed the top of her head.

Savannah could feel the slow and steady beat of his heart beneath her hand and a feeling of such contentment seeped into her heart that she sighed and then kissed his cheek.

"I've never felt like this, Savannah," Luc said, and raised his head and looked at her.

"Oh, Lucio . . ." Savannah kissed him softly and then scooted up to a sitting position. Placing a hand on his chest, Savannah said, "I know what you mean. So then why didn't you come to dinner the other night? Why did you push me away?"

Luc sat up and then said, "Stupid insecurity. I knew I was falling for you, but I was afraid of taking a backseat to your career." He reached over and touched her cheek. "I always felt as if I lived in the shadow of my sistas and I didn't want that feeling again."

"So what changed your mind?"

Luc shrugged. "I'm no longer an insecure kid who needs to worry about what other people think of me. I should have been supportive and proud of M. J. and Sophia instead of distancing myself from them. I can't go back and change that, but that doesn't mean that I should ruin my future with you."

"If it makes you feel any better, M. J. told me that she knew that you were a believer. She said that you've always been there for them when they needed you the most."

"You make me feel better. Ya know that?" He leaned in and kissed her.

"She also said that we're soul mates. Do you believe that?"

"Yeah, I guess you're stuck with me." Luc traced his finger down her cheek. "How'd I get so damned lucky to have you?"

Savannah pointed up to the sky and laughed softly. "I guess it's written in the stars." She grabbed his fingertip and kissed it. "You know, for a long time I've dreamed of being a big country singer. I thought that reaching my dream would make me happy, but as exciting as the past couple of weeks have been, I wasn't happy without you. Lucio, my career might take flight or I might flop, but I'll be able to handle anything with you by my side."

"You're not gonna flop."

"You never know. This is a competitive and fickle business . . . but it is just *business*. You mean more to me than a hit record."

Luc pulled her close and held her tight. "You can have both, ya know."

"That would be nice," she said with a low chuckle, and leaned back against his chest. "Oh my gosh, did you see that flash of light? Was that a shooting star?" Savannah pointed to the center of the lake. "Hey, there it is again!"

Luc frowned at the tiny light bobbing and weaving

near the surface of the lake. "I don't know what it is. But it sure is beautiful." Luc held Savannah close, and together, they watched the bright but tiny light stop and sort of hover near the center of the lake before shooting skyward, leaving a trail of shimmering light that sparkled against the inky black sky before fading away. . . .

Photo by Portrait Innovations

✳ About the Author ✳

LuAnn McLane lives in Florence, Kentucky, just outside Cincinnati, Ohio. When she takes breaks from writing, she enjoys going on long walks with her husband, watching chick flicks with her daughter, and trying to keep up with her three active sons. Visit her Web site at www.luannmclane.com.